Dear Readers,

Many years ago, when I was a kid, my father said to me, "Bill, it doesn't really matter what you do in life. What's important is to be the *best* William Johnstone you can be."

I've never forgotten those words. And now, many years and almost two hundred books later, I like to think that I am still trying to be the best William Johnstone I can be. Whether it's Ben Raines in the Ashes series, or Frank Morgan, the last gunfighter, or Smoke Jensen, our intrepid mountain man, or John Barrone and his hardworking crew keeping America safe from terrorist lowlifes in the Code Names series, I want to make each new book better than the last and deliver powerful storytelling.

Equally important, I try to create the kinds of believable characters that we can all identify with, real people who face tough challenges. When one of my creations blasts an enemy into the middle of next week, you can be damn sure he had a good reason.

As a storyteller, my job is to entertain you, my readers, and to make sure that you get plenty of enjoyment from my books for your hard-earned money. This is not a job I take lightly. And I greatly appreciate your feedback—you are my gold, and your opinions *do* count. So please keep the letters and e-mails coming.

Respectfully yours,

William W. Johnstone

WILLIAM W. JOHNSTONE

BLOOD BOND
GUNSIGHT CROSSING

PINNACLE BOOKS
Kensington Publishing Corp.
http://www.kensingtonbooks.com

All Kensington Titles, Imprints, and Distributed Lines are available at special quantity discounts for bulk purchases for sales promotions, premiums, fund-raising, and educational or institutional use. Special book excerpts or customized printings can also be created to fit specific needs. For details, write or phone the office of the Kensington special sales manager: Kensington Publishing Corp., 850 Third Avenue, New York, NY 10022, attn: Special Sales Department, Phone: 1-800-221-2647.

"Texas, by God!"
John Wesley Hardin

Chapter 1

"Do you have any idea at all where we might be?" Sam asked.

"Of course I do," Matt said with a smile. "We're in New Mexico Territory."

"You said that last week!"

"It's a big territory."

And it was hot. The hard-packed and rutted road upon which they traveled eastward flung the heat back at them. They had seen jackrabbits, a few eagles soaring high in the brilliant blue of the sky, and nothing else for two days.

"But I think it's time to cut south," Matt said.

"I think it's time to do something," Sam Two Wolves agreed. "We're running out of food, and if we don't find water soon, we're going to die out here in this godforsaken place."

Matt laughed at his blood brother, but he knew the truth lay like shining steel in his words. They were going to be in serious trouble if they didn't find water, and find it very quickly.

Matt Bodine and Sam August Webster Two Wolves were blood brothers, bonded by the Cheyenne ritual that made them as one. They were also Brothers of the Wolf; they were Onihomahan: Friends of the Wolf. The two men could and often did pass as having the same mother and father—which they did not. Both possessed the same broad shoulders, lean hips, and heavy musculature. Sam's eyes were black, Matt's were blue. Sam's hair was black, Bodine's was dark brown. They were the same height and very nearly the same weight. Both wore the same type of three-stone necklace around their necks, the stones-pierced by rawhide. Both were ruggedly handsome men. Both had gone through the Cheyenne Coming of Manhood; they had the scars on their chests to prove it.

"You really think God has forsaken this country?" Matt asked.

"No. Of course not. But I think that perhaps He ignores it more than other sections."

The brothers cut south.

The horses suddenly pricked their ears and became restless.

"Indians?" Matt asked.

"I hope not," Sam replied. "This is Comanche and Apache country—I think." He stood up in the stirrups and sniffed the air. It was moist. "Water," he said.

"What do you mean, 'I think'? You don't know what tribes are around here?"

"I am Northern Cheyenne, idiot! From a thousand miles north of this desolation. Am I supposed to know everything about every tribe in North America?"

A stranger would think the two disliked each other. They loved each other as brothers. The constant poking and ribbing was their way of showing the affection both felt for the other. As many trouble-hunters had learned painfully, quickly, and sometimes fatally, mess with one and you had the other with whom to deal.

"You're half Cheyenne," Bodine corrected. "And I don't expect you to know anything. Without me, you'd have been lost two weeks ago."

"Bah" Sam said contemptuously. "You couldn't find your way to an outhouse if you had the squirts."

Both men were excellent trackers and woodsmen, and both had the reputation of gunfighters, although neither had ever sought nor wanted that title.

The next day, the young men crossed a road that headed south by southwest. It looked well-traveled, but neither Matt nor Sam were looking for company, so they elected to go on for another day. They topped a ridge and saw another road, this one running north and south, and just beyond that, a river.

"What river is that?" Matt asked.

"I have no inkling whatsoever. Texas was your idea, not mine." Sam sat his saddle and tried to look solemn. But his dark eyes were twinkling at the thoughts of whatever adventure lay ahead of them. The two young men were full of the juices of youth and had never run from anything in their lives.

Matt called him a very vulgar name in Cheyenne and with a whoop, they went galloping their horses toward the beckoning waters of the river.

Matt stood guard while his *I-tat-an-e,* Cheyenne for *brother,* took a bath, soaping himself generously and diving under the waters several times to rinse off. He climbed out, dried and dressed, and Matt took his turn. They both needed it: it had been about ten days since they'd bathed and shaved. But a shave was going to have to wait.

It was growing late in the afternoon, and both men were weary from the long, hot, almost waterless miles and days behind them. Sam made camp while Matt rode out to shoot some rabbits for their supper. Their supplies were growing dangerously low.

Matt killed two jackrabbits, and Sam had the last of their potatoes and onions ready for stewing when his brother returned. While the stew was bubbling and thickening, the young men drank coffee and relaxed.

"You have any idea what this river is called?" Sam asked.

"I hate to say it, but it may be the Pecos."

"The Pecos!" Sam sat up. "If that's the case, we're almost out of New Mexico."

"Yeah. Want to cut south and follow the river come first light?"

"Why not?"

The two young men were wandering, entirely aimlessly, trying to get their minds settled before returning to their home range in Montana. They had witnessed the awful carnage at Little Bighorn the past year, the battle in which Sam's father, Medicine Horse, had charged Custer with a deliberately empty rifle and counted coup on Custer—striking him with his coup stick—before dying. Matt and Sam had laid on a ridge and watched through the swirling dust as the troopers of the Seventh fell.

Even though both young men were moderately wealthy in their own right—they both owned ranches and Sam's white mother had left him quite an estate for the time—Matt and Sam knew they had to drift for a time. After seeing the slaughter at Little Bighorn, neither man felt at peace with himself.

"Riders coming," Sam said, his palm to the ground. "Several of them."

"I heard them before you did," Matt lied.

"Ha! You couldn't hear a bumblebee until it stung you on the rear."

Matt and Sam got to their boots. Both men wore two guns. Matt carried both of his in leather, tied down, while Sam carried one in leather on his right side and another butt-forward on his left side, tucked in a sash he wore around his waist.

"They don't look friendly," Sam observed.

"Looking for trouble, I'd say." Bodine moved away from Sam to lessen the odds of both of them being taken out at once should shooting start.

"Slow it down!" Bodine yelled. "We don't need all that damn dust in our stew."

Instead of easing up, the four riders kicked their horses into a gallop and came charging into the camp, knocking over the stew and scattering the blankets. They made their mistake when they slowed, turned around, and came back for another go at the camp.

Bodine reached up and jerked one out of his saddle while Sam was doing the same thing to another. The men hit the ground hard, on their backs, jarring their teeth and having the wind knocked from them. One mounted cowboy made the mistake of grabbing iron. Bodine put a .44 slug in his shoulder. The last rider sat his saddle, wanting to get into action, but not in a terrible hurry to get shot.

The shoulder-shot cowboy moaned and passed out, falling from his saddle.

A big black-headed fellow got to his boots cussing. While Sam kept a .44 on the last cowboy in his saddle, Bodine hit the big fellow twice in the belly and then came up with an uppercut that stretched him on the ground.

"You want a piece of it?" Bodine asked the other cowpoke, who was getting up.

"I reckon not. But John Lee ain't gonna like this a-tall."

"I don't give a damn what John Lee likes or dislikes," Bodine told him. "But I'll tell you what you're going to do."

"Oh, yeah?"

Bodine stepped forward and knocked the man on his rear, bloodying his mouth and momentarily crossing his eyes.

"Yeah," Matt told him. "You ready to listen?"

"I reckon so. Beats gettin' my lights punched out."

"Coffeepot's smashed and the cook pot fell into the coals. Heat cracked it," Sam said.

Bodine reached down and removed the man's guns from leather. "Now listen carefully. You ride—I don't care where— and you get back here with a new coffeepot, a new cook pot, and some meat and vegetables to go in it." He pointed to the shoulder-shot puncher. "And take that punk with you. The others will stay here for insurance."

"Are you crazy, man?" Bloody-mouth asked. "Do you know who you're foolin' with?"

Matt jerked iron and jacked the hammer back, placing the muzzle of the .44 on the man's forehead. The sharp odor of urine filled the late afternoon air as Bloody-mouth peed in his long-handles.

"If I have to tell you again, I'm going to be talking to a corpse," Matt told him. "Now ride, you bastard!"

Bloody-mouth got gone. Matt boosted the shoulder-shot puncher into his saddle and slapped the horse on the rump.

Matt turned toward the kid in the saddle as the black-headed man moaned and started to rise. He looked down the muzzle of the .44 in Sam's hand and changed his mind. "You guys are crazy! Where's Val?"

"He went to get us some food," Sam told him. "After a brief altercation with my brother, he quickly realized the boorishness of your actions and felt very apologetic about it."

"What the hell did you say?"

"Shut up!"

"I understood that."

"Get off your horse," Matt told the young puncher. "Now, use your thumb and forefinger only and toss your guns over to me."

Two revolvers hit the ground.

"What's your name?" Matt asked him.

"Childress."

"What the hell was the point of coming in here and hoorahin' us?"

"Just funnin', that's all."

"You call destroying someone's camp fun?"

"You shouldna oughta told us to slow up. You don't tell Broken Lance riders to do nothin'. And you're gonna find that out the hard way damn quick."

"I doubt it," Matt told him. "Now get that coffee pot you got tied behind your saddle and make us some coffee."

"I'll be damned iffen I will!"

Bodine moved toward him. "Do it!" his cohort yelled. "We ain't got a whole lot of choice in the matter. And be sure to get that coffee sack outta your saddlebags."

Both Sam and Bodine smiled. Childress probably had a spare six-shooter in there and black head was telling him to use it.

Sam put the muzzle of his .44 against the black-haired man's ear. The sound of the hammer jacking back was very loud in the quiet. "If he comes out of there with iron in his hand instead of coffee, you're dead."

"Forget it, Childress," the man called. "Just make the damn coffee."

"Do you have a name?" Sam asked him.

"Blackie."

Childress slowly took his coffee and his pot and made coffee, using water from his canteen. The aroma of the spilled stew wafted deliciously around the camp.

"I was looking forward to that stew," Bodine remarked, sitting on a weathered log that had drifted down the river from only God knew where and how long ago.

"You ain't gonna look forward to John's visit," Blackie said. " 'Cause shortly after he gets here, you both gonna be dead men rottin' on the ground."

"You'll be right there with us," Matt told him, then his gaze cut to Childress. "And so will you."

The bullying punchers exchanged worried glances. There was something in Bodine's manner that led them both to believe he meant exactly what he said. And Sam Two Wolves had the same demeanor.

"You two related?" Blackie asked.

"Brothers," Sam told him.

"Don't see too many men wearin' necklaces," Childress said with a nasty smirk.

"They show us to be members of the Cheyenne tribe," Bodine informed him. "We've both endured the Coming of Manhood."

"Is that 'posed to mean something?" the young punk asked.

"It means something," Blackie said, the words softly spoken. "Now shut your mouth, Childress. We're in a lot more trouble here than you might think."

"Wise man," Sam told him. "You want some coffee?"

"I'd appreciate a cup."

The men drank coffee and lounged for nearly an hour. They all heard the thunder of many hooves long before the riders topped the crest of the hill and stopped, looking down at the small camp. Sam and Bodine stood up and picked up Henry rifles, chambering rounds and keeping the hammers back.

"Don't do nothin' stupid," Blackie said. "If John was comin' in hostile, he'd done been shootin'. Just relax."

"I'm very relaxed," Bodine told him. "Are you relaxed, *I-tat-an-e?*"

"I am so at ease I might fall asleep any moment."

"You guys are crazy!" Childress said. "John Lee is one of the fastest guns ever. And that's Rawhide O'Neal next to him. Down at the end there, that's Pen Masters—"

"Shut up, Childress!" Blackie told him. "Just shut your damn mouth!"

"You know somethin' I don't?" Childress asked.

"Yeah," Blackie said sourly. "I shore do. Just be quiet."

The cowhand Matt had sent for the pots, pans, and food rode beside John Lee as the men left the column and headed down the slope. Four riders fell in behind them.

"I sent you for pots and pans and food," Matt told Val. "And you bring back an army. Tell me, do you know the difference between a cow's tail and a pump handle?"

"Huh?" Val asked.

"You don't?"

"I don't understand the question."

"I'd hate to send you out for water, then," Matt grinned the words.

Sam laughed. John Lee and the others did not see the humor in it. John Lee said, "You boys need to be taught a lesson, I'm thinking."

"You're wearing a gun," Matt told him. "Why don't you get your butt and your mouth out of that saddle and let's see what you can do besides flap your gums."

John looked like he was about to have a stroke. He sputtered for a moment. Nobody talked to him like that. He'd show the young pup a thing or two.

"That's Matt Bodine, boss." Blackie tossed the words out before John could leave the saddle.

One of the riders behind John expelled air slowly. Another one grunted. All of them kept their hands in sight.

"So it figures that's got to be Sam Two Wolves with him," Blackie added.

John Lee was a man used to getting his own way. He'd come out to that part of New Mexico and Texas years back, when life on the frontier meant facing death every day. It took hard and rough men to stay. The graveyard at his ranch was filled with men who'd died riding for the Broken Lance. But John Lee was not an ignorant man. He knew that if anyone started shooting, he'd be the first one Bodine would blow out of the saddle.

Everyone in the West had heard of Matt Bodine. Killed his first man at age fourteen. A year later, the man's brothers came to avenge the killing. When the smoke drifted away, Matt was standing amid the bodies, both hands filled with Colts. When he was sixteen, rustlers hit the ranch. Matt killed two more and wounded two others. He'd lived with the Cheyenne for more than a year. Then he was a guard, riding shotgun for gold shipments. Four more men went to rest in lonely graves. He scouted for the Army and put more so-called bad men in the ground.

Sam Two Wolves was just as fast as Matt Bodine and jut as quick on the temper as he was on the trigger. John had heard the stories about Sam's high education at an Eastern university and about his white mother's wealth. John quickly surmised he was in the middle of a very volatile situation there.

"We didn't bring any cookin' utensils," John said.

"That's too bad," Bodine told him. " 'Cause we're getting hungry."

"And when we get hungry our tempers get short," Sam added.

"Why didn't you bring what I asked for?" Matt's eyes met those of John Lee.

John wanted to tell him to go right straight to hell. But he wisely kept his mouth shut.

"I'll tell you why," Matt said. "Because you allow your men to ride roughshod over anything and anybody and think it's funny when other people's possessions are destroyed. You thought you were going to come out here with your pack of hyenas and leave our bodies for the buzzards and the coyotes. You think you're God Almighty. Untouchable. I don't like people like you. At all."

Pen Masters rode down the slope. "Come on, Matt," the gunfighter said. "You and me know each other from our days back on the Tongue. I don't want this to turn into no shootin'. Not over some damn pots and pans."

"It isn't about pots and pans, Pen," Matt told him. "You know that."

"Matt," the gunfighter said, "you're the fastest man with a gun I've ever seen. But you'll be shot to ribbons if you start anything here."

"And you'll all be dead," Sam spoke. "And Lord of the Manor there," his eyes touched John, "will be the first to go."

"Copper!" John said. "Go on back to the ranch and fetch a goddamn coffeepot and other crap. Bring some food. We'll wait here for you."

The puncher left at a gallop. John's eyes were hard and mean as he looked at Bodine. "I don't take water from no man," he told Bodine. "Maybe my boys were wrong in what they done. So I'll replace your gear and provisions. Then you best ride on out of this area. No man wants to die before his time, Bodine. But if you ever brace me again and talk to me like you just done, as God is my witness, one of us will die. Come on, boys. Copper don't need no nursemaid to find his way back."

He wheeled his horse and rode away. Pen stayed for a moment, looking at Bodine while Blackie and Childress mounted up and rode off.

"Back off of this one, Bodine," he warned, not in an unfriendly tone. "John Lee runs this part of the country. He owns everything and everybody. John Lee says 'frog,' people jump."

"Then maybe he needs somebody to muddy up his pond," Matt replied.

Sam grinned. He had a hunch that he and Matt were going to stick around for a time.

Chapter 2

"So what's the plan?" Sam asked, as Pen rode away.

Matt shrugged his shoulders. "What plan? I just took a dislike for the man, that's all."

"He's easy to dislike," Sam agreed. "Be interesting to see if our gear is replaced."

"Oh, I think it will be. I'm sure he considers himself to be a very honorable man . . . and he might be in a very peculiar and self-serving fashion. I think as soon as our gear is replaced, we'd best pull out. That fellow back on the trail told us there was a little two-bit town about ten miles south of the New Mexico line. Half a dozen stores and a fleabag hotel. What do you think?"

"I'm game."

Within the hour, the puncher called Copper rode back in and dropped a sack on the ground. "I ain't got a thing in the world agin you fellers, so I'm gonna give you some friendly advice. Get gone. John Lee is all of a sudden hirin' hardcases and payin' fightin' wages. And it ain't 'cause of the Comanches neither. Quanah Parker and his bunch shot their wad a couple of years back. They's still Injuns around, but not many. I don't know what's goin' on, but was I you boys,

I wouldn't stick around and get caught up in the middle of it."

Copper turned his horse and rode off.

"The Southern Cheyenne rode with Quanah and his bunch for a time," Sam said. "But not many of them. Most of the others were Kiowa, Kwahadi, and Arapaho."

"What do you think about Copper's claim to know nothing about what John Lee is up to?"

Sam did a squatting motion, cupped his hands to indicate a large mound, and made a mooing sound. Cheyenne for *bullshit*.

John Lee had returned more than had been destroyed. There was a side of bacon, some flour and beans, potatoes and onions, and a skillet, cook pot, and coffeepot. Matt and Sam quickly packed up and headed south.

It was well after dark when they rode slowly into the town. A sign had proclaimed the town's name as Crossing.

"Crossing what?" Sam questioned.

"First town after crossing the territory line, I reckon," Matt replied.

"That is as good a reply as any," Sam said.

Crossing had a big general store, a bigger saloon, a blacksmith shop/livery stable, a combination saddle and gun shop, a barber shop, a café, a marshal's office, and a hotel that was over the saloon. "Bustling little place, isn't it?" Sam said.

They had seen no signs of life. The only building lit up was the saloon.

"Let's see to our horses," Matt suggested.

They swung into the livery stable and dismounted. A middle-aged man who smelled like he slept inside a barrel of whiskey walked out and greeted them sourly.

"Treat them right," Sam told the man. "All the corn they want."

"You got any money?"

They paid him in advance and the man grumbled something under his breath.

"What was that?" Matt asked, taking his saddlebags and rifle.

"I said: you boys ain't got no sense. John Lee told you to git, you oughtta git!"

"News travels fast," Sam said.

"John Lee don't just own the biggest spread in the county, he owns the county. You're not welcome here, boys."

They found that out when they tried to register at the hotel.

"Full up," the desk clerk told them.

The saloon was on the other side of a partition. No sounds came from the saloon area.

Matt spun the registry book, glanced at it, then lifted his eyes to meet the nervous eyes of the desk clerk.

"I got orders, boys," he said, his voice breaking.

Matt took the pen, dabbed it in the ink bottle, and started to register.

"I wouldn't do that, Bodine," the voice came from behind him. It was a familiar voice. John Lee.

Matt turned, surprised to see the man alone. The surprise must have been quite obvious, for John smiled.

"Did you think I have to have bodyguards around me at all times?" he questioned.

"The only thing I know about you is that I don't like you."

John's smile widened. "You don't even know me, Bodine."

Matt studied the man. A big man, wide of shoulder with hard-packed muscle and lean of hip. Big hands, thick wrists, heavily muscled arms. Matt guessed him to be in his early forties. "I know the type."

Sam had given the outside a careful once-over. "He's not alone."

"I didn't expect him to be."

This time, John's smile vanished. "The hotel is closed to you boys. But without malice. I have guests coming in, that's all there is to it."

"All right," Matt said with a shrug. "We understand that. You object to us sleeping in the stable?"

"No. Just be gone by morning."

Riders pulled up in the front of the hotel. Their horses moved like they were weary. John Lee's back was to Sam, and he didn't see the hand signal Sam gave Matt. Trouble.

"Mind if we have a drink in your saloon?" Matt asked.

"I'd deny no man a drink to cut the dust of the trail." John's smile was once more in place. "As a matter of fact, I'll buy the first one."

"Kind of you."

"Tell the barkeep."

He seemed anxious for them to leave the small lobby of the hotel, so they accommodated his silent wishes. "Thank you," Sam told him. Saddlebags and rifles in hand, the men walked into the bar. It was empty except for the barkeep.

"Evenin', gents. What'll it be?"

Neither was a hard-drinking man, so they both ordered beer. "Got some eggs and bread and cheese left from lunch," the barkeep told them. "It'll have to do for supper, seein' as how the café's closed."

"That'll be fine," Sam told him, as they sat down at a table next to a rear wall. The table was farthest away from the lanterns and in the shadows.

The barkeep brought their beer and food. Setting the mugs down on the table, he whispered, "I heard the exchange in the lobby. All hell's fixin' to bust loose around this part of the state. Ride south in the morning until you come to the Circle S spread. Ten miles south of town. They set a good breakfast and will turn no man away from a meal. Talk to Jeff Sparks."

After the barkeep had returned to his position behind the long bar, Sam whispered, "Now what was that all about?"

"I don't know. Some damn weird things going on around this place. Makes me curious."

"Me too. And I do admire a hearty breakfast."

The blood brothers grinned at each other and fell to eating, both of them conscious of the talking going on in the lobby of the hotel. A lot of voices. Hard voices, profane language. The men from the lobby began drifting into the bar in pairs. They were uncurried and uncouth, with most of them packing two guns in leather and another six-shooter tucked behind the gunbelt.

"Well, now," Bodine said softly. "Would you just look at that."

"I see it. I know a couple of them. You?"

"Yeah. Harry Street's the biggest one. Dean Waters is the one with a scar on his face. The two standing near the batwings are Carl Jergens and Dexter Campbell. That's as worthless a quartet as ever wore boots."

"That's Jack Morgan and Jim Johnson sitting at the far table. Arizona gunfighters. Pukey Stagg is the little one off by himself. He's vicious and snake-quick. I don't know the other one."

"His name is Mack. If he has a last name, I never heard it. He's out of Utah. Gunfighter."

"Any of them know you?"

"Several of them. And I'm not on their list of best-liked people."

"I can certainly understand that," Sam needled him. "You have such an abrasive personality."

"Look who's talking," Matt fired back. "Everywhere you go you start trouble."

"What are you two a-whisperin' about over yonder?" Big Harry Street bellered.

"None of your damn business," Sam told him.

"See what I mean?" Matt said.

The no-counts all stopped talking and looked at the two men sitting in the shadows.

Big Harry turned slowly from the bar, looking hard at Matt and Sam. He was a huge man, about six inches over six feet and weighing a good two hundred and fifty pounds. And he was as worthless a human being as they came. A killer for hire who would kill a baby as quickly as he would an adult. He enjoyed killing children's pets just to see the child cry.

Matt took the handles of the beer mugs in his left hand, got up, and walked slowly to the bar, his spurs jingling softly as he walked. The crowd of crud fell silent as they recognized him. The room got very silent when they heard Sam jack back the hammer on his Henry.

"Relax, people," Dean Waters said. "We ain't here to start no trouble with Bodine or his half-breed brother."

Sam laughed softly. But Bodine knew that behind that laugh was no humor.

"Nothin' meant by that, Two Wolves," Dean said. "I just called you what you is."

"If I called you what you are," Sam retorted, "I would probably be put in jail."

"Fill them up," Matt told the barkeep.

"You a long way from Wyoming, Bodine," Harry said.

"Quite a ways, Harry."

"You still rescuin' kids and dogs and cats and little old ladies, Bodine?"

"You still hiring your gun out to shoot people in the back, Harry?" Matt fired back.

Dean stepped between the two men before Harry could think of a comeback. He needn't have hurried, for thinking was not one of Harry's strong suits.

"Stand easy, Harry," Dean told him. He turned to face Matt. "What the hell are you on the prod about, Bodine?"

"I'm not on the prod about anything. I'm just passin' through, Waters. Having a couple of beers before turning in. But I'm not going to take a lot of mouth from this buffalo here." He looked at Harry.

"Who you callin' a buffalo, Bodine?" Harry blustered.

"You. I don't see anybody else around that looks and smells like one."

The barkeep laid a sawed-off shotgun on the bar. "No trouble in here, boys. And I mean it. I just had this floor mopped and blood is hard to get up."

Dean jerked his head at a couple of gunslicks and they led Harry off to a table, the big man mumbling and cussing. He turned to Bodine. "I hope you're not buyin' into this, Bodine. This is none of your damn affair."

"I don't even know what you're talking about, Waters. But don't crowd me. Just leave me alone and everything will be jam-up and jelly."

Matt took his refilled mugs and walked back to the table.

"Whatever is going on, it's big," Sam said. "Do we want to stay in the middle of it?"

"No. Tomorrow we'll ride out to the Circle S and look it over. At first guess I'd say that John Lee is land hungry and wants to swallow up the Circle S. But he just might be finding it tough chewing."

"And you intend to put a couple of more rocks in the stew?"

Matt smiled. "Yeah. Like you and me."

"And you call me a troublemaker."

The blood brothers rode out of town before dawn began streaking the eastern skies. The lamps were lit at the café, but while both men longed for a cup of coffee, neither man wanted to push their luck. A dozen more men, hardcases all, had ridden in during the night and put up their horses, obviously thinking the stable was deserted. They had talked and confirmed what Matt and Sam had already guessed: John Lee wanted the Circle S spread and was hiring gunslicks to help him get it.

Among the newly arrived gunmen were Bam Ford, Bob Grove, Mark Hazard, and Dave Land—all Texas gunslingers from around the Big Thicket area. Jack Lightfoot and Gil Lopez had come in around midnight. They worked as a team, both of them notorious ambushers and back shooters. Leo Grand had come in alone. He was from up around the Four Corners. And the Oklahoma gunhawk, Trest, had ridden in with Lew Hagan.

"The scum are gathering," Matt said, after about a mile on the trail.

"Yes. And it's costing John Lee a good deal of money for those men. They're all top guns."

"And I'll bet there are more coming in."

"If so, then he's building an army. But why all this to take over a ranch? According to the talk, Jeff Sparks barely has enough hands to run his ranch, much less fight."

"Maybe we can find that out over breakfast."

"I hope they make good coffee."

"I hope they don't shoot us before we can find out!"

They left the road at a battered hand-painted sign that was just legible. Circle S—3 miles. An arrow pointed the way. About an eighth of a mile from the ranch house, a closed gate blocked the way.

"Now what?" Sam asked.

"We wait."

It wasn't a long wait. Less than five minutes had passed before a tall old man with a handlebar mustache that was wider than his face rode out. He did not immediately open the gate. He sat his horse and stared at the blood brothers. He gave them the once-over very slowly and very carefully, his sharp eyes not missing a thing, and Matt knew he had pegged them as gunfighters right off the bat.

"We got the reputation of gunslingers, mister," Matt told him. "But it isn't something we wanted or work at. The barkeep at the saloon in Crossing told us the Circle S set a fine breakfast."

"Did he now?"

"Yes, sir," Sam said, and the old man picked up on the "sir" and smiled.

"Them's Cheyenne necklaces."

"Yes, they are. We're blood brothers."

"You got names?"

"I'm Matt and he's Sam."

"How come you didn't grub in town? You broke?"

Matt smiled. "We still have some coins to rub together." Fact was, Bodine and Sam had quite a bit of money in belts around their waists. "We had a run-in with a bigmouth name of John Lee yesterday. After his hands trashed our camp. We shot one and unhorsed the others. . . ."

"Rather rudely," Sam added, and the old man looked like he was going to bust out laughing.

"Sent one of them back to see his boss with orders to replace our busted gear. Mr. John Lee himself came back, with a whole bunch of hands. Had a gunfighter I knew years back with him. Name of Pen Masters. John Lee talked and we listened, then we talked and he listened. He replaced our gear."

"Do tell. Come on up to the house. I can't wait to hear the rest of this tale."

He pushed open the gate and latched it securely as soon as the brothers were inside. "Name's Dodge," he told them. "I'm the foreman." He pointed to a battered basin and a pump by what looked like the bunkhouse. "Wash there. I'll tell the boss we got two more for breakfast." He looked at Matt. "You ain't got no Injun in you, and your brother ain't got that much either."

"My mother was white," Sam said. "Their marriage was done legally and with prayers from the white man's god and from my father's gods. I was educated at a university back East."

Dodge nodded his head. "Wash up and come to grub. And watch your language. The boss's wife and daughters will be at the table. The hands has aready et and gone."

A man met them on the front porch of the large roomy and airy home. It was a long, low home, built in the Spanish hacienda style. "Jeff Sparks, boys," he said, holding out his hand. "Which one's Matt and which one's Sam?" Jeff was in his late forties or early fifties. His red hair just graying a mite.

He led them into the house and the men could see this was a home that was lived in. It had many nice furnishings for the frontier, but the chairs and couches were to sit on, not for show.

"Girls!" he hollered. "Got two mighty handsome young men in here. Come look 'em over!"

Matt and Sam exchanged glances, unaccustomed to being viewed like sides of beef. They both wished they'd shaved that morning when the girls came into the room.

"Lisa and Lia," Jeff said, obviously enjoying himself. "Matt and Sam."

The girls smiled at the boys and the boys blushed.

Lisa was a redhead and Lia was a strawberry blonde. Both of them were shapely and very, very comely. They were wearing something that neither Matt nor Sam had ever seen before. Split skirts. They weren't britches and they weren't skirts. The brothers didn't know what the hell they were.

"You boys had coffee?" Jeff asked.

"No, sir," Sam said.

"Hell's fire!" he hollered. "That ain't decent. Girls, go fetch the pot and some cups and tell your mama to come in and meet our guests. Tell Conchita to start rattlin' them pots and pans. She's got some hungry men salivating out here." He pointed to the couch. "Sit."

Matt and Sam sat. Before they could get comfortable, the girls were back with coffeepot and cups. Before they could take the first sip, a very handsome lady entered the room. No split skirt for this one. A full dress and a nice one at that.

"My wife, boys. Nancy."

Matt and Sam were already on their feet. "Pleasure, ma'am," they said.

"Sit and drink your coffee, gentlemen," Nancy said, taking a seat. "Dodge told us you had trouble with John Lee. Why should we believe you?"

"Mother . . ." Jeff said, putting out a hand.

"No, let me finish," she persisted. "We know that John has been hiring gunfighters. These young men are gunfighters. They have the stamp upon them. How do we know John didn't send them here to kill us in our own home?"

Matt's gaze cut to Dodge standing off to the side of the room, his hand on the butt of his pistol. Another man was on Sam's right, also ready for action.

"Yes," Nancy said. "You can have a good meal, then if you're here to cause trouble, you can be buried with a full stomach."

Matt grinned. "You have a right to be suspicious, but I can assure you all that we don't work for John Lee."

"Those are good questions, ma'am," Sam said. "And you're right on one count: we have used a gun a time or two. But we don't hire them out—ever!"

"Never seen that brand before," Dodge said.

"We're from up Wyoming, Montana. Both of us own ranches up there—paying ranches. Both of us were scouting for the Army when Custer was killed at Little Bighorn. Sam's father was killed there, too. He rode in, unarmed except for a coup stick. He did not want war."

"My mother left me an inheritance," Sam said. "While I am not wealthy, I am comfortable. So is my blood brother." He smiled. "Matt Bodine."

"Hell's fire!" Jeff shouted. "Matt Bodine!" He dropped his coffee cup.

Chapter 3

After the family settled down, Matt told them all that he and Sam had heard from the gunfighters while in the loft of the stable, then told them what had taken place at their campsite on the Pecos.

"John Lee's boys ride roughshod over everybody," Jeff said. "Except for me and mine," he added. "His spread is three times the size of mine, and still he wants more. He's either run out or killed the smaller ranchers in the area. Only a few farmers left. And why he's doing it is something none of us understand."

"Gold, silver?" Sam asked.

"No," the rancher shook his head. "Nothing like that around here. Water is the most precious thing in this part of the country, and both of us have about an equal supply of that. He's power hungry, I reckon."

"Has he always been like this?" Matt asked.

"Pretty much so. We come into this area at about the same time. Back in '55. We fought Indians and outlaws and comancheros while we built our spreads. I got along with my neighbors, he didn't. John thrived on other folks' misfortune. Drought would come and he wouldn't share his water or graze when he had it to spare. Bought people out for a nickel or dime on the dollar. Burned a few out, too; although that couldn't never be proved up in a court of law."

"Married?"

"Was. His wife died and he raised the boy himself. Mean kid. Same age as our boy Gene. But that's where the resemblance ends. Nick is worse than his dad, if that's possible. Quick with a short gun and likes to use it. He used to try courtin' Lisa here. She wouldn't have nothin' to do with him. I finally run him off 'bout two years ago and he swore he'd kill me someday."

"Where is your son?" Sam asked.

"Gone down to the settlement on the Pecos 'bout thirty miles south of here for supplies. Little place is called Pecos, but it isn't a real town yet. I can't buy nothin' at the Crossing. John Lee owns it all. Lock, stock, and horse troughs. He's run off or killed most of my hands. I'm down to five punchers, not countin' Dodge. Hell, you boys know you can't run a spread this size with five hands. It's impossible."

"The law?" Matt asked, knowing full well what the answer would be.

"There ain't no law west of the Pecos, boys. It's gun law out here. Survival of the fittest . . . or the meanest."

"What are you planning on doing?" Sam asked. "I mean—"

"I know what you mean," Jeff said. "I don't see that I got a choice. I'm not a poor man, and I can afford to hire guns. I don't hold with that. But . . ." He lifted his shoulders in a gesture of "what else can I do?"

"Who has more money?" Matt asked. "You or John Lee?"

"Oh, John does. After his wife died he come into a wad of money; she was from a wealthy family in Louisiana. French. Just the nicest person a body would ever want to meet. I don't know how in the hell she ever got tied up with John."

"She fell in love," Nancy said simply.

"Then she must have had a taste for horse crap," Jeff summed up.

The girls giggled.

Matt and Sam exchanged glances. Sam shrugged. "Show us the boundaries of your spread," Matt said. "It's time me and Sam did some honest labor for a change."

"What do you mean?" Jeff asked, a puzzled look on his face.

"Why, you just hired yourself a couple of new hands, Mr. Sparks."

Matt and Sam met the other Circle S hands that evening over supper. From now on, unless invited to do so, they would take their meals in the bunkhouse with the crew—it was all prepared by Conchita anyway and the hands took turns going to the big house and bringing it back.

All the remaining hands, except one, were men in their forties. Solid hard-working cowboys. Not fast gunhands, but men who had handled guns all their life and usually hit what they were shooting at with the first shot. They met Lomax, Tate, Bell, Red, and Jimmy. Jimmy was maybe nineteen, and that was iffy. If he was nineteen, he was a young nineteen.

"His pa was one John Lee's men kilt," Tate told them. "His ma died shortly after that—heart attack. Bein' a only child, Jimmy was pampered as much as that can be out here. He wears a gun, but he ain't much good with it. Crack shot with a rifle though, and he'll do what you tell him to do."

"Jimmy's a good boy," Lomax said. "But he's swore to kill John Lee. We can't keep nursemaidin' him, Matt. He's a man growed. You know well as me—probably better—how 't is out here."

"Oughtta let him go on and kill the dirty son," Red said. "John Lee crossed the line a long time ago. He's no good."

"Maybe that's what the boss hired these two to do?" Bell spoke for the first time. He had not been overly friendly with Matt or Sam.

"You got something stuck in your throat, Bell," Matt told him, "spit it out."

"I don't like gunfighters. Never seen one yet who was able to do an honest day's work."

"Neither me nor Sam asked for the name of gunfighter, Bell. And as far as work goes, both of us own ranches up north. Working ranches, paying ranches. I can ride anything with hair on it, rope just as good as the next man, and just to set the record straight, I'd rather take a beatin' than have to string wire."

Bell looked at him for a moment, then a slow grin creased his lips. "I reckon you'll do, Bodine. I've just heard some bad things about you is all."

"What things?"

"That you like usin' them guns of yours."

"I can't say that I haven't enjoyed killing a few men. Child rapers and torturers. Back-shooting cold-blooded murderers. That type."

Bell slowly nodded his head. "I hope you gut-shot 'em," he said and put the issue to rest.

For the next several days, Sam and Matt rode the sprawling range of the Circle S, familiarizing themselves with as much of it as possible. They talked as they rode.

"There's got to be more to it than what we've been told," Sam opined.

"Maybe not," Matt disagreed. If he didn't disagree most of the time Sam would have thought him ill.

Sam waited, then looked at him. "Is that all? 'Maybe not' doesn't tell me much. Of course, that may be all that you have on your mind—considering the usual state of your mind." He smiled.

"All you have on your mind is Lisa," Matt shot back. "And you'd better be careful, brother." The last was said without a trace of humor.

"I know," Sam said. "It is very difficult being part of two

worlds. It is a harmless flirtation, nothing more. I will not permit anything more."

"You might not have a say in the matter if she begins taking it seriously."

"I know. But what am I to do, ignore her?"

Matt grinned. "No. 'Cause if you do that, you'll make her mad, and then you'll really have hell to pay."

"After all is said and done, there is no difference between women, red or white."

They rode on for another mile or so in silence. Early summer, and it was already hot. After awhile they turned and began moving a herd of cattle—really more than two men could handle—heading them back toward a range closer to the big house. It had been a very dry spring, and the cattle were ranging all over the place looking for graze.

Sparks and Dodge rode up and pitched in, giving the brothers a hand with the herd.

"I got to sell some," Sparks said. "Got too many on the land."

"Let's round them up and drive them to market," Matt replied.

Sparks chuckled without humor. "Can't get hands, Matt. Nobody wants to buck John Lee. He's put the word out that ridin' for me is dangerous for your health."

"How long can you hold on, Jeff?"

"Not long. They cut back on the garrison at Fort Stockton, and Fort Concho buys beeves from ranchers around there. I got to ship them by railroad. That means a long drive. And I'd have to leave men behind to guard the ranch. John would burn me out."

"Then that doesn't leave you but one option, does it, Jeff?"

"What do you mean, Matt?"

"If John Lee won't let you and the others live in peace, then you've got to get together and take out John Lee."

"I been tryin' to convince him of that for months," Dodge said with a grunt. "Like talkin' to fence post."

"I do know that feeling," Sam said with a straight face.

"I won't start the war, Matt," the rancher said. "I just can't do it."

"Seems like to me it's already started."

"I told him that, too," the foreman said. He looked at Sparks. "Jeff, we've been through too much to see it all go down like this."

"I'll not hire professional killers." The rancher held on to his views.

"What if he makes a hostile move against you?" Sam questioned. "What then?"

"Then . . ." the rancher hesitated, "we'll see." He rode on ahead to take the point.

"He's a good, decent, honorable man," Dodge said. "Very high principled. And those are the very things that's gonna get him killed."

"Has he tried to talk to John Lee?"

"Many times. Jeff called John out last year. Said they could settle it this way without anybody gettin' kilt. Took off his gunbelt and called him out in the street in Crossing for a fight. Stand-up, bare-knuckle, kick and gouge. John wouldn't do it and he lost a lot of face that day. Lots of snickerin' went on and still goin' on behind his back."

"Is he insane?" Sam asked.

"No. I don't think so. I think he's just a low-down and mean-spirited man. Hell, boys, this ain't nothin' new on John Lee's part. He's always been thisaway to a degree. He's just got worser over the years is all."

"I notice that no one rides alone," Matt said.

"Boss's orders. Good orders. Couple of hands have been bushwhacked. One was roped and drug, busted him up bad. The whole shebang ain't but days from comin' to a head. I 'spect since John's hired all them gunslicks it'll pop anytime now."

"Is that the reason Jeff sent his son for supplies? For food and ammo?"

"Yep. The only other rancher standin' up to John sent his boy with young Gene. Ed Carson owns the Flyin' V. His property butts agin the Circle S on the east side. He's down to three hands. They're good boys, but they ain't gunhawks. Just damned good punchers."

They pushed the cattle onto new graze and left them, then rode for the ranch, reaching home just as the shadows began to lengthen in purple hues.

"You boys come to supper at the house tonight," Jeff told the brothers. "Gene's back and I want you to meet him and Ed Carson and family. It's a once a month doin' for the ladies. Life's hard on the women out here. See you shortly."

Both Matt and Sam took good-natured kidding from the other hands about the Sparks girls batting their eyes at them and swishing their skirts around. If there was any animosity about Sam's being half Cheyenne, the brothers had not felt it. And that was probably because Sam did not look like an Indian.

Sam's eyes were black, but without the cold obsidian look of a full blood. He had the high cheekbones of an Indian, but they were softened by some of his mother's features. Sam was just a handsome man by anybody's standards.

The brothers bathed and shaved and slicked up well by frontier standards. They blackened their boots and dabbed some sweet-smelling cologne on their faces.

"You boys cast your peepers on Cindy Carson," Red told them. "We'll tell you now that she's sweet on Nick Lee. And we think she's feedin' him information about her daddy's spread and to Circle S. Don't say nothin' to her that you don't want repeated."

"Does her father know this?" Sam asked.

"No," Dodge told him. "She's the apple of her daddy's eye, that girl is. She can do nothin' wrong. And Jeff don't be-lieve it, neither. We've all seen where she meets that little punk; tracks don't lie. She's got herself a paint pony that can damn near fly. She holds the reins in her right hand; she's left-handed. You're a tracker, Matt, you know that causes the pony to throw its gait peculiar. We've all trailed her to their meetin' place over near a grove of cottonwoods by a crick. And they don't hold hands and look tenderlike into each other's eyes, neither. They get right down to business like married folks with the lamp out. Disgustin'."

"She's a no-count whoor is what she is," Tate said. "Sellin' her daddy out. She ought to have a buggy whip taken to her backside."

As the brothers walked toward the big house, Sam said, "This Cindy throws a kink into matters."

"Sure does. Business plans are sure to come up at the table, and if the boys are right in their thinking, she's sure to report what is said to Nick."

"Want to see if we can't cut her trail in the morning?"

"You're reading my mind, brother."

Ed and Nettie Carson were good people trying to live decently in the face of hard times. Their son, Noah, was a good-natured young man with a fast grin and a sense of humor. He and Gene Sparks shared a lot in common. Cindy was quite another story. She was a pretty but pouty thing with too much rouge on her cheeks and a smart-aleck mouth. Neither Matt nor Sam trusted her any farther than line of sight.

"I never sat down at the table with no Injun before," Cindy said, glaring at Sam.

"I shall endeavor to master the complicated art of eating with knife and fork, miss," Sam said. "However, don't be alarmed if my savage heritage soon overcomes genteel manners and I begin to eat with my fingers."

Gene and Noah busted out laughing.

Cindy glared hatred at Sam.

No points gained there, Matt thought.

"So you're the famous gunfighter," Cindy said, directing

her venom toward Matt. "You'd better watch your step around these parts. There are men around here who'll take those guns away from you and feed them to you."

"Cindy!" her mother said, giving her a look that should have shut the brat's mouth immediately.

It didn't. But before she could spew any more poison, Matt said, "There are men who have tried that," as he spooned mashed potatoes on his plate and covered them with chicken gravy. "I'm still here and they're cold in the ground. Now why don't we move the subject to something more appropriate for the dinner table?"

"I agree," Nettie said, looking at her daughter. "Cindy, tuck your napkin in your bodice and fill your mouth with food!"

Noah grinned and winked at Matt.

"What's the word down at Pecos?" Jeff asked the boys.

"Saw half a dozen hardcases head out, riding this way," Noah told the man. "Saloon man said one of them was Hart, that Oklahoma gunslinger."

"Then Kingman won't be far behind," Matt said. "They're buddies."

"You know them?" Ed asked.

"I put lead in Kingman a few years back while I was scouting for the Army." He was very aware of how attentive Cindy had become. "Hart backed down. Both of them despise me. Did the bartender know any of the others?"

Noah shook his head. "No. But he said he'd heard that Dan Ringold was comin' in."

"That's bad news," Sam said.

"You know him?" Jeff asked.

"We both do. He's poison mean and a back-shooter. Uses a .44-.40 and is a crack shot."

"That's a pretty dress you have on," Lia said to Cindy, in an attempt to change the subject.

"It's old," the girl pouted. "I wanted a new one. Maybe I can have one for the dance."

"What dance?" her father asked.

"The shindig John Lee is throwing at Crossing," Gene said. "We heard about it all the way down to Pecos."

"We sure won't be going to that," Ed said quietly but very firmly. "Besides, I doubt that John Lee will offer any of us invitations."

"I don't ever get to go anywhere!" Cindy shouted, her face turning red. She threw down her fork, splattered mashed potatoes on the table, shoved back her chair, and stomped out of the room, swishing her butt like a hurdy-gurdy girl.

"I apologize for her behavior," Nettie said. "It's very lonely for her out here."

"Why don't you send her to a finishing school back East?" Sam suggested.

"You know," Ed said, laying down his eating utensils. "That's the odd thing. We were going to do that. Had it all arranged. Then she refused to go. I swear, I don't know what's come over this younger generation. I think they're goin' to wrack and ruin."

"You think I should go talk to her?" Lia asked her mother.

"No!" Ed said, before the mother could reply. "She'd probably give you a cussin'. That girl's gettin' a bad mouth on her. Pass some of them beans, please."

Red came into the dining area, hat in hand. "Boss, that girl's done throwed a saddle on a horse and tooken out. Hiked her dress plumb up to her—" He cleared his throat. "Anyways, she's gone."

Ed waved a hand. "Don't let it worry you, Red. She's gone back to the ranch, cuttin' cross-country. I just hope there ain't no renegade Comanches roamin' around this night."

"They wouldn't catch her," Red said, a mournful expression on his face. "She throwed that saddle on Lightning."

"That bitch took my horse!" Lia squalled, jumping up from the table.

"Lia!" her mother said, fanning herself vigorously with her napkin.

"You watch your mouth, young lady!" her father told her.

"What'd she call our girl, Mother?" Ed asked, looking a bit confused.

Lia didn't pay any of them the slightest bit of attention. She turned to face Red, preparing to let him have ol' Nick for letting Cindy take Lightning. But Red had seen it coming and had hit the air.

"We'll just take our plates and sit out on the porch," Matt said, both he and Sam rising—quickly—and grabbing another couple of pieces of chicken.

"Did she call our girl a bitch, Mother?" Ed said.

Jeff waved Sam and Matt out of the bunkhouse early the next morning. "Lightning didn't come home last night. Lia loves that damn horse more'un she does me, I think. She and Lisa are having horses saddled up now to go searchin'. You two go with them." He grinned. "How was your supper last night?"

"Excellent," Sam said. "Once we got out on the porch."

Jeff walked away chuckling.

The brothers were sitting their saddles when the girls came out. They knew then what those split skirts were for. Riding astride.

"Lord have mercy," Matt said.

It didn't bother Sam at all. Indian women always rode astride. But his mother never did. She always rode on a sidesaddle.

"We don't need nursemaids!" Lia fired the first salvo. The brothers could tell she was in a dandy mood.

"Your daddy told us to come along, so we're coming along," Matt told her.

"Well, you better tell the cook to fix you something to eat in case we have to noon. We only brought enough for the two of us."

"We did," Sam said.

"Well, aren't you the smart one?" Lisa said, swinging into the saddle. "Let's ride!"

The girls were gone in a cloud of dust.

"We'll just poke along behind," Matt said. "Their horses can't take much of that. They're just showing off for our benefit."

The brothers fell in behind the girls, riding at an easy canter, keeping them in sight but staying far back until the girls stopped their showing off and gave their horses a chance to blow. It didn't take long. The girls reined up at the crest of a long-swelling hill.

The day was one of those Texas days, the sky so blue it hurt your eyes and the visibility so fine you'd think you could see for a thousand miles.

"It's a good two-hour buggy ride from ranch to ranch," Lia said. "But we'll cut that in half going cross-country."

"Ever see any hostiles out here?" Sam asked innocently.

"You mean Indians on the warpath?" Lisa said.

"Yes."

"Not in about a year. There are a few renegade Comanches left and some Apaches, but the 'Paches usually stay well south of here. They still have some trouble along the border, but up here we've been lucky—so far," she knew to add. She looked at Sam, questions in her eyes. "You would kill an Indian?"

"Hell, yes!" The question startled him. "Would and have. Color has nothing to do with staying alive. My father, Lisa, banished me from the tribe, declaring me forever to be a white man. He knew that for me to get anywhere, as far as having any kind of future, I would have to adopt the white man's ways. I'm not saying he was right, or that I agreed with it, but I did it out of respect for my father."

"Riders coming," Matt said, shielding his eyes against the glare of the sun. "About a half a dozen of them."

"It's a cinch they aren't our hands or any of the boys from the Flyin' V," Lia said.

"They're Broken Lance riders," Lia said, standing up in the stirrups and squinting her eyes against the sun. "And they're on Circle S land."

"Blackie, Val, and Childress," Sam said. "Those are hired guns with them."

"Things are about to get real interesting," Matt said, slipping the hammer thongs from his .44's.

Both Lia and Lisa shucked rifles from saddle boots and levered in a round. Lia said, "My sister and me stood beside our parents since we were old enough to handle a rifle and fought Apaches, Comanches, and outlaws when they attacked the ranch. I'll be damned if we'll back down from a bunch of scum workin' for John Lee."

Sam smiled. "About to get very interesting, I should say."

Chapter 4

Bam Ford was one of the hired guns. Neither Matt nor Sam knew the other gunslicks. All told there were six Broken Lance riders: three punchers and three gunhawks. And none of the six liked those Winchester rifles in the hands of the girls—especially since they were pointed at their bellies, the hammers back.

"We was just cuttin' across your range, missy," Blackie said.

"This range is posted and has been for years. Can't you read?" Lia challenged.

"You need to have your butt jerked outta that saddle and spanked," a gunslick told her. "You got a smart mouth and a real bad attitude."

Lia shot him. She gave no warning, did not change expression, and did not flinch when she pulled the trigger.

The slug hit the hired gun in the shoulder and knocked him slap out of the saddle.

Matt and Sam had cleared leather before the gunhawk left the saddle. Bam Ford had a very sorrowful expression on his face as he looked down the muzzles of two rifles and two six-shooters. He and the others had been caught flat-footed and knew it.

Bam said, "He spoke for hisself, missy. I ain't never abused no woman in my life, nor talked ugly to one." Which was probably true. Bam was a hired gun, but like most Western men, had a deep respect for women . . . especially one who was as quick on the trigger as this young hellion.

"Fine," Lia told him. "I'm glad to hear it. Now get that thug back in his saddle and get off the Circle S range."

"John Lee will not like this one bit," Blackie said.

Lia proceeded to tell Blackie where John Lee could put his opinions, his gunhands, his ranch, and his horse. It would have been a very tight fit, unpleasant for the horse, and extremely uncomfortable for John.

Bam's mouth dropped open at her language. Blackie's eyes widened in disbelief. The other punchers and gunhands sat in their saddles and stared and listened in awe. This little lady knew all the right words and got them in proper order.

When Lia wound down, Bam said, "Missy, you ought to be ashamed of yourself."

She levered another round into her carbine.

"Whoa!" Bam said. "We're gone!"

And they got gone, the shoulder-shot gunhand holding onto the saddle horn and hollering in pain.

Matt looked over at the strawberry blonde. "You'll do," he said, paying her one of the highest compliments that could be offered on the frontier.

She smiled at him.

Matt blushed.

Lisa giggled and batted her eyes at Sam.

"Oh, my word!" Sam said.

"Figured you'd be over today," Ed said to Lia. "Lightning's all right. He's in the barn. Nettie put Cindy to bed. She come down with the vapors or something. Probably caught it from the night air. She's been vomitin' in the mornin's."

The girls exchanged glances. Matt and Sam just stood there looking stupid and wondering what was going on.

It was obvious that Ed was still miffed about his daughter being called names by Lia. He did not invite them in nor did Mrs. Carson make an appearance.

Standing outside the barn, the girls told Noah what had happened on their range that morning.

"So it's started," Noah mused. "Hell, it's time, I reckon. Lia, you know John will strike back. He's got to do it or lose face."

"You better warn your dad, then. He's not very happy with me as it is."

"All you did was call her what she is," Cindy's brother said. "She sure has been actin' funny for the past month."

"How long has she been throwing up in the mornings?" Lisa asked.

"Several weeks. Every morning. Mama looks real worried about it and pa don't seem to know what's goin' on." He shrugged his shoulders. "Neither do I."

"Sounds like to me she might be pregnant." Lia dropped it bluntly on him.

Noah jerked his hat off his head and threw it on the ground and cussed. When he wound down, out of breath, he said, "Boy, that's all we need. That'll really put the icing on the cake, light the candles, and blow them out."

"It's just a guess," Lisa said.

"But probably a good one. Mama will take to bed and Daddy will get a gun and go lookin' for Nick, sure as the world, he'll do that."

"That's crazy!" Lia told him. "It takes two, Noah. It can't be done alone, you know. Or maybe you don't."

Noah blushed a deep crimson, starting at his neck and traveling all the way to his forehead. He grinned and shuffled his boots in the dirt.

"That's all right, Noah," Lia told him. "That just means you're a good boy and you've stayed away from the shady ladies at drive's end."

"I reckon," the young man said. "I'll go fetch Lightning for you."

On the way back, Matt said, "You girls had best talk to your mother about Cindy's . . . ah . . . suspected condition. Maybe she can get through to your dad about how serious this thing is."

"I shouldn't have shot that gunfighter this morning," Lia said. "I may have gotten us all killed. But no man talks to me like that. Especially some low-down hired gun who's out to destroy everything my family has worked for."

"I think you did just fine," Matt told her.

"It might just make John Lee step back and think about what he's doing," Sam said. "Or," he added, "he might decide to attack the ranch tonight."

"You're just a real bundle of joy, aren't you?" Lisa asked.

Sam smiled. "I wouldn't use that term around Cindy if I were you."

Jeff was shocked when Lia and Lisa told him what had happened on the range, and he was speechless for a few minutes after they told him—at their mother's urgings—that it was a good chance his best friend's daughter was pregnant by the son of the man who had vowed to destroy both ranches.

"Ed'll kill that snot-nosed smart aleck," Jeff finally said.

"Or get killed," his son told him. "Nick's fast, Dad. Real fast. And he likes to use those guns."

"Who knows about this?" the father asked.

Lia said, "Me, Lisa, Matt and Sam, Noah, and now Dodge." The foreman was in the living room with Matt and Sam. "But it'll get out, Papa. You know that. Tomorrow, next week, next month. She's gonna start pokin' out any time."

Jeff grimaced at his daughter's language. None of the

others dared tell him what she had suggested that John Lee do with ranch, opinions, gunhands, and horse.

"I have a suggestion," Sam said.

"I'm sure open for one," Jeff looked at him.

"We can't bunch the cows close in; it probably takes fifteen acres of graze for one steer in this part of the country. Let Matt and me ride for hands. If you're willing to pay fighting wages."

"Gunhands, Sam?"

"No, sir. Just punchers who are willing to ride and fight for top wages."

"We need ten, but eight will do it," Matt said. "I know you're paying the hands that are left top wages, so they'll be no hard feelings there."

"Where will you go?"

"East. Dodge says there's little settlements all along the stage road east of Pecos. If you decide to do it, we'll leave first thing in the morning. We'll have to have some cash up front so the punchers will know we mean business."

Jeff sighed heavily and pushed up from his chair. He went into his study and came back with a small leather sack filled with greenbacks and gold coins. He tossed it to Matt. "Don't whitewash nothin', boys. Level with these men. Tell them there's a damn good chance they'll be buried right here on Circle S range."

"We'll leave before first light," Sam said.

"I'll have Conchita fix you a bait of food," Lisa said. "We'll have breakfast ready for you at four."

Jeff turned to Dodge. "Have the boys stay on our range, Dodge. Ride in pairs and have plenty of .44's and .45's. Tell them to put an extra six-shooter in their saddlebags, loaded up full. You and me, ol' hoss, we've seen range wars in our time. I don't think any of them have. Not like the bloody one that's about to erupt around these parts. I want every barrel filled with water and situated around the buildings in case John tries to burn us out. Get to it."

Matt and Sam left their own mounts stabled and chose two horses out of Jeff's herd. They were animals bred in and for this part of the country. They were gone long before first light.

They crossed the Pecos and headed south by southeast, moving across country. By midafternoon they swung down from the saddles at a small settlement many miles from the home range of John Lee. They walked into the saloon part of the big general store and ordered beer.

"You boys look like you been hard-travelin'," the barkeep remarked.

Matt drank half his beer before replying. "Yeah, you're right. We're looking for punchers with a good sand bottom who aren't afraid of a fight if it comes to that. And we're payin' top dollar."

A chair was pushed back within the shadows of the room and jingling spurs approached the bar. Matt turned around. A cowboy who looked to be in his late forties or early fifties was staring at him.

"Name's Barlow," the cowboy said. "I drifted up this way from down on the Rio Grande. Ranched down there for ten years. Fought Apaches, Comanches, and outlaws. Damn drought finally done me in where nothin' else could. Who you boys ride for?"

"The Circle S. Up on the Pecos northwest of here. Range war shaping up there."

"Is that right? Tell me more."

"Want a beer?"

"I'd drink one. Let's sit over yonder."

The conversation was short and blunt. Matt and Sam pulled no punches.

"This John Lee shapes up like a rattler that needs stompin' on. But then, I ain't heard but one side of the story."

"I'm not known for telling lies. My name's Bodine. Matt Bodine."

"Heard of you. I ain't no fast gun."

"We're not looking for fast guns. Just punchers."

Barlow sat for a moment, then drained his mug. He looked at Sam. "You got Injun blood in you?"

"I'm half Cheyenne. That make a difference to you?"

"Not unless you try to lift my hair some night. Then I might get hostile." He smiled. "If we leave now we can make a little no-name town east of here by evenin'. I know an ol' boy over there name of Gilley. He can ride anything with hair on it, he's good with a rope, there ain't no back-up in him, and he's a fair hand with a gun."

"You got a horse?"

"I damn shore didn't walk up here!"

They made the settlement just at dusk and stabled their tired horses. The three of them arranged with the hostler to sleep in the loft and then went to the saloon for a drink before eating supper at the small café in the settlement.

"Lookin' for a cowboy name of Gilley," Barlow told the saloon keeper.

"He's around. Tryin' to find work. I think he's choppin' wood for his supper."

"Got a swamper you can send to fetch him?" Matt asked, placing a coin on the bar.

"You bet."

Gilley was in his late thirties. His boots were patched and run down at the heels, and his clothes were old, but he carried himself proudly and wore his six-shooter like a man who knew how to use it. And more importantly, would use it.

After the introductions, Barlow said, "Hard times befall you, Gilley?"

"You might say that. Man I was ridin' for lost it all and I ain't found steady work since. You hirin' your gun out, Barlow?"

"I ain't no gunslick; you know that. Man up north and west of here got range trouble. He's payin' top dollar for men who won't back up. You interested?"

"Only if you feed me first," Gilley said with a grin. "I ain't et since yesterday."

The four of them pulled out the next morning. They rode nearly forty miles before finding a small five-building town with a saloon.

They had a beer and a cold roast beef sandwich while they were looking around the saloon.

"I'm looking for punchers," Matt said, and the room fell silent. "Men who don't look under the bunk every night for ghosts and who don't have to be nursemaided. Is there anybody like that here who wants to earn top dollar—fighting wages?"

"Feller was in here about six weeks ago, sayin' the same thing," a cowboy said. "I didn't like him a-tall. His name was Lee. John Lee, I think it was."

"I ride for the brand John Lee is trying to put out of business," Matt told him. "John Lee's hired him about fifteen top guns and looking for more. If you sign on, it's for the duration, and you best notify your next of kin."

"You talk mighty tough, mister. You got a name?"

"Matt Bodine. This is my blood brother, Sam Two Wolves. You got anymore questions?"

The man stood up and his buddy rose with him. "My name's Compton and this here is my pal, Tony. I'm with any man who stands up to that damn arrogant John Lee. Are we gonna stand around here all day or ride?"

Six men rode out of the town, looking for about six more. Anyone looking at the riders knew at first glance they were men with a mission. Before leaving town, Matt had spent some of Jeff's money outfitting the new hands. Every loop was filled on their gunbelts, the brass twinkling in the hot Texas sun. Their saddlebags were filled with supplies and clothing and other possibles. They rode abreast, unless meeting a wagon, a stage, or other riders.

They cut south, heading for a settlement that Compton

knew about, where a friend of his was working as a smithy's helper, and hating every minute of it.

As soon as the men reined up, the blacksmith knew he'd lost a helper.

"You got a horse, Beavers?" Compton said, swinging down from the saddle and shaking hands with the young man with the easy grin.

"That's about all I got, Compton. Had to sell my saddle. What's goin' on?"

"Mind if he takes a break?" Matt asked the smithy.

"Wouldn't do no good if I did, would it? Take off, Beavers."

Beavers drank a beer and listened. When Matt finished, the young man nodded his head. "You stake me for a saddle, Mr. Bodine?"

Matt tossed money on the table. "We ride in an hour."

Then there were seven. They continued south. Tony thought he knew of two men working on a ranch down near the beginning of the Middle Concho. If they were still there, they'd ride in a heartbeat.

"I wouldn't appreciate anyone else comin' here and takin' my boys," the rancher said to Matt. "But I've heard tell of John Lee. Man's swingin' a mighty big loop and from what I hear, he needs his comeuppance. You boys get done up yonder, come on back. Your jobs is a-waitin'."

Taylor and Cloud joined the group. Cloud said he knew of a man who just got out of jail for whippin' a man who had beat a plow horse to death. Horse was so tired it just couldn't work no more. His buddy just didn't like to see an animal mistreated and he beat the crap out of the farmer.

"I like him already," Sam said.

His name was Denver and they found him after two days of searching. He was camped by a little crick looking sadly at the holes in his last pair of socks.

"If you ain't the most pitiful sight I ever seen," Cloud

said. "I oughta just shoot you and put you out of your misery."

"Feed me first," Denver said. "My belt buckle is rubbing agin my backbone."

Sam gave him a fresh pair of socks and Denver saddled up. The group began angling west and slightly north. At a campsite near a small copse of trees, Matt reined up and started laughing. The two men looked up and grinned at him.

"Matt Bodine!" one hollered. "Light and sit. We would offer you some coffee, but we ain't got airy."

"We've got plenty of coffee and food, Chookie. Let's make camp here, boys. We've found the hands we need."

Over hot food and hotter and stronger coffee, Matt laid it out for Chookie and Parnell, two men who had worked for his dad a few years back up in Montana.

"We seen Tanner and Peck the other week," Chookie said. "They was makin' their brags about goin' to work for some big shot rancher name of Lee. Drawin' top wages."

"They said they was meetin' up with Roberts, Windlow, and Dusty Jordan," Parnell added. "That's a whole slop-jar full of top guns."

"You boys in with us?" Matt asked.

The punchers grinned. "Just try to keep us away!" Chookie said.

Chapter 5

The men headed back for Circle S range. Matt had noticed that the remuda of the Circle S was not up to snuff, so he stopped along the way and bought a dozen horses from two different ranchers. The horses he bought would not win any beauty contests. They were tough working horses, trained to work cattle.

Exactly one week after the brothers had pulled out, they rode into the ranch yard of the Circle S. Someone had spotted the dust long before the riders reached the ranch, and everyone was out, waiting for them.

They were a rough-looking bunch, and that included Matt and Sam. Their clothing was caked with dust and stiff from days of sweat; they had not shaved in a week.

"Barlow," Dodge said. "Ain't seen you in a spell."

"'Bout ten years, Dodge. You ramrodding this outfit?"

"That I am."

"Good workin' with you again."

"The same. Matt and Sam lay it on the line for you boys?" He watched the riders nod their heads in understanding. "Fine. This here," he pointed, "is the boss and his lady. Jeff Sparks and his missus. These are his younguns. This fine lookin' boy here is Gene Sparks, and them two gals yonder is Lia and Lisa Sparks. The cook is Conchita. Don't make her mad or we'll all be gnawin' on armadiller. Which ain't that bad, by the way. Boss?"

Jeff stepped up. "I'm grateful to you men. More than I can say. With you here, we all stand a fightin' chance of pulling this thing off. And I won't forget you. Now, you boys go clean up and tonight we'll have us a little yard party and roast a beeve." That was met with cheers. "Tomorrow, the work begins."

The bunkhouse had been built to house twenty-five or more men—that many usually was needed at roundup and branding—so it was no problem getting settled in. Many of the new hands were either familiar with the names of the regulars or knew them outright, so an easy camaraderie was quickly arranged.

Matt and Sam and those who just rode in took turns in the wooden tubs out back of the bunkhouse, with fresh water being added often. After Matt bathed and shaved and put on clean clothes, he walked up to the main house.

Lia showed him to the study. Jeff pointed to a chair and Matt sat. Lia left the room, closing the door behind her.

"I don't guess the news of Cindy's, ah, condition has reached her father yet. Least there hasn't been any killin's that I'm aware of."

"How'd the dance go?"

Jeff looked confused.

"The dance that Cindy talked about over supper."

"Oh! I don't know; hadn't heard anymore about it. I hope he called it off."

"Might be kind of fun going."

Jeff noticed the devil-may-care twinkle in Matt's eyes. "Pull in your horns, boy. They'll be plenty of action for everybody soon enough. How much of my money did you spend?"

Matt tossed the leather sack on the desk. "Maybe a third of it. I outfitted some of the boys and advanced them some coins to rattle in their pockets. I've got it written down in my tally book. We're gonna need a lot of supplies for this crew, and if it's all right with you, why not take several wagons into the settlement and get it all done at one shack before John Lee hears about the new hands."

"Good idea. I'll send Red over to Carson's place and ask if he wants to send a wagon with us. Gene and Noah can drive two of the wagons. Will you and Sam go with them?"

"Sure. What's been the reaction from John Lee over the gunhand that Lia shot?"

"None, so far. But from what the boys hear, the gunslick is out of action for a long time. That .44 slug did some terrible damage."

"When do you want us to leave for the settlement?"

"I'll send Red over to the Flyin' V first thing in the morning. Probably pull out the next day." He smiled. "But for tonight, let's relax and have a good time."

But cowboys being what they are, the new hands did not lounge around that afternoon. They roped fresh mounts from the corral and rode out onto Circle S range, getting some feel of the land. The holdings of Jeff were so vast it would take them days to ride over all of the range, but they checked out what they could that afternoon and were back in time to knock the dust from their clothes and enjoy the party.

With so many hands to feed, Mrs. Sparks and Lia and Lisa pitched in to help Conchita, while Jeff manned the steer over the cook pit, turning it often on the spit to insure even cooking. The party went off without a hitch, with everybody having a good time and everybody eating too much. Loud rumblings in the bunkhouse that night awakened the punchers often, with many rude comments made about the gastronomical escapings of certain people.

Breakfast was served and over with before dawn. Dodge stepped into the bunkhouse carrying a sack and the place fell silent.

"No ridin' alone," the foreman ordered. "Everybody works

in pairs. Make sure your rifle is loaded up full, as well as your short guns." He placed the sack on a scarred and uneven old table. "Sack's full of boxes of .44's and .45's. Everybody put a box in your saddlebags. Red, you and Jimmy ride over to the Flyin' V this morning and see if Carson wants to send a wagon to the settlement to fetch supplies. Take off. The rest of you listen up."

The gist of it was a roundup. While Matt and Sam had been gone, Jeff had received a reply to a letter he'd sent some weeks before. It was from an Army procurement agent agreeing to buy cattle from both Sparks and Carson. The army was sending in drovers to take the cattle to railhead. If they were heading west, it would be Dodge City. If the cattle were due to head east, they would be driven to Fort Worth.

All knew that the drovers would be left alone by John Lee and his hired thugs. He swung a big loop, but he also had sense enough to leave the Army alone. But the move would be sure to anger the man, for he would know that now Jeff and Ed would have plenty of cash money to operate.

"Just as soon as the Army's drovers have left," Sam said. "John Lee will strike."

"That's my thinking, too," Matt agreed. "He'll either do a first strike—an all-out attack against the ranch—or he'll start picking us off one at a time."

"He'll hit Ed Carson first," Sam said. "The smaller number of men to fight."

"Not if his son knows his girlfriend is with child. Not unless he's crazy. He won't want her harmed." Matt was thoughtful for a moment. "Or perhaps he would, to hide his guilt. Think about that."

"It would take a low-down man to do something like that."

"Let's talk it over with Jeff."

* * *

The rancher sighed heavily. Drummed his gloved finger-tips on his saddlehorn. Shook his head. "You boys sure like to bring me problems," he finally spoke. "But you're right. Nick is crazy enough to do something like you suggest. He don't love the girl. Never has. He's said it often enough when drinkin'. She's just an . . . object to him. Terrible thing to say, but it's true. But look here, if I tell her father what we all suspect, he'll go crazy. Killin' crazy. You boys don't know him the way I do. Ed's tough. He planted some of them god-damn Northern reconstructionists who come in hereafter the war, blowin' off at the mouth about what they was goin' to do."

"It's your decision, Jeff," Matt said. "I suppose this puts you in one of those damned if you do and damned if you don't positions."

The rancher nodded his head. "I'll think on it. Red's back. Ed will send Noah with a wagon for supplies. You boys be ready to pull out early in the morning and be prepared for trouble in Crossing."

The Circle S was sending three wagons, the Flying V two wagons. Gene, Red, and Matt would each drive a wagon, with Sam on horseback, scouting, and Noah and Sonny would drive the Flying V wagons. The Circle S crew breakfasted at Carson's place, arriving just after dawn. Neither Cindy nor her mother made an appearance. As soon as the men had emptied the big pot of coffee and shoved in the last of the beef and potatoes, they were on the road. They expected to be gone the better part of two days. A day down and then load up and catch some sleep, then a day back with the heavily loaded wagons.

The trip down was boring. But as soon as they pulled into the settlement, all knew boredom was over. Half a dozen Broken Lance horses were tied up at the hitchrail in front of the saloon. And several more horses wearing the brand were tied across the street.

They pulled the wagons around back of the huge general store and grouped up.

"We're not here to start trouble," Matt told the men. "But if it comes, be ready for it. And it will probably come."

"I'd like a beer to cut the dust," Red said.

"Sounds good to me," Matt replied. "After we get the supplies loaded."

Red grinned. "I had a hunch you'd say that."

"I don't want no trouble in my store, mister," were the first words out of the shopkeeper's mouth as soon as Matt walked in the door, followed by Noah and Gene. He was speaking to Matt but his eyes were on Noah and Gene.

"There won't be any problems," Matt told him, laying several sheets of paper on the counter. "Just fill that order." He had noticed two men lounging at the rear of the store, and they weren't there to play checkers and gossip. Their tied-down guns and smirky faces gave them away.

"That's the problem, mister," the shopkeeper said. "I can't fill that order."

"Why not?" Matt looked around. The shelves were filled with everything imaginable: bolts of cloth to boots; canned goods to corsets; ammunition to hernia aids; nostrums to cure everything from hangnails to flat feet and medicines for various ladies' woes. "You seem to have everything we need." Matt casually pulled an axe handle out of a half barrel as if inspecting it.

"Hey, you!" one of the gunslingers said, walking up to him. "Are you deaf? Carry your damn business elsewhere."

"Why should I?" Matt asked.

The gunny grinned at him. He had bad teeth. Matt had a hunch he was going to make them worse in a few seconds—or make them better, depending on one's point of view. " 'Cause I said so, cowboy. Now rattle your hocks on outta here, before I take them guns of yourn and feed 'em to you." His buddy moved in closer.

Matt hit him with the axe handle. Right in the teeth just as hard as he could swing the wood. The gunhand was stone cold out before he hit the floor.

His buddy was jerking iron when Matt drove one end of the axe handle into his belly. The air came whooshing out as he doubled over, and Matt conked him on the noggin with the business end of the wood. The gunslinger kissed the floor.

"Load up the supplies, boys," Matt said, just as Sam and the others came in through the back door to see what the holdup was.

"Tsk tsk," Sam said. "I can't leave you alone for a moment without you getting into mischief."

"Take their guns," Matt told Red. "We can always use spare six-shooters."

"Oh, Lordy," the shopkeeper moaned. "Man, don't you know who them two is? That's Terry Perkins and Jay Hunt. They work for Mr. Lee. Them's real bad men, mister. I bet they kilt a hundred men between them."

"I'm impressed," Matt told him. "You best be keeping a tally of what we're taking instead of running your mouth."

That snapped the man out of it. He began frantically writing down what the boys grabbed up.

Matt cut himself a wedge of cheese and got a handful of crackers. He kept the axe handle close by and his eyes on the front door. It paid off. Just as he was finishing his snack, a man stepped out of the saloon and began walking across the street.

"Drag these two out back," Matt said to Noah and Gene. He turned to the shopkeeper. "Where's all your customers?"

"These gunhands run 'em off. Told 'em not to come back 'til they was gone."

"When'd the gunhawks get into town?"

"This mornin'. They knew you boys was comin'. I hear 'em talkin' about it."

"That . . . obscenity of a girl!" Sam said. "She tipped off Nick knowing it might get her brother hurt or killed."

"Yeah. She's a real sweetheart." To the shopkeeper: "This one of them coming across the street?"

"Yes. I don't know his name. He threatened me."

"Did he now?" Matt leaned against the counter and waited, his guns loose in leather.

"What the hell!" the gunhand said, stepping into the store. "Where's Terry and Jay?"

"They were tired," Matt said. "I suggested they take a nap. They thought it was a good idea."

"Who the hell are you?" the hard-faced man demanded.

"Matt Bodine."

The gunny drew and Matt shot him in the belly before his Peacemaker could clear leather. He hit the floor moaning, both hands holding his .44-caliber-punctured belly.

The saloon emptied of men, all running for the general store and all with guns in their hands. Matt pulled his other .44, stepped to the door, and emptied both .44's into the knot of gunslicks. When he was through, not a man was left standing, and several weren't moving.

"Are you really Matt Bodine?" the shopkeeper asked. "The Wyoming gunfighter?"

"I'm Matt Bodine," he said, reloading.

"Holy crap!" Gene said, running inside and looking out at the bloody, body-lined street.

Sam looked. "That's my brother," he said. "Subtle is his middle name."

"Shore cut the odds down some," Red remarked.

"Oh, God!" the gun-shot gunny on the floor moaned. "Get me a doctor."

"We ain't got none," the shopkeeper told him. "Had one, but he moved down to Fort Stockton. Sorry, mister. Got a barber with some leeches, though."

"Hell with you," the man groaned.

"Leeches!" Sam looked at the man. "Nobody bleeds people anymore."

"Well, he does!"

"Get the stuff loaded up," Matt said and stepped out into the street, walking over to the men lying moaning and twisting in the dirt.

One pointed a .41 derringer at him. Matt kicked it out of his hand. It went off as it hit the ground and shot a shoulder-wounded gunhand in the leg.

"Goddamn you!" the twice-shot man hollered.

Matt didn't know if the man was cussing him or his buddy. He counted three dead and four wounded, one of them hard hit.

"You played hell, mister," the hard-hit man gasped, looking up at Matt. "I'd be obliged to know the name of the man who done me in."

"Matt Bodine."

"Damn my luck!" the man moaned. "At least it weren't no tinhorn." He closed his eyes and died.

Sam walked across the street to his brother's side. "An ugly day, *I-tat-an-e.*"

"Yes. And this is sure to blow the lid off. But damned if I was going to let them reach the store."

"I would have done the same."

A crowd had gathered around, gawking and whispering.

A portly man shoved his way through the crowd. He was a part-time undertaker, part-time preacher, part-time water-finder, and part-time rainmaker. He was, Matt was told, a fair undertaker, a pretty good preacher, a better-than-average deviner, and a lousy rainmaker.

Little boys and girls peeked around their mothers' skirts, staring at Matt Bodine and Sam Two Wolves.

No one noticed the lone rider walking his horse showly from the east side of the settlement.

"What the hell are we supposed to do with all these wounded men?" a man asked.

"Patch them up or let the hogs have them," Matt said shortly. "I really don't care."

"Pretty tough way of lookin' at it, son," a soft-spoken voice came from behind Matt and Sam.

They both turned. The small man—not more than five feet six or seven and slender built—stood alone, but the guns belted around his waist made him larger than life, and the badge pinned to his vest said it all: Texas Ranger.

"They opened this dance," Matt told him.

"Is that right? I heard the shootin' a mile out of town. Thought I'd see what was happenin'. Who are you?"

"Matt Bodine."

The Ranger nodded his head. "Heard of you. Wyoming gunhand."

"I'm a Wyoming rancher who happens to be blessed—or cursed with the ability to use a short gun."

"Blessed or cursed," the Ranger said. "Interestin' way of puttin' it. I'll have to remember that."

"Help me!" a gunhand shot in both legs hollered.

"Shut up," the Ranger told him. "I'll get to you in due time." He looked at Matt. "I'm Josiah Finch. Texas Rangers. I'm trackin' two murderers. Been after 'em for three weeks. I ain't particular interested in your doin's, but it's a rare thing to see one man standin' and six or seven on the ground, some of them gettin' stiff."

"I'll tell you what happened, Ranger!" a citizen yelled.

"I don't want to know what happened," Finch told him. "You tell me and then I'll have to spend hours writin' out a damn report. 'Sides, I ain't seen no complaints in anybody's hand."

"No complaints on this side of the issue," Sam said.

Finch cut his hard eyes to him. "I reckon you'd be Sam Two Wolves."

"That is correct."

"Heard of you, too. Your daddy was a Cheyenne chief name of Medicine Horse; educated fine back East."

"That's right."

"I'm bleedin' to death!" a gunslick bellered.

"No, you ain't," Finch told him. "Wound's damn near closed up. Terrible wounds do that. You'll probably die, but it won't be from bleedin' to death."

"Well, the hell with you, too!" the gunhawk told him.

"Get the wagons ready to roll," Matt told Red.

As Red walked away, Finch said, "You come into a town, leave three or four dead a-layin' around, and then just leave like you would a church picnic when the fried chicken run out. I find that interestin'."

"What do you want me to do?" Matt asked. "Squat down here in the street and hold their hands?"

Finch took off his hat, wiped the sweat from his forehead, and chuckled. "I've known a bunch of hard men, son. Sam Bass, Hardin, Baker, Allison—to mention a few. You're a hard man, Matt Bodine. I think we better talk."

"Is that an order?"

"It could be," Finch said softly. "If you push me to it."

"You a drinking man, Ranger?"

"I have been known to tipple now and then."

"Let's find us a quiet table and a cool beer."

"That's the best offer anyone's made me in some time."

The wagons were moved to a shady location just outside of town while Matt and Sam talked with the Ranger.

"Yeah," Finch said, draining his beer mug and wiping his mouth with the back of his hand. "John Lee's name has been mentioned around headquarters more'un once. The governor is gettin' tired of people sayin' there ain't no law west of the Pecos. I'm a-fixin' to change all that."

"By yourself?" Sam asked.

"Yep," the small quiet man said. "Soon as I track down these murderers."

"Finch," Matt said, "John Lee probably has fifty gun-hands on his payroll . . ."

The men looked out the window as Terry Perkins and Jay Hunt rode slowly out of town. Perkins had a bloody rag tied around his mouth and Jay Hunt's hat was sitting his head cockeyed from the big knot put there by an axe handle.

"I guess you done that, too?" Finch questioned.

"Me and an axe handle," Matt said.

Finch sighed and shook his head.

"As I was saying, Lee has a lot of men on his payroll. Some of them snake-mean. How do you propose to bring law and order when you're looking down the barrels of that many guns?"

"You don't shoot a Texas Ranger, son. Makes other Rangers irritable. I know a Ranger tracked a man for five years. Finally found him in a fancy eatin' place in New York City. Whupped him right there in front of God, the mayor, and everybody else. Throwed him on a train and brung him back to Texas. We allowed him a fair trial and then hanged him. Bad business shootin' a Texas Ranger."

Matt then realized all the wild tales he'd heard about the Texas Rangers over the years were more than likely true—or at least had a vein of truth running through them. Matt had a hunch this small, quiet Ranger would track a man through the gates of Hell and if braced would kill you in a heartbeat.

"Jeff Sparks and Ed Carson are good decent men, Finch. If they weren't, neither Sam nor me would have thrown in with them."

"I don't doubt that at all."

"And as you saw today, if lead is to fly, then so be it."

"I shore enough seen that. But you hear this: if the governor has to send in the militia, he's gonna be one irritated man. It's bad enough we had all them goddamn Yankee carpetbaggers and reconstructionists in here; now things are gettin' back to normal and we're beginnin' to run our own lives. The last thing he needs is a range war."

"He's got one," Sam said bluntly.

"I'll be along in about a week," the Ranger said. "I found out where these murderers is hidin' and I'll head there. I hope to take them alive, but I ain't countin' on it. I figure they'll go down smokin'. If that's the case, I won't have to tote them back, and that'll save me some time."

Sam looked at the man closely to see if he was kidding.

He was not. If Finch even had a sense of humor, he kept it well hidden.

"You married, Finch?" Sam asked, interested in this small intense lawman.

"Was. Outlaws killed her back in sixty-six. I'd just come home from the war and we was tryin' to pick up the pieces of our lives. We was just kids when we got married. Took me four years to track those no-goods down. But I done it. Found the last one in a canyon in Idaho. Shot him in the belly and left them there. I hope it took him a long time to die. I don't like outlaws. At all." He pushed back his chair and stood up.

"Have you heard that some learned people are saying that home environment has a great deal to do in the making of a criminal?" Sam asked.

Finch blinked. "Hell's fire! That's the silliest damn thing I ever heard of. I didn't even have shoes when I was a-growin' up and I never stole nothin' nor done a harmful thing to no innocent person in my life."

Josiah Finch walked out of the saloon. The way he walked told anybody with a lick of sense that this was a man to be given a wide berth. Josiah might be small in stature, but he was one hell of a big man.

"That, brother," Matt said, "is one man I would not want on my trail."

"Nor me. You ready to head out?"

"Yeah. We'll camp alongside the road—well off the road. John Lee is liable to go on the warpath after today."

"If we're lucky, he'll wait until Josiah Finch returns. I have a hunch Finch would willingly take on the entire bunch of them and come out on top!"

Chapter 6

"I already heard what happened," Jeff said, meeting the wagons as they came to a stop in front of the house. "John Lee sent a rider over early this morning. His message was short and sweet. He's ordered any Circle S or Flyin' V rider shot on sight if they come into Crossing."

"If I'd a backed down, we wouldn't have any supplies. John Lee's boys were waiting and had already told the shopkeeper not to sell to the Circle S or the Flying V."

"I understand. I'm not blamin' you. It had to come at some point. We'll just stay out of Crossing." He smiled, a grim moving of the lips. "I told the messenger that any Broken Lance riders found on my range will be shot on sight."

"Do you mean it?" Matt asked, after climbing down from the wagon seat.

"Yes, I do. Ever seen a range war, son?"

"Not really."

"They're mean and ugly. And a lot of blood will be spilled on each side. The blood of men and women. I've ordered the girls to stay within sight of the house when they ride. You've seen how this land can fool you. You think you're alone on the range and the next instant fifty riders come out over a swell not three hundred yards away from you."

"Will they pay any attention to you?" Sam asked, a dubious note in his voice.

"Yes. They know how serious this is. Now tell me this: how did the Broken Lance gunslicks know we were going to the settlement for supplies?"

"I imagine Cindy tipped off Nick," Matt said.

"Ed just left here. He thinks the same thing. He got the same message I got this mornin'."

"His reaction?"

"Open the chute and let 'er bump. I 'spect right now Cindy's rear end is on fire. He was talkin' strong about takin' a razor strop to her butt."

"That would be a sight to see," Gene said with a grin. "If anyone deserves it, she does."

"I hate you!" Cindy screamed at her father. "You can't whup me like a damn plow horse!"

Mrs. Carson had left the room in tears.

"Don't you even care that because of you your brother might have been killed?"

"Nick'll kill you for slappin' me around!" she screamed at him.

The father stood dumbfounded, staring at his girl. "Is that what you want, Cindy? Me dead?"

"Yes!" she screamed. "I despise you. I love Nick. I'm carrying his baby."

"I know that." The father spoke with a calmness he did not feel. "I've known it for several weeks. Pack your bags, girl," he told her. "Take the buggy. Leave it in town. I'll pick it up someday. I want you out of this house in one hour. I'll give you money to get you a room at Fanny's. She takes in boarders from time to time. The baby I could live with and love, if that was all there was to it. It would be my grandbaby. Your treachery is something I can't and won't abide. I'll arrange to have money sent to you from time to time—"

"I don't need your goddamn money!" she screamed at him. "Nick will take care of me."

Ed shook his head. "You poor little fool. That punk doesn't care about you. He used you like a whoor. He told ever'body in the damn county about it. I've known it for months. But I never let on to your mama; I didn't know that she knew too. Now listen to me. I'll see that you get proper care and arrange for you to go on to an unwed mother's home. I think there's one in Fort Worth. I—"

She started cussing her father. She cussed him until she was breathless. She sucked in air and started all over again. She was still cussing and screaming when Ed left the room, closing the door behind him.

"Hitch up the buggy for your sister, Noah," he told his son. "She'll be leavin' us." He turned to go into his office to get Cindy some money.

"For how long, Papa?" the young man asked.

"Forever." The man's words were just audible over the sobbing of his wife in the bedroom.

"Boss," Red said, standing in the doorway, hat in hand. "I was over by the road about an hour ago. Cindy Carson come along drivin' a buggy. Eyes all red from cryin'. Buggy was loaded down with trunks and valises."

"Which direction was she headin'?"

"Toward Crossing."

"She's either run away from home or Ed's tossed her out. Thank you, Red."

The puncher nodded and walked back to the bunkhouse to clean up for supper.

Jeff turned to his family. "I'd like to comfort my old friend," he said. "But I don't know what to do or what to say."

"If Cindy thinks Nick is going to welcome her," Lia said, "she's sure in for a rude surprise there."

"I think we're all in for a whole bunch of surprises, girl," father said, his face grim. "None of them are goin' to be much fun."

The drovers hired by the Army showed up early the next morning and that day was a busy one, with no one allowed much time to ponder the fate of Cindy. Jeff put the money from the sale of his cattle into his big safe and breathed a little easier. Now he had some working capital, hands to help fight John Lee—whenever the man made his move—and a thousand less head of cattle to worry about. There was nothing he could do now except wait. And worry and wonder.

John Lee sat behind his desk and smiled at the news. His son sat before him, looking very unhappy.

"I guess you're gonna tell me marryin' her is the honorable thing to do?" Nick finally broke the silence.

"Honor has nothing to do with it," his father said. "But you are going to marry her."

The young man cussed.

"Use your head for a change," John admonished his son. "Think. If something were to happen to the Carson family, you would own the Flying V."

Nick lifted his head, and the eyes of father and son met. Hard eyes, cruel eyes.

John said, "It's a good thing to have a wife and children. Makes a man respectable. After a time you can keep you a woman in town for variety. Just as long as it's a discreet affair. I'll ride in and talk to Cindy. It wouldn't be proper to have her staying out here before the wedding. But the wedding will take place here, of course. We'll invite all the townspeople. They'll come, don't worry. Is Cindy showing yet?"

"Huh?"

John grimaced. "Is her condition noticeable?"

"Oh. Naw."

"Good. I'll have the dressmaker do it up right then. Oh, it'll be a grand affair, son. A grand affair."

"If you say so," Nick said.

John Lee smiled. "I'll be a grandfather. My, my. If it's a boy, he'll be named after me, of course. If it's a girl, we'll name her after your mother. No finer woman ever lived than your mother. Go get my horse saddled, son. And tell the boys we're riding into town. I love parties," he mused. "And I'll make sure this party is one that the townspeople will never forget."

He was right on that count.

"I'd a not believed it," Jeff said, when he heard the news of the upcoming marriage. "John's pulled in the horns of his gunfighters and his son is getting married. Incredible."

Matt and Sam were sitting in the big den of the ranch house with the Sparks family, having coffee. The foreman sat on the lower outer hearth of the cold fireplace.

"Oh, perhaps it's not so incredible," Sam said, after taking a sip of coffee.

"How do you mean?" Jeff asked.

"Should something happen to the Carson family, the Flying V is John's without his having to fire a shot."

The rancher said a very ugly word that caused his wife to give him a dirty look and his girls to giggle. He nodded his head in agreement with Sam. "Of course. You're right. I never thought of that.

"You don't really think John would stoop that low, do you?" his wife asked.

"Oh, Mother!" Lia said.

"Lia's right, Nance. John Lee would do anything to gain

total control of this area." He stopped, looking at Matt, who was sitting with a smile on his face. "What are you grinnin' about, boy?"

"So you heard that everybody in the town of Crossing is invited to the wedding, right, Jeff?" Matt asked.

"That's right."

"And they'll go?"

"Everybody but Al. He's the bartender at the saloon and he hates John Lee. Always has. I think John keeps him on for his amusement."

"The townspeople . . . they'll go because they're afraid of John, or because they like him?"

"Mostly because they're all just like him. Petty, mean little-minded people. Used to be a lot of good folks made up that town. No more. They all left, scattered around from the settlement to Fort Worth. What are you gettin' at?"

"So the town will be deserted, right?"

"Just about. Might be a travelin' drummer at the hotel. But I 'spect the town will just shut down."

"That's interesting. Very interesting."

Sam looked at his brother. The very devil seemed to be popping out of Matt's eyes. "Oh, Lord, Matt! Am I reading you right?"

Matt just grinned.

Ed Carson sat down on his front steps and howled with laughter. It was the first time he'd laughed since he'd banished his daughter from his house and life. Noah sat beside him and laughed until tears ran from his eyes. Mrs. Carson could not contain her laughter and soon they all were laughing.

"It might work," Ed said, wiping his eyes. "By God, we might be able to pull it off."

"It'll be worth the effort just to see the expression on John's face," Noah said.

"I got the boys scouring the area for wagons," Jeff said. "Folks left behind a lot of wagons when they pulled out . . . or were killed," he added. "The boys are patchin' them up. Weddin's next week. We got lots of time to plan this out."

"I love it!" the owner of the Flying V said.

"We'll use those big Missouri mules the farmers sold me," Jeff said, getting more and more into the spirit of the thing. "I never seen nothin' that could pull like those mules."

"To make it even better," Dodge said, "John Lee has declared the whole week before the weddin' peaceful. No trouble as long as we stay out of Crossin'." The foreman started chuckling and the chuckling soon changed into full blown laughter. Between his snorting and bellering, he gasped, "And we'll damn sure stay out of Crossin' 'tween now and the weddin' day!"

That started everybody off again. The usually poker-faced Sam was caught up in it and he was soon chortling and howling. One of Ed's hands rode in and sat his saddle in amazement, looking at the men and women practically screaming with laughter.

"What the hell's goin' on here?" Lee hollered during a break in the merriment.

"We're gonna go steal something, Lee!" Noah yelled.

"Steal something? Steal what?"

Noah told him. Lee's mouth dropped open. He sat his saddle, speechless. When he finally found his voice, he said, "You can't do that! Nobody ever stole a whole damn town!"

While John Lee was all caught up in planning for the wedding and the party afterward, the men and women of the Circle S and the Flying V were making plans of their own, and doing so with all the cunning of generals planning a major offensive.

"Wagons?" Jeff asked.

"Twelve," he was told.

"Mules?"

"Eight. And enough horses to take up the slack."

They had sent Parnell into town, since no one knew he worked for the Circle S—that plus the fact he lost the draw when they drew cards.

"They're shuttin' 'er down for the day and the night," he reported back. The only person who ain't goin' to the shindig is Al, the bartender."

"We'll have a place for Al when the new town is built," Jeff said with a smile. "And won't John be happy about that?"

"I hate to poke holes in all this happy planning," Sam said. "But tell me this: what is to prevent John Lee from building another town?"

"Nothing," the rancher told him. "But he'll have to have the lumber brought in by wagon. From the time he sends in the order, to the time the material actually arrives will be weeks. Maybe months. This range war will be over, one way or the other, long before then."

"But this victory will be ours," Lia said. "And pulled off without firing a shot. That's what makes it so nice."

"They'll be plenty of shots fired after those penny-pinchin' weasels in town come back from the weddin' and find the whole damn town gone!" Jeff said.

"I just hope that when this is reported—if it is reported—that the Rangers don't send in Josiah Finch to investigate it," Sam said.

"There ain't no law out here, Sam," Jeff told him. "The nearest law is a hundred miles away. Report it? I don't think so. John doesn't want Rangers in here. But he'll be plenty mad about it. Killin' mad. Oh, it's a fine plan, and in the long run—if we win—it'll benefit us. But once it's done, the lead is gonna start flyin'."

"So let's have some fun before the real shooting starts," Matt said with a grin, and it was an infectious grin.

The closer the date drew, the more frenzied the work

around the Circle S and the Flying V became. The cowboys were all caught up in it, for once not griping about work they had to do out of a saddle. The wagons and harnesses were checked out; spokes and rims and reins and buckles and collars and hobbles were repaired or replaced. And always somebody was chuckling at just the thought of what they were going to attempt to pull off, and it was no certainty they could do it. They were going to have about twelve hours to take down a town and transport it and all the goods within the buildings.

Cindy's name was not mentioned in the Carson house. As far as Ed was concerned, his daughter no longer existed. Her being with child out of wedlock had nothing to do with it. That she would consort with the enemy was the straw that overloaded the camel. Whatever she had left behind at the house was removed and burned at Ed's orders. Her name was removed from the family Bible. In Ed's mind, Cindy Carson was dead.

Chapter 7

On the night before the wedding, the lamps went out early in the ranches of Sparks and Carson. And everyone went to sleep with a smile on their lips. Cowboys occasionally chuckled in their sleep.

Long before dawn tinted the horizon with day's rebirth, the wagons were rolling slowly toward Crossing. The drivers wanted to be in as close as they dared when the exodus of the townspeople began.

At nine o'clock, the air hot and still, the first buggies and men on horseback began leaving the town. Matt lay on the crest of a low hill, on his belly in the short grass, watching the town through field glasses.

"Get them ready," he told Tate. "It won't be long now."

At nine-thirty, Matt watched as Al the bartender walked through the silent town. He made his loop, returned to the end of the street, and waved a white handkerchief.

"Let's go!" Sam yelled.

Whooping and hollering, the cowboys slapped the reins on the horses' butts and the wagons rolled into Crossing.

"We'll take no one's personal possessions," Jeff ordered. "But I helped build this damn town—put up some of the money to buy the lumber—so I figure at least a part of it belongs to me. Take it down."

It wasn't as difficult as it might have seemed. With a few braces knocked out, several ropes in the right places, and cowboys on horseback with the rope around the saddlehorn, a wall came down. As soon as that was done, teams began dismantling the wall and stacking the lumber in wagons.

"How 'bout the boardwalk?" Gilly asked.

"Take it," Ed ordered.

The sounds of protesting rusty nails being pried up with crowbars filled the air. The first wagons left the town within fifteen minutes, the wagons filled with merchandise from stores. The town was being moved eight miles south, onto Circle S property. With people working frantically, the job did not take nearly as long as some had imagined.

They left behind them a very strange sight: beds and feather ticks and chamber pots, cookstoves and washtubs and dressing tables, dressing screens and parlor lamps and corset chairs, spittoons and foot warmers and mop buckets, all sitting forlornly on the rolling prairie.

The men left the outhouses intact, and that only added to the bizarreness of the sight.

Sometimes when the sides of structures were jerked out, the roof fell in and landed intact. If the building had been small enough, mules were used to simply pull the roof away from the town's rapidly vanishing site to be dismantled later.

By midafternoon, the town of Crossing no longer existed. Eight miles south of the site, hammering and banging and sawing had been going on for hours. All hoped that no stiff wind would suddenly spring up, for the new town, for awhile at least, was going to be flimsily built.

Stocker's General Store and Emporium was changed to Lia's Family Store. Crossing Stable and Livery was changed to Dodge's Barn. Harris's Saddle Shop was now Gene's Leather Goods. Crossing Hotel and Saloon was changed to the Pecos Rooms and Bar. The café was now the Eats. The barber shop was now the Hair Palace (that was Lisa's idea). Matt Bodine was now the new town marshal, elected to the office in the same election that made Jeff Sparks the new mayor.

"What are we going to call it?" Sam asked.

"Name it," Ed said.

"OK. That's good enough," Matt said.

Nameit was about to be born.

"What's good enough?" Sam asked.

"The new name."

"What new name?" Sam yelled.

"Nameit."

"You want the town to be called *Nameit?"*

"Why not?"

"Sounds good to me," Jeff said.

"I'd like to call it Prairie Flower, or something like that," Lisa suggested.

"I ain't bein' the mayor of no damn town called Prairie Flower," her father said.

"Why don't we just stay with Nameit?" Sam said wearily. He walked off muttering, "Prairie Flower?"

Nick and Cindy were united in holy matrimony—more or less, since there was no preacher and John Lee married them after reading a few words from the Good Book. The party got underway. About seven o'clock, he sent riders into town to bring back more whiskey. They returned in a cloud of dust and confusion.

"There ain't no town!" Pen told John.

"I beg your pardon?" John looked up at the man, still sitting his saddle.

"There ain't no town!" Pen repeated.

"Are you drunk?" John yelled, as a crowd began gathering around.

"Hell, no, I ain't drunk! I'm tellin' you what I seen with

my own eyes." He paused. "Or what I didn't see, I reckon would be the way to put it. There ain't no damn town left."

"Towns don't disappear!" the man who used to be the owner of the general store said. "You must have got lost."

"I ain't lost, you igit!" Pen hollered. "Even the dogs is gone."

In the new town of Nameit, hammering and sawing and banging and cussing were still going on. Shelves were being restocked and signs painted. The men and women all knew they were working against time.

". . . The privies is still standin'," Pen said. "Tables and chairs and chamberpots is there. Clothes all over the place, blowin' here and yonder. But there ain't a buildin' left standin' nowheres and dammit I know what I seen."

Sam drew up papers proclaiming the town of Nameit legal and binding—sort of. He dated the paper a year back. "Does anybody here know what the governor's signature looks like?"

"I don't even know if he can write," Ed said.

Sam scrawled the governor's name on the bottom of the page and held it up for all to see. "This town has been in existence for one year, folks."

As tired as they were, they all cheered and applauded.

John Lee looked over what was left of his town. He had a pretty good idea what had happened and where it was. For this to have been done this quickly also told John that Sparks had indeed hired himself a bunch of new hands, and they wouldn't be fresh-faced greenhorns either. They might not be gunslicks, but they would be men who knew what a fight was all about and who would fight and die for the brand.

He also saw the fine hands of Matt Bodine and that damned half-breed brother of his in this work.

John sat his saddle and sighed as he watched the bewildered-acting people who once owned businesses in the now-gone town wander around trying to salvage something—anything. There was damn little to pick up. And no goods at all. Jeff and Ed and the others had not only taken the buildings, they'd also taken all the damn merchandise that had been in them.

"This is flat-out stealin'!" the man who had run the general store hollered.

"Prove it," Bam Ford said quietly. "That is, if you want the law in here."

John glanced at him. "There is that to consider, for a fact."

"Well," Bam said, trying awfully hard not to smile. "It ain't all bad. They did leave the folks a pot to pee in."

John jerked the reins and rode off. He was in no mood for any jokes.

"Man just don't have no sense of humor at all," Bam said to Kingman.

"I don't like you, Bam," Kingman said shortly. "And I don't trust you. You was always a little wishy-washy to my way of thinkin'. I just don't know what side you're on in this fight."

"I'm takin' John Lee's money, Kingman. I made it clear to him from the start that I fight growed-up men. Not women and kids and children's pet animals. I'll leave that up to people like you."

"I oughta kill you right here and now!" Kingman snarled at him.

Bam met him look for look. "Anytime you feel like dyin', Kingman, just make your play."

"The day will come, Bam," Kingman said. "Bet on it." He turned his horse and rode off.

Pen Masters had been listening. He walked his horse over to Bam. "What's the matter, Bam?"

"The same thing that's been gnawin' on you, Pen. I ain't fightin' no women and kids."

"We ain't fought no one yet, Bam."

"John Lee's a ruthless man, Pen. A man used to gettin' his own way, anyway he sees fit. You and me, Pen, we rode out of that mess up in Utah, remember?"

"Yeah. I remember. I need the money, Bam. It's just that simple."

"I need money, too. But I also need sleep at night. I ain't never killed no women or kids and I ain't gonna kill no more cattle or sheep. That made me sick up in Utah. I just ain't a-gonna do it no more."

"Let's stick this out for a few more days, Bam. If it gets to where innocents is gonna get hurt, we'll pull out."

"Deal."

The next morning, John Lee, accompanied by his small army, headed south, following the wagon tracks from what used to be Crossing. Over forty strong, they kicked up a powerful lot of dust as they rode. They reined up at a freshly painted sign nailed to a fence post.

Nameit, Texas—one mile.

"Nameit?" Lopez said, taking off his hat and scratching his head.

Bam and Pen both ducked their heads to hide their smiles.

"Very amusing, I'm sure," John said. He lifted his reins and paused, watching a large group of riders heading their way. They were all carrying Winchesters.

"We got 'em outnumbered two to one," Lightfoot pointed out.

"And he didn't even have to take off his boots to use his toes," Bam said.

Pen laughed and Lightfoot gave them both dirty looks.

"Nobody wins in a fight with this many people, this close up," John said, knowing full well that if a fight started, he'd be the first one dead. "Just stay calm and let's see what they want. But spread out just in case."

As John's men spread out, the riders coming from the

south broke out of their bunch and spread out. It was a sight that caused even the most hardened gunhand to wonder why he didn't pursue some other line of work.

The line of riders stopped about twenty feet from John's army. Jeff and Ed, flanked by Matt and Sam and Gene and Noah, sat their saddles and stared at John Lee. Various hands formed a line behind them.

Nick had been so hungover and sick he'd been unable to ride that morning. Cindy hadn't helped matters by vomiting while Nick lay abed moaning about his head hurting.

"This is a public road, Jeff," John pointed out. "You have no right to try to stop us from using it."

"That wasn't my intention at all. With all the dust, we thought it might have been the Army coming to visit our town, or a band of outlaws," he added.

"We just thought we'd pay your new town a visit, Jeff."

"New town?" Jeff looked puzzled. "What new town is that, John?"

John was not a patient man. He had very little in the way of a sense of humor. He struggled to keep his temper in check as he pointed to the sign by the road. *"That* new town."

"Nameit? Why, John, Nameit's been here for near 'bouts a year. We just had an election. Matt Bodine is the marshal and I'm the mayor. You boys are welcome in Nameit. Just don't start any trouble."

"A . . . year?" John said.

"That's right, John," Ed said. "You need to get out more, see all the changes that are takin' place around you."

"Broaden your horizons," Sam said with a straight face.

"You won't get away with this, Jeff. None of you. What you done was stealing."

"Get away with what?" Jeff asked. "Stealing? What did any of us steal?"

"How are things in Crossing?" Matt asked. "Is business good or are conditions a little . . . vacant?"

John drummed his gloved fingertips on his saddle horn.

He just didn't know what to do. He'd always been in command, always taken charge. This new development had caught him off guard and he wasn't sure how to handle it.

"The . . . ah . . . town of Nameit, is it on your property, Jeff?" John asked.

"Oh, no!" the rancher said with a serious look. "I deeded the land to the town. A hundred acres. All legal and proper. We expect Nameit to grow with the times. Things are changing, John. Even you must see that."

"Some mighty good people lost everything they had back at Crossing," John pointed out.

"Did something happen at Crossing?" Sam asked. "Tornado touch down maybe?"

"Yeah," Jimmy said, hatred for the man who killed his father very evident in his eyes, "I seen a funnel cloud yesterday—'bout noon, I think it was. I told ever'body I thought it musta hit Crossin'. But since you think you're Lord God Almighty, and forbid any of us from visitin' Crossin', there wasn't much none of us could do about it, since we shore didn't want to do nothin' that might upset you. You bein' such an important man, an' all."

"Except pray," Sam said.

"Yeah," Dodge said. "As soon as we seen the funnel cloud, we immediately got together and held a prayer meetin' for all the good people of Crossin'."

"It was wonderfully inspirin'," Chookie said. "Brought tears to my eyes. 'Specially when we all lifted our voices in song and sang "The Mighty Winds Do Blow.""

"No play on words intended," Sam added.

John Lee kept his face bland. But inside he was boiling and burning with fury and hatred. John Lee did not like to be the butt of jokes. But this time there was nothing he could do about it, except take it.

"Have your fun, boys," John said, in a voice that was choked with rage. He lifted the reins and all could see his hands were shaking. Then his anger boiled over. "I'll pay your town a visit some night and burn the goddamn thing to the ground! Let's ride, men!"

They left in a cloud of dust.

"That's a mighty upset man," Dodge said.

"Hell with him," Ed said. "Right now, we got to spread the word we need a barber and a blacksmith and a dressmaker and so forth for our town." He turned to one of his hands. "Gary, ride for the settlement and start talkin' it up. It won't take long for folks to come in."

"Go with him, Bell," Jeff ordered. "And you boys watch yourselves."

"See if you can find a piano player for the saloon," Al said. "Nothin' like someone poundin' the eighty-eight's to liven things up."

"And a preacher," Dodge added. "Tell him we'll build him a church and a house for his family if he'll come live here. We got to have a church to make the town respectable."

The men would provision up at the ranch and then head out, looking for citizens to inhabit the new town.

Ed lifted the reins. "Let's head back for Nameit, boys. We've still got a lot of hammerin' and sawin' to do to make the town look right."

"Not to mention to make it able to stand up agin any kind of stiff breeze," Chookie added.

Chapter 8

John Lee paced the floor in his study. His rage mounted with every step. He wanted to strike out, destroy, hurt, kill. But how? He had looked over the new hands Jeff had hired and saw wang-leather toughness in them all. These were men his hired guns would not intimidate. His men might be faster on the draw, but that alone would not cause Jeff's new punchers to back up. He knew only too well that many fast guns put their first shot into the dirt. And Jeff's new men, although slower on the draw, would not miss their first shot. And he knew, too, that tough men could take two or three slugs and still stay on their boots, firing with deadly accuracy. He'd personally witnessed that more than once.

And there was nothing he could do about the stealing of Crossing. He didn't want the law in here.

But to steal a whole damn *town!* Incredible.

John Lee ceased his angry, restless pacing and sat down behind his desk. He had to think. He'd offered up his brags, but Jeff and Ed, with the help of Bodine and Two Wolves, had turned his brags into so much hot air.

And stolen a whole damn town.

That rankled John Lee. Crossing was his. He frowned,

thinking: or rather it used to be his. Bunch of outhouses was all that was left.

And the people he'd brought in to run it were gone or in the process of leaving. Bunch of whiners and quitters. He was glad to be rid of them, tell the truth.

He sighed. But now where the hell was he going to buy supplies? He shook his head in disgust. Damned if he'd go buy supplies in Nameit. Stupid name for a town. He'd just have to send wagons to the settlement. That's all there was to it.

"Come in!" he called out at the knock on the study door.

Nick walked in, his mouth all poked out in a pout.

"What's wrong with you?" John asked.

"Cindy don't want to perform her wifely duties," the young man said, sitting down.

John glanced at the clock. "At two o'clock in the afternoon? What's the matter with you? Things like that are done at night. Not in the middle of the day. Damn, boy!"

"Marriage ain't what it's cracked up to be," Nick griped.

His father chuckled, thinking: you haven't seen anything yet, boy. "You talk to any of the hands?"

"Yeah. They told me the town is gone. Now what?"

"I honestly don't know. Do you have any suggestions?"

"Kill Bodine and the Injun."

"Matt Bodine is a skilled gunfighter, son. And Sam Two Wolves is nearabout as good as he is. Don't tangle with either of them."

"I could take both of them."

"Did you hear what I just said?"

"Yes, sir."

"Fine. Now leave me alone and let me think. We've got to come up with a plan."

"Dad, we're payin' them gunslicks out there in the yard fightin' wages. They ain't done no fightin' yet. Turn 'em loose and let them earn their money."

John leaned back in his chair and folded his big hands across his hard belly. "Go on, boy. I'm listening."

"Peck told me that we ain't been banned from the town, right?"

"That's right."

"Them new hands are gonna be ridin' in for drinks come this weekend, right?"

"Go on."

"Ambush 'em."

"Just like that, eh?"

"No, sir. We wait until they start the ride back home. They'll be full of beer and whiskey and a whole lot more careless than they was ridin' in. We hit them fast and hard and then get the hell gone."

John thought for a moment, then slowly nodded his head. "I like it, son. I like the way you think. Let's add this: two groups of men. One to hit the punchers on their way home, the other lying in wait for those left in the saddle when they come chasing after our people. A double ambush."

"Yeah!" the son said. "I like that."

"I'll ramrod the first bunch, you can lead the second bunch. Agreed?"

"Agreed."

The father rose and took a map of the area from a drawer and laid it out on a table. "Let's plan where we're going to hit them."

"What would you do if you were in John Lee's shoes. brother?" Sam asked.

"I've been thinking on it. I'd strike and I'd hit hard. That's the how of it. Where and when is the unknown."

"He threatened to burn the town."

"Temper talk, I think. It wouldn't accomplish anything. Not as far as lessening the odds anyway."

"He was looking over the boys today, for a fact. I don't think he liked what he saw."

"I'm sure he didn't. Jeff's got a fine crew now, what with those four men he just hired from up Kansas way who left their crew when the herd they were supposed to take back fizzled out. You met them. What do you think?"

"I think they're stayers."

"So do I. But John's still got us badly outnumbered with the money to hire a hundred more men if need be. But maybe we're looking at it from the wrong angle."

"What do you mean?"

"We're thinking and talking about a full-scale attack. Maybe that isn't the way John's thinking. Let's think like an Apache, Sam."

"Ambush?"

"That's right."

"Yeah," Sam said, shifting himself to a more comfortable position in the saddle. "You're right. And with some of the pressure off, and a place to go and relax—namely Nameit," he said with a grimace, "the boys will surely head for the saloon come Saturday night."

"That's when it might be."

"Let's go talk to Dodge."

"Not Jeff?"

"No. Jeff's still holding on to hope that this can all be settled without gunplay. And that just might get him killed. If we go to him with our thoughts, he might try to keep the boys on the ranch come Saturday night."

"Let's go see the foreman."

"I'm glad you come to me with this instead of goin' to Jeff," Dodge said, moments later. "I hate to hold back from him, but until he gets it through his head that we're in a real life-and-death struggle here, that's the way it's got to be."

"How many men does he have to lose before he understands that?" Sam asked.

"This ambush oughta do it." Dodge smiled. "I know how

you boys operate. I heard about that business with the kids west of here. You boys like to ride in all lathered up and hell-for-leather. I was your age I'd probably do the same thing. Age tempers things. Now you boys go talk to the hands while I ponder on this theory of yours. I was fightin' Apaches twenty-five years before either of you was born. Don't worry. I'll set it up right."

"That's a tough old man," Sam said, walking to the bunkhouse. "I have a hunch that he's going to get down and dirty with his planning."

"I think you're right."

They gathered the hands around them and discussed it over supper.

"I think you boys hit on something," Barlow said. "For sure we was all plannin' on ridin' into Nameit come Saturday night for cards and drinks. Look here." He got a pencil and a piece of a paper. Barlow drew the meandering lines of a creek about three miles from the town. "Road takes a sharp bend right there at this crick. Good cover in the bend. That's the only place 'tween the town and the ranch they could pull it off."

Matt and Sam nodded their agreement, Sam saying, "And if I was planning this, I'd set it up to hit us after we've spent half the night drinking in the saloon, riding along half-asleep in the saddle."

"Right," Chookie said. "So what's the plan?"

Matt shrugged. "Dodge is thinking on it. If it were up to me, I'd get there before Lee's men and blow them out of the saddle."

Gilley grinned. "I do like the way you think, Matt."

"Sounds good to me," the foreman said, later that night. "Anyway we cut it up, John Lee's men have to ride onto Circle S range to get to that crick. They been warned what would happen. So to hell with them."

"Who stays behind to guard the ranch?" Sam asked.

"We'll draw straws," the old man said. He smiled. " 'Ceptin' you boys and me, that is."

* * *

The Circle S men left their horses behind a bluff on an old dry creek bed and walked to the cottonwoods, getting into position just at dusk. Dodge had strapped on another long-barreled Peacemaker and the old foreman looked right at home wearing the guns. Matt had told Sam that he suspected Dodge had not always been a foreman, that there were things in the foreman's past that were dark. Sam agreed.

Crouched behind the bank of the creek, enjoying the coolness of dusk, Dodge turned his eyes to Matt, who had been studying him. "Think you got me pegged, eh, boy?"

"I don't believe you've spent all your life looking at the rear end of cows, if that's what you mean."

Dodge chuckled and spat a stream of tobacco juice, knocking a frog off a flat rock about five feet away. "I traveled here and there in my youth. I scouted for the Army and I've rode with mountain men and wintered with Injuns. I've been the marshal of more than one wild town that people said couldn't be tamed. I tamed 'em. But I never rode on the hoot-owl trails. Never stole nothin' and don't have no use for them that do. I own a percentage of the Circle S, Matt. So this is personal for me."

"Vonny Dodge," Matt softly pegged him, "the man some people say was the first to use a fast draw."

"That's what some people say, all right."

"You dropped out of sight more than twenty years ago, according to my dad. The word is that you're dead."

"That's the way I like it, boy. I had too many young punks lookin' for me, wantin' to make a reputation. Got mighty tired of lookin' over my shoulder all the time. So I left the gold fields and come east, landed here and here I'll die— tonight, next week, ten years from now. Who knows? Listen to me. Hang up them guns of yourn, boy. Before it's too late. You've already got the name, and it'll haunt you. You and Sam go on back to your ranches, marry up with good women, and settle down. I used to be just like you, Matt. It's in the walk, the way a man carries hisself. I could clear a barroom of some of the most saltiest ol' boys west of the Mississippi just by walkin' in there. I liked it, and so do you. I lived for that cotton-dry mouth seconds before the lead started to fly. And I knowed no one could beat me. I knew it. Just like you know it. Has to be that way. When you lose that confidence, that's the day you'll die."

"Did you lose it, Dodge?"

"Nope." He chewed and spat again. The frog had gotten the message the first time and moved to another rock, farther away. "I got smart, boy. Just like you'll get smart on down the road. If you don't, you'll die. It's just that simple."

Sam was on the other side of the old foreman, listening intently. Dodge cut his eyes to him.

"You got the same bearin' about you as your brother, Sam. I knew what you boys was the moment I laid eyes on you. I'm forty years older than the both of you. And I know what I'm talkin' about."

"We'll drift back to Wyoming sometime," Sam told him.

"Maybe," Dodge countered, "but I wouldn't bet my last chip on either of you doin' it anytime soon. You both got the mark on you. But for now, I'm glad you're here. Enough talk. We best start listenin'."

"If the Broken Lance riders come," Sam said, "do we give them any breaks at all?"

Dodge looked at him, and the old man's eyes were as flat and hard as a rattler's gaze. "Hell, no! When they get into range, we just stand up and blow 'em out of the saddle."

Sam grinned. "You're a randy old bastard, aren't you?"

"I'm alive, son. And I didn't get to my advanced age by doin' no damn favors to the crud of this earth."

Matt and Sam both grinned at him in the gathering gloom along the lazy-flowing little creek.

The men waited. Stars were out and the moon up before the sounds of hooves reached the men. All the punchers jacked back the hammers of the six-shooters. The riders were walking their horses very slowly, to keep both the dust and the noise down. Just outside of effective pistol range, the riders pulled up. The sounds of low talking reached the ears of the men waiting by the creek, but they could not make out any words. Then a lone rider left the bunch and walked his horse toward the thicket.

He walked his horse up and down the road by the creek. But the men from the Circle S were all wearing dark clothing and none of them moved. Most breathed through their mouths to cut down even that slight sound.

He walked his horse back to the bunch and talked for a moment. "Let's get into position." The clear sounds of John Lee's voice reached them.

When the Broken Lance gunhands were no more than twenty-five yards away, Vonny Dodge opened the dance by blowing a gunhand clean out of his saddle.

The creek bank blossomed with streaks of fire, the violent sounds shattering the quiet night. The frog who had been watching the men leaped for the water and sank out of sight.

Horses were rearing and bucking and screaming in fright. Half a dozen saddles were empty, some slick with fresh blood. The air was thick with the combination of kicked-up dust and gunsmoke. The sounds of wounded men moaning and calling out for help was lost in the frantic melee. Those still in the saddle—and some of them were wounded and just hanging on—got their animals under control and hit the air.

"That's it!" Dodge called. "Load up in case they double back and try it again. But I think that's doubtful."

When the sounds of running horses could no longer be heard, Matt called out, "You boys on the road, keep your hands empty and sit up if you're able. Anyone who comes up with a fistful of iron gets dead."

"Dirty murderin' ambushin' bastards!" a wounded man moaned.

"That's what you were going to do to us, wasn't it?" Chookie called.

"That's different," the man groaned.

"I fail to see the distinction," Sam said, spinning the cylinder of his pistol. "But then, I'm just a poor ignorant savage."

"Stinkin' redskin," another said.

"May I borrow your knife, Matt," Sam said. "I think I'm going to take a scalp."

"Now wait just a damn minute!" a new voice was added. "You make sure you're peelin' the right feller. I ain't said nothin'!"

"Is that you, Dallas?" Chookie called.

"Yeah. Who am I talkin' to?"

"Chookie. You sure picked the wrong side, Dallas. You hard hit?"

"Side and leg. But I can sit a saddle. How about it?"

"Can you trust him not to come back?" Dodge asked.

"Oh, yeah. I been knowin' him for years. If he gives his word, he's gone."

"Tell him."

"I want your word on it, Dallas," Chookie called.

"You got it. I'm gone if I can find my horse."

"Just pick one," Matt called. "They're all probably stolen anyway."

"Mine ain't! I worked all summer last year to buy that horse. Honest work." He whistled softly and the animal came to him, nuzzling him. The puncher turned hired gun climbed painfully into the saddle and rode out.

"You better shoot me," the original mouthy gunhand popped off. " 'Cause when I get my hands on a gun, I'm comin' back and finishing this job."

Dodge stepped out into the road and kicked a fallen six-shooter to the man. It landed right by his hand and shone dully under the stars and moonlight.

Dodge's guns were in leather. "Pick it up, loudmouth," the foreman told him.

"Why, you lousy old fart!" the gunhand said, and grabbed for the gun.

Dodge was smooth and quick and sure and deadly. With absolutely no emotion on his face, he shot the man right between the eyes, and then, with a very faint smile showing under his snow-white handlebar mustache, he spun the long-barreled Peacemaker a couple of times before shoving it back into leather.

"Vonny Dodge," a wounded man breathed, being very careful not to move his hands. "Got to be. That was shore his trademark. I thought you was dead, Vonny."

"I heard that myself a time or two. I know that voice. Who you be, boy?"

"Hazelton. From up on the Tongue. I was tryin' to homestead up there when you kilt them three in that tradin' post."

"Can you ride?"

"I can."

"Git your horse and git gone and don't come back to this part of Texas. I know your face and your voice. If I see you again, I'll kill you."

"I'm gone, Vonny."

"And keep your mouth shut about seein' me. You hear?"

"I'll go to my grave with it, Vonny. You got my word."

"Five dead, Dodge," Tate said. "Two more look like they ain't gonna last the night. Five can ride, I reckon. What the hell do you want to do with them?"

"I know what I want to do," the old gunslinger said. He looked at Matt. "Suggestions?"

Matt smiled. "Well, I am the marshal."

"Shore enough," Dodge said with a smile. "I plumb forgot about that. And we got plenty of lumber left to build a gallows."

"Now wait just a damn minute!" a shoulder-shot gunhand bellered.

"I ain't been to a good hangin' in, oh Lord, I reckon it's been fifteen years," Dodge said.

"Will y'all hush up that hangin' talk?" another hollered. "Just let us ride and we're gone with the wind, boys. That's a promise."

Another drummed his booted feet on the hard-packed road and died.

"Get 'em on their horses and get 'em out of here," Dodge said. "Throw them dead men across the saddles and rope down good. I don't feel like diggin' no damn holes this night."

The hired guns gone, Matt said, "You don't suppose we were lucky enough to get lead in John Lee, do you?"

"No," the foreman said. "He was gone in the first bunch. Least I think I seen him hightail it out."

"What now?" Beavers said, as he kicked dirt over a bloody spot in the road.

"Well," Dodge said, smiling. "Let's ride into Nameit and have us a beer."

Chapter 9

John Lee sat in his study and assessed his damages. He and his men had ridden straight into an ambush and had paid the price for it. But how did Jeff know they were coming? Did he have a leak? He immediately dismissed that. Only he and his son knew where they were going and what they planned to do; he had told the others during the ride over to the creek.

Jeff—no, probably Bodine—had made a lucky guess. That had to be it. Once back on home range, John had only then realized how lucky he had been. His bunch of hired guns had been shot to ribbons. Only he and Dusty Jordon had escaped uninjured. Several of the men who'd ridden back to the ranch were in bad shape, not expected to make it through the night. The others had suffered only minor wounds.

He dismissed those unfortunates from his mind. They were only hired guns and he could hire more. What was important was the blow John Lee had suffered to his ego. He felt the beginnings of dark savage hatred growing within him. He never thought about calling off the war. He never thought about why he was doing it. He didn't even know. He just knew that he wanted all the land around him, thousands and thousands of acres, to be his to do with as he saw fit.

And he was going to get it. Even if it meant killing everybody that opposed his grand plans.

Jeff Sparks stood on the front porch of his house, standing in his long underwear—but with his hat on his head—and listened to Dodge's report about the ambush.

When Dodge finished, the rancher nodded. "It had to be, I reckon. They couldn't have been ridin' on our range with nothin' else on their minds. All right, Dodge. From now on out it's war and I realize it, so don't never leave me out of plannin' again."

"You have my word on it, Jeff."

"Any of our boys get hurt?"

"Not a scratch."

"Get some sleep. You can bet that John Lee is makin' war plans right this minute."

Sunday dawned hot and those who weren't riding the range stayed inside the bunkhouse to escape the heat. They mended socks, patched boots, checked equipment, played cards, told lies to one another, and relaxed.

The men who had been sent to the settlement returned with the news that people were on the way. About twenty-five or so—counting the kids—to run the stores, work the saloon, the blacksmith shop, the barber shop, and so forth.

"Did you find a preacher?" Ed asked his hand.

"Sure did. And his wife's a schoolteacher, too. We're gonna have to build a school."

"Church can be the schoolhouse Monday through Friday." Ed smiled at Jeff. "We got us a town, partner. A real town with honest-to-God hard-workin' real people."

"I posted a notice in several places announcin' the town," Bell said. "The north/south stage is gonna schedule the town for a stop, the stationmaster told me."

"We're on the way to bringing law and order to this part of the country," Jeff said. "It's a grand day, boys."

They all looked up as the very faint sound of a single gunshot drifted to them.

"Let's ride," Matt said, running for his horse.

They found Sonny, one of Ed's hands, dead on the ground, his horse standing over him, nuzzling the man who'd been his master for years.

Sam rolled him over. A bloody hole was centered in the man's back. The slug had cut the spinal cord and probably busted the heart.

"Goddammit!" Ed swore, and he was not a man who often used strong language, "Sonny had been with me for years. He was one of the finest men I ever knew. Like one of the family."

"Dan Ringold," Matt said. "You dig that slug out and it'll be a .44-.40. Bet on it. That back-hooter has gone to work." He looked at Ed. "Me and Sam will pick up his trail. You can bet on that, too. We'll be back when you see us, Jeff."

"Now, boys . . ." the rancher started to protest. He shook his head, his features growing hard. "Be careful," was how he ended it.

"We'll bury Sonny at dusk," Ed said. "He liked that time of day. He used to sit outside the bunkhouse and play his guitar and sing songs. He had a good voice."

Matt swung into the saddle. "Family?" he asked.

Ed shook his head. "If he did he never talked about them. He was a quiet man."

"Burn that on the marker," Sam said. "Here lies a good quiet man." He looked at Matt. "Let's go find the man who killed him, brother."

They began working in long slow circles. It did not take them long to pick up the tracks. They found where the back-shooter had positioned himself, on the crest of a long low hill. And they found the spent brass, twinkling in the sunlight.

"Not enough to stand up in a court of law," Sam said.

"It's like they say, brother. There ain't no law west of the Pecos."

They followed the tracks back to the main road. There, they headed north.

"He sure isn't making any effort to hide his trail," Sam said.

Matt reined up.

"What's the matter?" Sam asked.

"He isn't making any effort to hide his tracks."

Sam frowned. "Yeah. I see what you mean. It's too obvious."

"He's leading us into a trap."

"Feel like heading cross-country to get ahead of him?"

"You're reading my mind, brother."

The brothers crossed the road and rode for about two miles, then cut north, keeping their horses moving in a distance-eating lope, slowing them often to save them.

"We've got to be ahead of him," Sam shouted after a time. "What do you think?"

"Let's cut back east."

They slowed their horses to a walk as they neared the road and reined up at the base of a small hill. Carrying their rifles, they ran up to the crest, taking off their hats to present less of a skyline, and peeked over the crest.

"Would you just look at that?" Sam said. "Like ducks in a row, just waiting for us to come riding along."

Matt smiled and they both eared back the hammers on their Winchesters, sighted in, and started making life miserable for the ambushers.

The range was too far for any kind of accurate shooting, but both brothers scored hits, both of them knowing that at this range the wounds would be very minor. The ambushers—including the two that were hit—used great agility in scampering over the crest of their hill, cussing and hollering as they went.

"Recognize any of them?" Matt asked.

"That big ass has to belong to Lou Witter. That's the only one I'd bet on at this distance."

"Bodine!" the call came to them.

"Right here," Matt called. "What'd you want?"

"I like to know a man's name 'fore I kill him!"

Matt laughed. "Who am I talkin' to?"

"Trest."

"You better carry your butt back to Oklahoma Territory, Trest. I'm gonna put lead in it if you hang around here."

Trest cussed him, the profanity drifting over the hot, windless expanse of short grass and prickly pear cactus.

"Is that the best you can do, Trest?" Matt hurled out the challenge.

"I'll meet you anytime, Bodine!" Trest yelled. "One on one."

"Name your spot, Trest."

Silence greeted the brothers.

"They're planning a setup, Matt," Sam said.

"Sure they are. I'd be surprised if they weren't."

A minute passed. A dust devil was spun up and went whirling and dancing across the little valley that separated the two factions.

"How about now, Bodine?" Trest called.

"Where?"

"In the road back of us."

"They're sure to have a rifleman getting in place now," Sam said.

"Yeah. But that ridge they're on is the highest point around here. Where would he be?"

"How about it, Bodine?" Trest called. "You turnin' yellow on me?"

"There were six of you when we started firing," Bodine yelled. "At the count of three, me and Sam stand up, and the six of you stand up. How about that?"

A long pause from the other side. Finally, Trest yelled, "What's the matter, Bodine, don't you trust me?"

"Hell, no!"

"They're stalling, calling the rifleman back, brother."

"Yeah." Raising his voice, Matt said, "Do it right now, Trest. Or it's off."

"Some other time, Bodine."

"I'll do you one better, Trest. I know you got that lard-butted Lou Witter with you. He fancies himself a good man with his fists. How about it, Lou—you think you could take me stand-up bare-knuckle?"

But only silence greeted his challenge. Lou wanted no part of Matt Bodine. After a moment, the men had reached their horses, hidden nearby but well in this deceptive terrain, and were riding off, heading north toward Broken Lance range.

"We follow them?"

Matt shook his head. "No. They're probably counting on that and will be waiting for us. Let's get back to the ranch. I imagine a lot of the boys will be wanting to go to Sonny's funeral. We'll stay behind as guards."

Jeff, his wife, and Lisa and Lia were going to stay over at the Flying V for the night, and the boys would ride back after supper. Matt, Sam, Barlow, Gilley, Compton, and Tony stayed at the ranch as guards.

"You think they'll hit us this night, Matt?" Tony asked, as they were eating an early supper.

"I'd bet on it. So let's play it this way: Sam and me will take the front porch of the house. It's got good cover behind that adobe and a good field of fire. Barlow, you and Gilley take the bunkhouse. Compton and Tony, the barn. Let's make sure we have plenty of water and our pockets stuffed with ammo. Let's load up the spare rifles we have and the short guns we took from the dead outlaws. I just think they'll hit us right after dark and they'll hit us hard."

"Conchita?" Gilley asked.

Sam smiled. "I'd hate to be the gunny who invades her kitchen. She's got a shotgun, a rifle, and a pistol nearby, and knows how to use them. The kitchen being where it is, she's well protected."

Matt sopped up the last of his gravy with a hunk of bread and pushed back from the table. He glanced out the window of the bunkhouse. The sun was setting. "Let's get into position, boys. I think we're going to have visitors pretty soon."

Tanner had worked his way as close to the ranch house as possible. He studied the tranquil-appearing scene through field glasses, then Injuned back to where the hired guns were waiting.

"They left behind some men," he told Trest. "Maybe a half a dozen. No more than that. They was just gettin' into position when I left. Got some men in the barn and on the front porch. I couldn't tell where any others was, but I 'spect they's some in the bunkhouse."

Trest turned to a man. "Stay with the horses and keep them settled down. Soon as it's dark, we'll work our way in and hit 'em. You boys get them torches soaked good now. We'll burn those bastards out. Let's get set."

The horses began restless movement in the corral and in the barn.

"You were right on the mark, brother," Sam said. "I think we're about to have visitors."

"Yeah, and they're all around us, too. Time to split up. See you in a few minutes."

"Right."

The brothers moved to opposite ends of the long front porch. The heavy wooden shutters of the house had all been closed to guard against torches being thrown into the house. Conchita had barricaded herself in the kitchen and was putting on a fresh pot of coffee. She knew cowboys and knew they would want some hot, strong coffee when this fight was over. That done, she stoked up the fire then broke open her shotgun to check the loads of buckshot. She checked rifle and pistol and placed them within easy reach. This was nothing new to Conchita. She'd been with the Sparks family since they came into the area. She'd stood alongside them and fought Comanches, Apaches, and outlaws. She'd killed before and knew she would probably kill again this night. She fixed her a sandwich and sat down at the table. Let the no-goods come on. She was ready.

Four Circle S rifles barked, from the bunkhouse, the barn, and the front porch, and one of John Lee's hired guns had no more roads to ride on this earth as the .44 slugs ended his life before he stretched out cold on the still-hot ground.

A slug howled over Sam's head and Sam sighted in the muzzle flash and returned the fire, smiling as his slug struck flesh and bone and the gunny screamed, pitching his rifle and falling face-first on the earth.

"I smell kerosene!" Matt called from the other end of the porch. "They're going to try to burn us out."

A slug knocked a board from the house, stinging the back of his head. Matt triggered off two fast rounds. He couldn't tell if he'd hit anything but he was certain he'd make life a little more exciting for the gunslick who'd shot at him. A running shadow caught his eyes and he fired. A man screamed, dropped his unlit torch, grabbed at his hip, and fell heavily. Matt sighted him in and ended his yelling for help.

From his position in the loft of the barn, Tony saw a torch burst into fire and he pulled the trigger, the slug doubling the man over and dropping him to the ground. He landed on the flaming torch and his clothing erupted into flames. The man screamed and rolled frantically, trying to extinguish the flames. Another ran to him and Tony cut him down. It was a quick shot, a hurried one, and not a killing shot. But the man was out of action for awhile, yelling and holding one leg.

The burning man screamed for a few more seconds and then was silent as his hair exploded in fire.

Tony felt sick to his stomach, fought it back, belched, and

took his eyes off the human torch, returning his attention to the battle.

A hired gun dived through a window of the bunkhouse, shattering glass. He landed on a bunk, rolled to the floor, and jumped to his knees just as Barlow ran to him and clubbed him with a rifle butt and Gilley turned and swung his rifle, triggering off a round. Gilley's slug caught the man in the throat, knocking him off his knees and back against the wall. John Lee's hired killer died with his eyes wide open, a horrible gaping wound in his throat and in the back of his neck where the .44 slug exited. There was no time to drag him out into the yard. He would have to wait. Both men felt the hired gun probably wouldn't even notice the short inconvenience.

"Burn the goddamned place to the ground!" Trest yelled.

Matt fired two quick rounds in the direction of Trest's voice, but was uncertain whether he hit anything except air.

Torches burst into flame, and the men carrying them ran toward their targets, one running toward the rear of the house where the kitchen was located. Where Conchita was waiting in the darkness, all lamps out. She sat in a chair facing the back door, holding the double-barreled shotgun, both hammers back.

The gunhand grunted in pleasant surprise when he found the door unbarred. He pushed it open and stepped into the darkened kitchen. John Lee's hired gun had only a very brief second to realize what he had stepped into and not nearly enough time to scream, pray, cuss, or wish he had stayed home in the Idaho Territory.

Conchita blew him in two, the force of the rusty nails, broken bits of metal, and ball bearings loaded in the shells slamming both parts of the man clear off the back porch and into the dirt where Conchita was trying to raise flowers.

Conchita reloaded then stepped out and threw dirt on the flaming torch until it was out. A gunhand ran around the corner of the house, a torch in one hand and a six-shooter in the other. Conchita showed him the twin muzzles of the shotgun. He lifted his pistol just as Conchita shot him. The blast caught him in the chest, lifted him off his boots, and slammed him backward, the torch falling into a water barrel and dying with a hiss.

She stepped back into the house, taking shells from her apron pocket and reloading. She poured a cup of coffee and sat down in her chair. No one else, not even Jeff Sparks, sat in that chair. "Come on, you sons of Hell," Conchita said. "I'm waiting."

"It ain't workin', Trest!" Pukey Stagg panted, sliding down beside the gunman behind a well. "The roof won't catch fire on the house and them ol' boys is dead shots with them rifles. I seen five of our people go down myself. They's someone with a shotgun behind the house and Benny and Frank don't answer to no one's call. I think they're dead too and I think we've had it for this night."

Trest looked around him. The torches had been put out by the men carrying them when they realized there was no way they were going to burn anything down except one privy behind the bunkhouse. It was still burning. The man who had torched the outhouse lay dead in front of it.

"Let's get out of here," Trest said, after some fancy cussing.

They lost one more man in leaving. Barlow drilled him dead center in the chest and that was the last shot fired that night. Before the men had left their positions, Dodge and the boys were galloping hellbent into the yard.

"I was afraid of something like this," the foreman said, swinging down from the saddle with the grace and ease of a man half his age. "When'd they hit you boys?"

"'Bout half an hour ago, I think," Matt told him. "I wasn't checking the time. It got a little busy around here."

"So I see," Dodge said drily.

"Conchita put the skids to two back here," Bell called

from the back of the house. "Blowed one plumb in half and damn near tore the other'n up 'bout as bad."

"She's hell with that shotgun," Dodge said. "And there ain't no back-up in that woman. Hell of a woman!"

Matt knew then that what the older hands said was true. Dodge and Conchita had quite a thing going for each other. Very discreetly, of course.

"We could probably catch 'em, Dodge!" Gene said. "Let's go after 'em."

"You just sit tight, boy," Dodge told him. "There ain't none of us goin' a-blunderin' around out yonder in the dark. We'd likely be ridin' right smack into an ambush. We got plenty to do here this night."

"Dodge!" Conchita called from the side of the house. "You get your old bones in here and sit and have coffee with me. I baked a cake, too."

Dodge grinned sheepishly. "Take charge here, Matt. I got cake on my mind."

"Among other things," Sam muttered, low enough so that Dodge couldn't hear him. In the West, a man had best be very careful how he spoke of another man's woman, even in jest.

"Got some wounded over here, Matt!" Lomax called from out of the darkness.

"Be right there." To Sam: "Let's go see what these yahoos have to say, brother."

"I have no doubts whatsoever that the conversation will be mentally stimulating."

"Sam?" Gene Sparks said, walking along with them. "Can you teach me to talk like that?"

"Certainly!" Sam grinned and looked at Matt who was shaking his head in disgust. "A small voice crying out from the wilderness for education. Isn't it wonderful?"

Matt reached over and jerked Sam's hat down over his ears.

Chapter 10

Matt knelt down beside a man who looked like he did not have long to live. He'd been shot through and through, from one side to the other. The pink foam leaking from his mouth indicated he'd been lung shot.

"You got anything you want to say?" Matt asked.

"Yeah," he whispered, "Go to hell, Bodine."

"You'll be there a long time before I make it, partner." He rose and walked to another, squatting down. He knew the man. "Jess. Long way from the Wind River Range, isn't it?"

"Far piece, Bodine. Looks like I hired my gun out to the wrong person this time, don't it?"

"I won't lie; you're hard hit and there's no doctor anywhere near here."

Matt could barely see the nod of the man's head in the darkness. "I figured I was. Hurts."

"Family?"

"Naw. Had a wife once. She got smart and left me. That was years ago. Took the kids. I don't know where they are."

"Don't that just break your heart, now?" another shot-up hired gun sneered from his position a few yards away. "I always knew you was a real sob sister, Jess."

Jess smiled through his pain and turned on his side. He palmed a derringer with his left hand and put a .41 slug into the outlaw's head. The tiny two-shot pistol fell from his suddenly very weak fingers. "I never did like him," Jess said. "I think I'll just close my eyes for a minute or so.

He never opened them again.

"Conchita is pretty good at patchin' folks up," Jimmy said, "But you'll never get her to work on this bunch."

"Who the hell wants a greasy Mex to work on them, anyway?" a gunhand said. "I'd sooner have a goddamn Injun medicine man helpin' me."

"You better be glad Dodge didn't hear that," Lomax muttered. "If he had, you wouldn't have to worry none about gettin' patched up."

The mouthy gunhand did not hear the last part. He was dead and cooling.

Dodge strolled out into the yard, a cup of coffee in one hand and a large piece of cake in the other. "Take all their guns and ammo," he ordered. "Store them. Put them that look like they might make it in a wagon. We'll drive them to where Crossin' used to be and leave them. If John Lee wants these gunslicks, he can come fetch them."

"That ain't decent!" a man shot in both legs hollered.

Dodged turned to Red. "Git a rope, Red."

"Now wait a minute!" the outlaw bellered. "I ain't real happy about that suggestion, neither."

"Then shut your damn mouth," the old foreman told him. "Open it up again and I'll hang you. Get this pack of crud out of here, boys."

The hands were sober and reflective the next morning. They had been very lucky so far, and they all knew it. That six men with rifles had managed to beat back an attack by three times that many was something just short of a miracle, and all knew that the next time the Broken Lance attacked, they probably wouldn't come out of it nearly so well.

After breakfast, the hands rolled the dead into blankets and buried them in unmarked graves. Jeff Sparks read from the Bible and the hired guns became one with the earth.

Matt and Sam accompanied Jeff and his wife and daughters into town. The ladies went shopping and visiting, while the men went to the saloon.

"Fifteen new folks pulled in yesterday," Al said with a big grin. "We got us a preacher and a schoolteacher. Got us two bar girls and a piano thumper. Folks to work the general store on shares and a smithy and leatherworker. Nameit's gonna boom, boys. I can feel it."

It would. But not under that name.

"How about supplies for the businesses?" Sam asked.

"Stage stopped by yesterday. Left word that the wagons are rolling from the settlement. Be here today."

"I reckon we better hang around and see this," Jeff said. "Big day for us."

Al turned to look at the clock. "Stage will be back in a couple of hours."

"How about some coffee, Al?" Matt asked. It was a little early for beer and the café wasn't open yet. No cook. But one was supposed to be arriving soon.

"Comin' up."

"What's the new buildin' over yonder?" Jeff asked, pointing across the street.

"That's the marshal's office," Al said. "With all these new people comin' in, don't you think Matt should stay in town?"

Matt felt eyes on him. He nodded his head. "That's probably the best thing," he said reluctantly. He hadn't wanted the job of marshal and had taken it only at the other's persistent requests.

"I'll stay on as deputy," Sam volunteered.

"I'd appreciate it, brother." Conversation stopped at the sounds of wagons rumbling up the street.

"Look at that!" Al said proudly. "The word has gotten out and people are comin' in. Five wagons with settlers and those are supply wagons behind them. We got us a town, boys. We got us a real town!"

Later, standing outside the saloon, Jeff said, "This ain't farmin' country. I got to get the word out about that. Them folks that come in today was merchants and the like. That's good. But this ain't farmin' country. It might be someday, but not now. People have tried and failed."

Jeff had jumped the gun on John Lee, ordering all available lumber from the settlement's supplier. Even if John Lee had plans to rebuild Crossing, it would be several months before any lumber order could be filled. He probably knew that by now and would be furious.

Sam pointed that out.

"John Lee can go straight to hell," Jeff said. "The rest of us are tryin' to look ahead and build for the future while he wants to destroy. Far as I'm concerned, there's no turnin' back now. It's come down to root hog or die for all sides. I'll have your things sent in this afternoon, boys. Good luck to you both."

The heavy hand of John Lee had been lifted from the area. The oppressive and deadly grip he had tried to maintain was, while not gone, at least softened. And the news quickly spread.

For the next several days, the sounds of hammers and saws filled the town. Buildings went up quickly with everybody pitching in to help. Jeff and Ed split their hands and sent half into town to help out. The town of Nameit no longer looked as if it might fall down in a stiff breeze. There was an air of permanency about it now. Women walked the boardwalks and kids played in the alleys and in front of tents that would soon be replaced by wooden structures.

Quarters had been built behind the marshal's office, and Matt and Sam settled in.

"I wonder just how far our authority reaches?" Sam wondered aloud.

"I asked Jeff that," Matt replied. "He said just as far as we wanted to push it."

"You're the only law between here and El Paso," Al said, joining them on the boardwalk in front of the saloon.

"No," Matt corrected. "There is one more badge-toter somewhere around here."

"Oh?" Al said.

"Yeah. A man by the name of Josiah Finch."

Josiah sat his horse and looked around him, momentary confusion stamping his face.

"Now, I know I ain't lost," he said to his horse. "I ain't been lost in years. I didn't know where I was a time or two, but I wasn't lost!"

He knew there had been a town here several weeks past. He'd stopped and had him a bite to eat and several cups of coffee. Now all that was visible to the eyes were half a dozen outhouses. Josiah's horse was named Horse. All of Josiah's horses were named Horse. It was easier to keep track of them that way.

"Horse," Josiah said. "Did you take a wrong trail somewhere down the line?"

Horse swung his head, a reproachful look in his eyes. A look that seemed to say: Don't blame me.

Josiah swung down from the saddle and ground-reined Horse. He studied the situation for a moment. The sounds of riders coming turned him around. A lot of riders. A big man leading them. They reined up in a cloud of dust. Josiah slapped the dust from his clothing and put a disgusted look on the big man.

"You got to be John Lee," Josiah said. "Anybody else would have showed some respect and common courtesy by not raisin' a dust cloud."

"Who the hell do you think you are, talking to me that way?" John blustered.

"I know who I am," Josiah said. "Name's Finch. Texas Rangers. And if that news don't suit you, get down off that horse and do something about it, if you think today is a good day to die."

John sat back in his saddle. He did not want trouble with the law, and he especially did not want trouble with the Rangers. Texas Rangers took a very dim view of people who inflicted bodily harm on one of their own. As a matter of fact, they could get downright hostile in reacting to news of one of their own being hurt or killed.

"Sorry about the dust," John mumbled, as if the words hurt his mouth.

"Where the hell's the town that used to be here?" Finch asked.

John sighed. Now he was caught in a bind. If he told his Ranger that someone had stolen the town, there would be an investigation. And he sure didn't want that. God*damn* Matt Bodine!

Finch saw several smiles among the hardcases that rode with John Lee. Two smiles, as a matter of fact. He knew both men. Pen Masters and Bam Ford. Ford was from the Big Thicket country and while he was known as a gunslinger, he was not really a vicious man. Neither, really, was Pen Masters.

"A . . . cyclone came up and blew the town away," John Lee finally said.

"A *cyclone?*" Finch said. "You mean it took down all the buildin's except the privies?"

"Looks that way," John said sourly.

"Blowed them about ten miles south of here," Pen said,

obviously enjoying John Lee's discomfort, for John twisted in his saddle and gave the man a very dirty look.

"Yeah," Bam picked it up. "Just set 'em right down on the ground just as pretty as you please. Folks down there give the place a new title. They call it Nameit."

Finch blinked. "Nameit? We got a town in Texas called Nameit?"

"Yeah."

"Who's the law in . . . Nameit?"

"Matt Bodine," John said, then spat on the ground.

Josiah Finch smiled. He now had a pretty good idea what had happened to Crossing. A cyclone hit it, all right, in the form of Jeff Sparks, Ed Carson, and a couple of Wyoming gunhands.

No, he corrected that. Bodine and Two Wolves were not gunhands in the ordinary sense. They were not coldblooded killers nor did they hire their guns. They just both happened to be very, very good with short guns and very, very bad men to fool with.

Josiah swung up on Horse and picked up the reins. He gave the gunhands a long slow once-over, then looked at John Lee. "For a prominent rancher, you sure keep strange company, John Lee. Word I get is that this is only about a third of the men you're payin' fightin' wages to. The last thing the governor wants is a range war. And if that happens, he's gonna be a mighty unhappy man, he is. Now, I'm gonna take me a ride over to Nameit and check into the hotel—if there is one—and have me a haircut and a shave and a hot bath. If you boys is plannin' on goin' over there, fine. Go on. But you'll by God follow me, 'cause I don't feel like eatin' your dust."

Josiah turned his back to the men and put Horse into an easy canter.

John Lee looked back at Pen and Bam. "You boys think this is funny, do you?"

They both grinned at him.

John backed his horse up and handed them both green-backs. "There's your pay. Don't let me see your faces around here again."

"Or you'll do what?" Pen asked him, his right hand close to the butt of his gun.

"Too close, boss," Bob Grove muttered. "'Way too close in here."

John Lee knew it. Packed in like the riders were, should gunplay start now, a lot of people would get hurt or killed. And John Lee knew he'd be the first one to take a bullet. He savagely swung his horse's head and galloped off toward Nameit.

"I hate to see a man treat a horse like that," Bam said. "A man who's mean to animals ain't much of a man."

"Yeah," Pen said, looking at the money in his left hand. "Well, what now, partner?"

Bam grinned. "We ride to the Circle S and ask for a job, after we stop off in Nameit and tell Matt what's happened."

"It might be interestin' to see what goes down in town."

"Yeah. Let's just poke along after our *ex*-partners and see what happens."

The men rode slowly along, heading south. Pen was the first to break the silence. "You know, Bam, the last two, three jobs I had, and they were fightin' jobs, I just . . . well, I wasn't very happy with myself. I felt all out of place. You know what I mean?"

"Oh, yeah. I been that way since Utah. I been thinkin' about gettin' a real job, an honorable one, and savin' some money. I'd like to head to California and start all over."

"Sounds good to me. You want a ridin' partner?"

"Sure. Pen, if we hook up with the Circle S, we're gonna have to kill some of them ol' boys ahead of us, you know that, don't you?"

"Most of them ol' boys up yonder need killin'," was Pen's reply.

Bam couldn't argue it. He knew it was fact.

* * *

"Boys," Josiah said, stepping into the marshal's office and startling Matt and Sam. The man moved like a damn ghost. "I got John Lee and his bunch about ten minutes behind me, all of 'em primed and cocked for trouble. So I think I'll wait 'fore I get all duded up at the barber shop. I do hate to get all cleaned up and then have to bathe again. Too much soap and water in one day is not good for the skin." He poured himself a cup of coffee and sat down. "What do you boys know about Pen Masters and Bam Ford?"

"I knew Pen from up north," Matt said. "He's a fast gun, but not a killer, if you know what I mean."

"I do. And Bam's the same way. Bam's really a pretty good ol' boy. But like a lot of young men after the war, he had a lot of violence in him and the damn Yankee reconstructionists didn't help none, struttin' around like God Almighty tellin' folks what they could and couldn't do." He sighed. "Oh, well, that's water under the bridge. While we're waitin' for John Lee and his bunch, you boys bring me up to date on what's been happenin'. All that you can talk about, that is," he added drily.

The brothers leveled with the man, leaving nothing out. They were just as anxious to bring this spreading range war to a halt as anyone.

Josiah Finch chuckled. "Vonny Dodge. Good Lord, boys! That man was supposed to have been killed years and years ago. He come west—according to the legends—back in thirty or thirty-five." Josiah's eyes twinkled. "Vonny got him a Spanish woman, eh?"

"It appears that way."

"Old goat! Did he twirl them six-shooters of his just once for you boys?"

"That he did," Sam allowed.

"I got to see that. Is he still quick, boys?"

"You're mighty right he's quick," Matt answered. "I wouldn't want to brace that old man," he added.

"High compliment, comin' from you. I think I'll just hang around for a spell. See if you get into action. I been hearin' that you're faster than any man alive."

"It isn't a reputation that I asked for," Matt said softly.

"Don't none of us ever do, boy," the Ranger told him. "But once it gets hung on a man, he never shakes it loose. Here comes John Lee and his bunch. Take some advice from a man who's been behind a badge for years, boys?"

"Sure," Sam said. "We'd be fools not to."

"Get them greeners outta them racks and load 'em up. There ain't nothin' like lookin' down the barrel of a sawed-off shotgun to take the heart out of a man huntin' trouble. Not to mention his guts and a lot of other awful-lookin' things when you pull them triggers," he added with a savage smile.

Chapter 11

Josiah had this to say before the brothers stepped out of the office. "I ain't here on no official business. My business is concluded. So I ain't gonna take no hand in this unless I personally see someone is breaking the law and I think you boys can't handle it. Course I will get into it if any of them hardcases out yonder lip off to me. And by the way, looks like Bam and Pen done left the crowd. They ain't among 'em."

"What happened to those murderers you were tracking?" Sam asked.

"I thronged dirt on 'em and read over 'em from the Good Book. I carry a Bible in my saddlebags. I like to read it when I got the light, usually while supper is cookin'. The night is quiet and all is peaceful. Makes a man feel plumb humble."

Josiah stepped out of the office and closed the door behind him.

Matt glanced at Sam. "Does it make you feel better just knowing that little man is staying around?"

"Infinitely so. That is, providing he's on our side!" He glanced out the window and counted the Broken Lance horses. "Twenty of them."

"I can't believe that John Lee is coming here to deliberately start trouble."

"I don't think he is. But neither do I believe he'd interfere if some of his hands wanted to mix it up."

"I think you're right." Matt hefted the sawed-off. "You ready?"

"Let's do it."

The brothers stepped out of the office and sat down on a bench on the boardwalk, the greeners across their knees. Josiah was across the wide and dusty street, leaning against an awning support, building a cigarette.

John Lee stomped up on the boardwalk. The carving on it, a small boy's name, looked familiar to him. He grimaced, thinking that it should look familiar; he'd walked on it dozens of times. "What's your stand in this matter, Finch?"

"The only stand I got is law and order, Lee." He thumb-nailed a match into flame and lighted up.

The rancher snorted his contempt and pushed past the batwings, walking into the saloon. Al stood behind the bar, polishing glasses and smiling at the customers.

"Afternoon, gents," Al said. "What's your pleasure this fine day?" He noticed Josiah Finch slipping quietly into the bar and taking a table.

Part of a wagon tongue was nailed over the long mirror behind the bar. John Lee stared at it. "What the hell is that thing doing up there?" he demanded.

"Saved my life," Al said, his expression serious.

"A wagon tongue?" young Childress blurted. His guns were polished to a mirror gloss and rested in black leather. Childress fancied himself a fast gun.

"Sure did," Al said. "When the big blow come up, I grabbed hold of that wagon tongue and held on. I tell you boys, it was a wild ride, a-flyin' through the air, miles high, holdin' on for dear life. I was talking to God, boys, let me tell you I was. But when the wind died down and I stopped spinnin', I was standing right in front of this very establishment, the wagon tongue lodged 'tween the awnin' and the second floor. Why, I just stepped off and walked down the stairs and grabbed me a broom and started sweepin' up. Yep. That's the way it was, all right."

"Gimmie a bottle," John Lee said wearily, shaking his head. "Good whiskey."

"Certainly!" Al said. He looked at Josiah. "And you, sir?"

"Beer. After you serve them others. They was here first. I wouldn't want no one to get their feelin's hurt."

"Coming right up."

John Lee looked out of the window. Bodine and Two Wolves were sitting on the bench, sawed-off shotguns across their knees. His gaze cut to Childress. The young gunny was drinking shots of whiskey and chasing them down with great gulps of beer. Maybe, John Lee thought. Just maybe he could at that. He walked over to Childress, Josiah's eyes following him.

"Just between you and me, Childress, and I wouldn't want the others to hear this," John said, whispering "I think you could take Matt Bodine."

"I know I could," Childress returned the low tones. "There ain't nothin' to him."

"Five hundred dollars is yours if you do. Just between us, now."

"When do you want me to brace him?"

"Anytime. But you better go easy on the hooch."

"Yeah. You're right." He pushed shot glass and beer mug away from him. "No time like right now, is there?"

"If you're ready."

"I'm ready," the punk said. "I owe him for that deal back by the Pecos, anyways."

"That's right," John rubbed it in, speaking in low tones. "I guess that was pretty damned humiliating, wasn't it?"

"He just got the drop on us, was all."

"But this time will be different, won't it?"

"Damn right, boss. Five minutes from now, you can think about buryin' Matt Bodine."

"Go get him, boy."

Josiah sat at his table by the window and watched John Lee speaking in low tones to the punk-lookin' young man. Josiah pegged the punk as maybe twenty-one or two. If John Lee was settin' up what the Ranger figured he was, the punk would never see another birthday.

But it ain't my show, Josiah thought, lifting his mug and taking a sip. Josiah watched as John Lee turned to a big, rough-lookin' fellow and winked. The big man—probably his foreman—nodded his head minutely and smiled.

Here it comes, Josiah thought.

The punk walked away from the bar and out onto the boardwalk, working his guns in and out of leather before he hit the batwings with his shoulder.

He leaned against a post and stared across the street at Bodine and Two Wolves.

"I believe that young man over there is looking for trouble, brother," Sam said.

"Sure looks that way, doesn't it?"

"You intend on obliging him?"

"If he pushes it, what choice do I have?"

"You have a very bad habit of answering a question with a question, are you aware of that?"

"Does it annoy you?" Matt said with a grin.

Sam muttered a very ugly phrase in Flathead.

"I speak Flathead, too, brother," Matt reminded him.

"Bodine!" Childress yelled. "I say you're yellow. I say you're afraid to face me without that express gun. And I say you're the son of a whore!"

The punk could have said a lot of things that Matt would have ignored. But not that last bit. No Western man would ignore that. Matt laid the shotgun aside and stood up, slipping off the hammer thongs from his guns.

In the saloon, Josiah pulled out a long-barreled Peacemaker and slowly spun the cylinder. He opened the loading gate and filled it up full with six. His message was silent but very loud: Interfere and someone dies in the saloon.

The town lay north to south. Matt stepped out into the street and put his back to the sun. Josiah smiled, watching him. The young man knew his business, all right. "If you can muzzle your dog, John Lee," Josiah said, "you better do it now. 'Cause if you don't, he's soon dead."

"I'm not his nursemaid," John Lee replied.

"Suit yourself," the Ranger told him, "but I hope you got enough money in your britches to bury him."

"Don't you worry about it, Ranger. You just mind your own affairs and stay out of mine."

Josiah drained his beer mug and set it down on the table. "And don't you tell me what to do, big mouth," Josiah said softly but with a deadly tinge to his words. "When it comes to law and order, I can damn well make it my affair."

Max, the big foreman, stepped in. He knew his boss's volatile temper. "There ain't no law about two men facin' each other in the street, Finch."

"That's right. Yet," he added.

John Lee turned his side to the Ranger and stared out over the batwings at the life-and-death scene building in quiet intensity in the hot street.

Childress had left the boardwalk and was walking to the center of the street, his boot heels kicking up dust, his fancy spurs jingling, cussing Bodine as he walked, both hands hovering over the butts of his guns.

Sam sat in his chair, watching, his face impassive.

"Now I'm gonna get to see what you're made of, Bodine," Childress sneered. "And I don't think you're made of very much."

"This doesn't have to be," Matt called, his voice carrying the distance between the men. "Just apologize for that remark about my mother."

"Hell with you, Bodine. And yeah, it has to be."

"Why?"

The question seemed to confuse Childress. He cocked his head to one side, a puzzled look on his face. " 'Cause of who you is, Bodine."

"What am I?"

"Dammit, you're a gunfighter!" Childress yelled.

"I'm a rancher," Matt replied.

"You're yellow!"

Matt stopped about forty feet from the young punk, his hands by his side. He could see the sweat forming on Childress's face. John Lee, Matt thought, you are one low-down person; you put this punk up to this. His death is going to be on your hands.

"Did you hear me?" Childress yelled.

"I heard you."

"Then draw, you yellow bastard!"

Matt waited.

"Drag iron!" Childress screamed.

Matt's hands did not move.

Cool, Josiah thought, watching Matt from his table. Very cool. He's a natural.

"You're gonna die!" Childress shouted. "I'll be known as the man who killed Matt Bodine."

"No," Matt spoke the words softly, but with enough force behind them to reach Childress. "All you'll have is an un-marked grave. Give this up."

In the saloon, everyone had left the bar to gather at the windows and the batwings, watching in silence. The hired guns were anxious to see what speed Bodine had, what accuracy. They knew their time with Bodine would soon come.

"Cool," Lightfoot said, his eyes on Bodine.

"The kid is losin' it," Pukey Stagg remarked.

Dusty Jordan said, "I think Bodine is scared of him."

"Then you're a fool," Trest told him.

Mark Hazard said, "Matt Bodine ain't scared. He knows he'll be standin' when it's over."

"Shut up." John Lee put an end to it.

"I said *draw*, damn you!" Childress yelled. "Come on, Bodine. Do it."

"I didn't start this, Childress. Just walk off and we'll forget it."

The punk cussed him. He cussed Matt, he cussed Two Wolves, he cussed Matt's mother and father, any sisters and brothers and ended up by calling his horse names. Still Bodine did not move. He waited.

Childress's hands flashed to his guns. Matt's draw was so quick the eye could not follow it. He drew, cocked, and fired all in one blindingly fast motion.

"Jesus," Lew Hagen breathed.

Matt's slug hit Childress in the belly and knocked him sideways, still on his boots. The kid had not fully cleared leather. One of the punk's guns fell to the ground. He managed to lift the other six-shooter and cock it. Matt shot him again, the .44 slug taking him in the chest. Childress sat down hard on the hot dirt of the street.

"Now we know." Dean Waters spoke the words softly.

The six-shooter fell from Childress's hand. It landed on the dirt and went off, the slug plowing up dust.

In the saloon, Leo Grand slipped his .45 from leather. He froze at the sound of Josiah cocking his Peacemaker. "Go ahead, hombre," Josiah said.

"I think I'll pass this round," Leo said.

"You ain't altogether stupid," the Ranger told him. "Just ugly."

Matt walked to where Childress had fallen, and rolled him on his back, his eyes staring up at the brilliant blue of the cloudless Texas sky.

Matt holstered his .44. "Anybody know where to write your kin?"

"You beat me!" the punk gasped, his hands clutching at his .44-slug-punctured belly.

"Where's your parents?" Matt persisted.

"You beat me!"

"Listen to me," Matt said, squatting down beside the young man. He wasn't worried about any of the other gunslicks. Josiah was in the saloon and Sam was watching his back. "You're dying, Childress. Your mama would want to know."

"I killed five men," Childress gasped. "I filed five notches in my guns. This ain't real." Then the pain hit him and he screamed, realizing then it was very real.

Matt stood up and turned, looking at the saloon. His eyes met those of John Lee. And John Lee's expression was one of shock. John was good with a gun, but he was not in Matt Bodine's class.

"Oh, God, it hurts!" Childress screamed. He tried to move but that only made the pain worse.

Men and women and kids began leaving their houses and tents and places of business. They gathered on the boardwalk and on the edge of the street, wide-eyed and watching.

"Somebody help me!" Childress screamed, blood leaking through his fingers. "Somebody give me somethin' for the pain. Please help me."

"You happy now, John Lee?" Matt called.

John Lee did not change his expression nor move from the batwings.

"Answer me, you sorry son!" Matt yelled.

Josiah smiled, thinking he knew what Matt was going to do next. And if one didn't work, the other would. This, he thought, was going to get real interesting, real soon.

The cries of Childress were growing louder.

"Somebody help that boy," a woman said.

"Why?" a man asked her. "He started it."

"I don't think I like it out here," the woman said. "This wouldn't have happened in Pennsylvania."

"This ain't Pennsylvania," another man spoke up.

"I can't die," Childress called. "I just can't. I'm too young to die."

The new preacher ran up, a Bible in his hand. "Have you been saved, boy?" he yelled.

"Can you help me?" Childress asked.

"Only God can help you now, boy," the preacher told him.

"John Lee!" Matt yelled. "Step out here, John Lee. This death is on your shoulders. Step out here and face me."

John Lee turned to Finch. The Ranger was smiling at him.

"Your move, Mister Hot Shot," Josiah told him. "Now we get to see what you're made of, don't we?"

John Lee flushed and cut his eyes to Bodine. "I'm no gunhand, Bodine," John Lee called.

"Sure," Matt yelled. "You just hire your killing done. Is there any honor among you boys working with John Lee?"

"What do you mean, Bodine?" Trest called. "Of course, we got honor."

Matt was slipping on leather gloves. Josiah smiled as Matt yelled, "Your boss is too damn yellow to meet me with guns. So I'm calling him out for fists. Are you boys willing to stand and let the chips fall without back-shooting me?"

Big Harry Street said, "I don't like you a-tall, Bodine, but I'll shoot any man who interferes. I swear that on my mother's grave."

"That's good enough for me, Harry," Matt called. "Come on, John Lee, or are you yellow through and through?" Matt took off his guns. Sam walked to him and took the twin .44's in leather.

John Lee smiled for the first time since he'd egged Childress on to meet his death. He had never been whipped in a fistfight. Not in his life.

"Don't nobody care nothin' about me?" Childress called weakly.

"I'll pray for you," Reverend Willowby said.

"We'll sing Christian songs," a woman said.

"Wonderful," Childress said. "I think I hear the angels callin' me home."

A horse tied to a hitchrail dumped a load of road apples in the street.

"Sing, ladies," Esther Willowby said.

John Lee took off his gunbelt and handed it to his foreman. "No one interferes," he gave the orders.

"Sing me home," Childress said.

John Lee pushed open the batwings and stepped out. "I'm gonna stomp your guts out, Bodine."

The church ladies lifted their voices in Christian song.

"Then come on and try," Bodine told him.

Josiah ordered another beer. Nameit was sure an interesting town.

Chapter 12

John Lee stepped up and tried to fake Matt out. Matt wouldn't have any of that. He sidestepped and popped John in the belly. It was like hitting a tree.

"When the roll is called up yonder," the church ladies sang sweetly.

"Bastard!" John Lee said, and swung a big fist. Matt ducked and popped the man in the mouth.

John's head jerked back from the impact and he glared at Matt, but with new respect in his eyes. Bodine could punch like the kick of a mule.

"Oh, Lord!" Childress hollered. "I don't wanna die."

"When the roll is called up yonder. . . ."

"Lord," Reverend Willowby prayed. "I ask You to take pity on this poor wretch of a man . . ."

John Lee hit Matt on the side of the head and knocked him sprawling. Matt scrambled out of the way as John tried to kick his face in. Rolling, Matt came to his boots, knowing that this was no simple bare-knuckle fight. John was out to kill him any way he could. If that's the way it was going to play, that suited Matt just fine.

". . . that will soon be entering the Pearly Gates," the preacher said.

"I ain't ready to go!" Childress said.

"Hush, boy," a citizen told him. "The man's prayin' for your evil soul."

John Lee charged in and Matt hit him twice, a left and right combination to the jaw that stopped the rancher cold in his boots, then backed him up, blood leaking from his mouth.

"This is becoming rather boring, brother," Sam called from his position on the bench. "Can't you pick up the pace some?"

"When the roll is called up yonder, I'll be there!" the ladies sang.

John swung a right, Matt ducked, and John's big left fist caught him on the side of the head and Matt heard birds chirping and singing. He backed up, shaking his head.

John sensed victory and came in swinging. Matt backheeled him and the big man hit the ground. Matt kicked him in the side, bringing a grunt of pain from the man. John rolled away, giving both of them time to clear their heads.

For all his size and strength, John was very quick on his feet and had obviously done some boxing in his time. He covered up and decided to duke it out for a change. That was a mistake, for Matt was not only a skilled boxer, but had grown up in Cheyenne villages, learning Indian wrestling.

Matt hit the big man twice in his already busted mouth and then ducked a looping punch and kicked the bigger man on the knee. John howled in pain and automatically grabbed at his knee. Matt grabbed the man's head with both hands and brought the head down and his knee up. Knee impacted with nose, and the nose spread out all over John's face with a crunch and a gush of blood.

John staggered back, fighting for time and for air, sucking it in through his bloody mouth. Matt didn't let up. He followed John's backing up, hammering at the man's belly with left and right punches, and occasionally busting John's mouth and jaw with solid connections.

In the saloon, Pukey slipped a .45 out of leather, after checking to see if the Ranger was looking. The menacing voice of Harry Street stopped him cold.

"I'll kill you, Pukey," Harry told him. "I gave my word and it stands."

"And I give mine," Trest said. "You shove that Hogleg back into leather or you'll die where you stand."

"Okay, boys," Pukey said. "I'm out of it."

What strange moral codes they live by, Josiah thought, then returned his gaze to the fight in the churned-up street.

"I ask that you accord the same saving grace to this poor wretch as you did the thief on the cross, oh Lord," Willowby intoned.

"Lead me Home, precious Lord," the ladies warbled.

"How about 'My Ship is on a Stormy Sea'?" Sam asked, getting into the spirit of things.

Willowby looked at him. "I thought you were an Indian?"

"Half. But I was baptized a Presbyterian."

"You don't say? Well, I'll be damned!"

Childress tugged at his leg. "Don't forget me, preacher."

John connected and knocked Matt flat on his butt, blood leaking from his mouth. John swung a boot at Matt's face, and Matt grabbed the boot and twisted, spilling the big man into the dirt. Matt was the first up and he kicked John in the belly as the rancher rose. The air whooshed out of him and he sat down hard on his behind.

Matt took aim and the toe of his boot connected with John Lee's chin. Teeth busted, and John fell back, blood pouring from his ruined mouth. His eyes rolled back into his head. He sighed and was out of it.

Matt walked over to a horse trough and stuck his head in the water, clearing the cobwebs from his brain and the blood from his face.

Max walked out of the saloon and motioned for some of the boys to help him. They carried John Lee off to the shaded boardwalk and stretched him out.

"Do you hear the mighty flapping of wings, boy?" Willowby asked.

"I hear them," Childress said.

"Those are the angels coming to carry you home, boy."

"Buzzards would be more like it," Josiah said, walking up.

"Angels, brother!" Willowby thundered.

"Angels don't want this trash," Josiah countered, pointing to Childress.

Childress spat a bloody glob at the Ranger's boots.

"Our Lord is a forgiving Lord, brother," Willowby said.

"I ain't your brother and don't give me none of that New Testament crap. I'm an Old Testament man. I believe in an eye for an eye and a tooth for a tooth."

"Vengence is mine, sayth the Lord."

"Mine too, if I find the son of a bitch who done me a hurt," Josiah told him.

"You heathen!" Willowby shouted.

"Windbag," the Ranger replied.

Childress died in the dirt while the Ranger and the preacher were debating theological differences. Josiah finally walked away from the sputtering preacher and went to Matt's side, looking at his face.

"He tagged you a couple of times," the Ranger observed. "But nothin' like what you give him." He looked down at the broken teeth that lay in the torn-up dirt. "He'll not forgive you for this, Bodine. I think John Lee is a mighty vain man about his looks."

"I hope he likes soup," Sam said. "He'll sure be eating it for awhile."

The church ladies hummed a sad melody as the body of Childress was toted off to be fitted for a pine box. His fancy guns lay in the dirt.

John Lee was still unconscious. A wagon was hired to carry him back to Broken Lance range.

"How do you like our little town?" Matt asked Josiah.

The Ranger grinned and cocked his head to one side. "Interestin' little place. First town I ever seen that was picked up and set down intact, lock, stock, and horse troughs by a cyclone."

"Strange things happen," Sam said. "I guess you might say it was done by the hand of God."

"Damn shore done by somebody's hands," Josiah said drily.

Not a shot was fired in anger for two weeks. The Broken Lance hired guns stayed out of Nameit and the town continued to grow as settlers moving west found it a pleasant place. Some of the smaller ranchers who had been driven out by John Lee returned to try to pick up the pieces of their lives. After a visit to the settlement, Josiah found he had orders and he drifted on, saying he would be back from time to time to check on things.

After careful interviewing and much thought, Jeff Sparks hired Bam Ford and Pen Masters. The men proved to be good cowboys with no aversion to hard work.

And Nameit had a doctor. Young Dr. Wilbur Winters with a fresh degree in medicine was on his way to El Paso, passing through on a stage. The stage stopped to change teams, Wilbur took a break, and decided he liked Nameit. With a preacher, a schoolteacher, and a doctor, the town of Nameit was solid settled now.

One of his first patients was Cindy Lee.

"You're pregnant," Wilbur told her.

"Hell, I knew that!" she said crossly. "When's the baby due?"

"You're asking me?" Wilbur said.

She had been driven into town in a buggy, accompanied by her husband and a dozen Broken Lance riders.

Dodge had ridden in, accompanied by half a dozen Circle S hands, among them, Gene and Lia and Lisa Sparks. The girls had come to town to shop.

"I'll stay with the Broken Lance people," Sam volunteered. "You stay with the Circle S bunch."

Matt smiled. "I might get the impression that you're avoiding Lisa."

"You'd be right. That woman has matrimony on the mind. And so does Lia. You be careful, brother, or you'll find yourself roped, tied, and branded."

"Not as long as I know the way out of town and have a fast horse."

The brothers had a lot of country to travel before they would entertain the thought of marriage.

It had been two weeks since any of the Circle S crew had visited town, and Matt was anxious to catch up on what had been happening at the ranch.

"Quiet," Dodge told him over beer. "Ever since you laid that whuppin' on John Lee, he's pulled in his horns. I'd a give a month's pay to have seen it."

Gene grinned. "That Texas Ranger stopped by the ranch. He said Childress won't be giving us anymore trouble."

"Childress was a loudmouth punk," Matt said. "John Lee put him up to bracing me."

"Josiah paid you a high compliment, Matt," Dodge said. "He said you're the man who is faster than him."

"That's a compliment I hope he keeps to himself."

"Oh, he will. But them gunnies out at Broken Lance won't. The word's already spread. Two of them guns John Lee hired pulled out. They hauled their ashes the day after you dropped Childress and whupped John Lee. Pen Masters said they was pretty fair hands with a short gun themselves."

"I wish they'd all leave," Matt said, after taking a pull of beer.

"Speaking of Broken Lance people," Gene said. "Here they come."

The batwings squeaked open and the saloon filled with Broken Lance guns, including Nick, who looked like he was on the prod. The young man gave Matt a dirty look and gave Gene an even dirtier one. Then his eyes touched on young Jimmy and a smirk crossed his face. He whispered something to one of the gunnies and both men laughed.

Jimmy flushed and tensed. Dodge touched his arm. "Just stand easy, boy," the foreman said. "You ain't no gunhand."

Matt put his back to the bar to face the Broken Lance crowd. Sam pushed open the batwings and stepped inside, holding a greener in his left hand.

"Cain't a man even sit down an' enjoy a drink without havin' to look down the barrels of a damn express gun?" Tanner griped from his chair.

"It isn't pointed at you or anybody else," Sam told him.

"I always figured a man who carried one of them was a coward," Nick sneered.

He was standing too close to Sam to have said that. Sam hit him with a right that knocked the smartmouth off his boots and stretched him out flat on the saloon floor. With a snarl and a curse on his bloody lips, Nick made a grab for his guns. He sighed and paled when Sam beat him to the draw in a no-contest show of speed.

Sam smiled at the young punk. "Take his guns out of leather," Sam told a Broken Lance rider. "Then get him to his boots."

Sam laid the greener on the bar, then took off his gunbelt and pulled his second .44 from behind his sash. Just as Nick was getting to his boots, Sam walked over and busted him smack in the mouth with a hard right fist. The rancher's son hit the floor for the second time in as many minutes. With blood leaking from his mouth, Nick shook his head and cussed, springing to his boots and wading in after Sam, both fists flailing the air.

Sam sidestepped and clubbed the punk on the side of his face with a right then followed that with a left to Nick's belly. He hooked a boot behind Nick's foot and sent him crashing to the floor.

Nick rolled and came up with a chair in his hands. He hurled the wooden chair at Sam. The chair missed and Al caught it before it could shatter the mirror.

Nick screamed his rage and frustration and charged Sam. Sam waited until the last possible split second, stepped aside, and Nick slammed into the bar, knocking the wind from him. Sam hammered at the punk's kidneys with hard fists, bringing a scream of pain from the young man.

Sam grabbed the punk by his long hair and jerked him away from the bar. With one hand in his hair and the other holding onto the seat of his jeans, Sam propelled the yelling and cussing punk out of the saloon and deposited him in a horse trough just as Lisa and Lia came walking up from one directon and Cindy waddling up from another.

The Broken Lance rider who had escorted Cindy to the doc's office grabbed for iron and Matt, standing by the batwings, drilled him dead center in the chest. The gunny tumbled off the boardwalk and died with his face in the dirt.

As soon as Matt jerked iron, Dodge cleared leather with both Peacemakers, holding the Broken Lance riders in the saloon at ease. Sam hauled Nick out of the water and threw him into the center of the street. The punk rolled in the dirt and came up looking like a mudball.

"Lousy greasy Injun bastard!" Nick yelled at Sam. "I'll kill you for this."

Sam walked over to him and kicked him in the mouth. Nick's front teeth now joined his father's front teeth, still lying somewhere in the dirt of the street. Nick stretched out in the dirt, unconscious.

"John Lee will hang your scalp on his saddle horn for this," Cindy squalled at Sam, her face becoming ugly and mottled.

"Pick up your rabid skunk and your dead gunslick and get out of town," Matt told the Broken Lance riders, turning from the batwings to face them. "I'll not bar any of you from town, but don't come in here looking for trouble. Pass the word, boys. No trouble in Nameit."

"You've played hell this time, Bodine," Harry Street said. "You know John Lee will not let this pass easy. And I ain't threatenin' you none by sayin' it. I'm just statin' a fact, is all. He's a revenge-seekin' man, he is."

"Harry," Matt said, "I'm going to give you and the other boys some advice. You know there's a Texas Ranger working slow circles around this area. If this situation busts wide open, he'll call for help and you all know what that means. Shoot a Texas Ranger and his buddies will track you through the gates of hell. Best thing you boys could do is draw your pay and ride."

Harry Street hesitated, then slowly shook his head. "I ain't never quit a job of work, Bodine. No point in startin' now."

"Attacking ranches and trying to burn them out, Harry? That's what you call a job of work? Attacking women?"

Harry Street's grin held little humor. "I heard about some ol' boys attackin' the Circle S. Course I wouldn't know nothin' about who done it. Seems they run up on a Mex cook with a shotgun. Them boys lost. 'Pears to me them women you speak of can take care of themselves."

"I've said all I can say then, Harry."

"If a couple of the boys escort Nick and his bride back to the ranch, you mind if the rest of us finish our drinks?"

"Don't mind at all, Harry. Long as there is no trouble."

"It won't come from none of us, Bodine."

"Nor from any Circle S hand," Dodge said.

"Fair enough. Enjoy your drinks, boys." Matt walked out on the boardwalk and stood with Sam, watching as the unconscious form of Nick Lee was loaded into the buggy beside his still-squalling wife. The body of the hired gun was tied facedown across his saddle, and the parade headed out of town, escorted by several Broken Lance riders.

"Wonder where the nearest dentist is?" Sam said.

"El Paso, probably. Maybe Fort Worth. Brother, if this doesn't blow the lid off things, I don't know what will."

"We said that when you whipped John Lee, remember?"

"Yeah, we sure did. What's he waiting on, Sam?"

Sam chuckled. "He might be waiting on some false teeth!"

Chapter 13

Matt and Sam were awakened about ten o'clock by Lomax banging on the front door. "They hit the Flying V 'bout two, three hours ago, boys. Burned down the barn, scattered the horses, and put lead in Ed Carson. He ain't a-gonna make it, I'm thinkin'. Chookie's over gettin' the doc now. Gary rode in to tell us, but he couldn't ride no more. He caught one in the shoulder."

"I'll saddle the horses," Sam said, stepping around Matt and slinging his gunbelt around his lean waist and sticking the second .44 behind his sash.

They were in the saddle ten minutes later, the doctor right behind them in his buggy. Jeff Sparks had left ten hands behind at his ranch, and he had led the ride over to the Flying V, Lisa driving her mother in the buggy, Lia on Lightning.

"I say we ride over to the Broken Lance and burn the goddamn place to the ground and kill every dirty son there!" Sparks said, his voice tight with anger.

"Not while I'm wearing this badge," Matt told him.

"Nor me," Sam told them.

"Whose side are you on?" Sparks yelled at the brothers.

"I won't even dignify that with a reply," Sam told the rancher.

Sparks's shoulders slumped and he shook his head. "I'm sorry, Sam. I truly am. But what the hell can we do?"

"Did you get lead in any of the attackers?" Matt asked.

"Killed four," Gary said, a bloody bandage on his left shoulder. Noah was inside with his father. "We stretched 'em out over yonder. John Lee's hired some new men, Matt. We ain't never seen any of them dead gunslicks before. And their horses got brands that we ain't never seen."

"He hired them especially for this job," Sam said. "And those that got away are still riding. Bet on it. Nothing left behind to connect the Broken Lance with this night's trouble. He's getting smarter."

"How many men were there?" Matt asked.

"Ten, I'd say," Teddy said. "They was all wearin' dark dusters and come out at us fast and hard. I'd guess that we wounded maybe two of them. How bad is anybody's guess."

"And they headed north," Mark said. "Straight for the New Mexico border."

Dr. Winters stepped out on the porch of the ranch house. "Gentlemen, Ed Carson just died."

Matt pulled Beavers over to one side. "Get you a fresh horse and ride for the settlement. Get a wire out or some kind of message to Ranger Headquarters. Advise them we need Josiah Finch in here and we need him right now!"

"I'm gone, Matt."

"I'm here now." The voice came from behind the bunch.

They all turned around. Josiah Finch sat Horse about twenty-five feet from them. Horse moved as quietly as the Ranger.

"I seen the fire from miles off," Josiah said. "Figured it had to be trouble." He looked at Matt and Sam. "By the power vested in me by the State of Texas I now say that you two is swore in Texas Rangers. Raise your right hands and repeat after me."

He swore them in on the spot. "Now, by God, you two will not be a-ridin' hellbent around for trouble. You're Texas Rangers now." He dug in his saddlebags and tossed the badges. "Pin 'em on, boys. You!" he pointed to Pen Masters. "You're now marshal of Nameit."

"Me?" Pen shouted. "The hell you say!"

"And you," Josiah pointed to Bam, "is his deputy."

"That's disgusting!" Bam said. "What'll all my friends say?"

"Knowin' the kind of people you been associatin' with for years, they'll probably shoot you on sight," Josiah said, his eyes twinkling with dark humor. "Matt, Sam, give them two new lawmen your marshal's badges and switch your saddles to fresh horses. We got some trackin' to do. First light, one of you boys ride to the settlement and send a wire to Austin—Ranger HQ. Advise them we got two new Rangers—Matt Bodine and Sam Two Wolves—and to put them on the payroll. Let's ride, boys."

Daylight found them closing in on the men who had attacked the ranch. The outlaws had ridden hard for ten miles, then rested and back in the saddle had been walking their horses.

"Does it bother you at all that we just might be in New Mexico?" Sam asked Josiah.

"Nope."

"But you have no arrest powers outside of Texas."

"I do as long as I keep the criminals in sight."

"But we haven't seem them yet!"

"Seen their tracks. Same thing."

"You are a very exasperating man," Sam told him.

"I'm a Texas Ranger. That says it all. And so is you boys. Bear that in mind."

"Smoke from a campfire up ahead," Matt said, spotting a thin line of smoke in the distance.

"That'll be them," Josiah said.

Sam looked at Josiah. The man's jaw was set and his eyes

focused straight ahead. "Why do I get this feeling that we're just going to ride right into the outlaw camp— if it is the men who attacked the ranch—announce who we are and demand their surrender?"

" 'Cause that's what's we're gonna do," Josiah told him. "Ain't no point in pussy-footin' around and bein' polite and all that. We'll know where we stand as soon as they jerk iron. If they don't jerk iron, we got the wrong bunch and we can step down and have coffee with them."

"And if they are the right bunch?" Sam asked.

"We shoot them and then drink their coffee. Lawin's easy once you get the hang of it."

"Incredible," Sam said.

"Thank you," Josiah replied.

Six men looked up from their breakfast as the three Rangers approached their camp. Two of them wore bloody bandages; one on his leg, the other arm-shot. All had dark dusters tied behind their saddles.

"Get ready," Josiah said. "We got two apiece."

"We have them outnumbered," Sam said, the sarcasm thick in his voice.

"Sure do," Josiah agreed. "Glad to see you're gettin' the hang of it so fast."

The three Rangers had the reins in their left hands. Their right hands were close to their guns. The outlaws were heavily armed, and the men brushed back their coats, exposing their pistols.

"Texas Rangers," Josiah announced. "Stand or deliver, boys."

The outlaws chose the former, grabbing for iron. The camp exploded in gunfire, gunsmoke filling the air with puffs of gray clouds. At that range, it was nearly impossible to miss. It came down to who cleared leather first, and the Rangers did. When the shooting stopped, three outlaws were stretched out in the dirt, dead. Two were hard hit and probably dying, and a third stood holding his one good arm in the air. His right arm dangled bullet-shattered by his side.

"You damn people are crazy!" the wounded outlaw said.

Sam wanted to tell him that he agreed wholeheartedly with that assessment, but held his tongue, figuring Josiah would take exception to it.

"Stand over yonder," Josiah told the man, motioning with his Peacemaker.

The man moved slowly back.

The Rangers swung down from their saddles and began checking the camp. Josiah tied the wounded man's good arm to his belt and poured himself a cup of coffee, using his own cup from his saddlebags.

"Might catch hydrophoby from them yahoos' cups," he said. He looked at the wounded man. "Talk to me, boy."

"Nice day, ain't it?"

Josiah smiled, the slight curving of his lips resembling a rattler's smile. "Now, boy, we can do this any number of ways. You can cooperate, and I might see that the judge goes easy on you. You can get smartmouthed, and I'll just leave you out here, without horse, guns, boots, or food. And if you think I won't do that, then you're a fool."

The outlaw nodded his head. "Man come up to our camp outside the trading post called Roswell. Up north of here. Must have been three, four weeks ago. It was at night. Never did get a good look at him. Said he wanted a job of work done. Wanted a rancher name of Carson burned out and his cattle drove off. Throwed a sack of money onto the ground and left. Took Steven there," he nodded at a dead outlaw, " 'bout a week to round up enough boys to pull it off. Then we done 'er. Now I'm sittin' here shot up lookin' at you. That's all I know about it."

Josiah sipped his coffee and stared at the man. One of the wounded men screamed horribly and then died. The other was lung shot and belly shot and wouldn't last much longer.

"It's my duty to tell you that you're under arrest for murder. That rancher died last night."

"You'll play hell provin' it was me that kilt him."

"That's a fact," Josiah agreed. "But you was a part of it, you confessed to it in front of three Texas Rangers, so that means you'll spend some years in prison. Which horse is yours?"

"The bay over there."

Matt saddled the bay while Sam collected the guns and personal effects from the dead. The men sat around the fire, for the morning was still cool, drinking coffee and frying bacon while they waited for the other outlaw to die. As soon as he passed, his body was dragged over to a ravine to lie with the others. A small bluff was caved in over them. Josiah got his Bible and the men took off their hats.

"Oh, Lord," Josiah said. "Do what you can for these sorry bastards. Amen. Let's ride."

They headed back to Texas.

They rode into Nameit, dirty and tired and hungry and wanting a hot bath, some food, and rest. The wounded outlaw—his name was Charles Gruen—was treated by Dr. Winters and tossed into one cell of the three-cell pokey.

"Now what happens?" Gruen asked.

"You get tried soon as I can get a judge over here," Josiah told him. "Might be next month, might be next year. Then we either hang you or you go to prison."

"I want a lawyer."

"Sure, you do. But they ain't no lawyers in this town. Thank the Lord."

"I was driven to a life of crime. I had a terrible childhood," Gruen said. "My daddy beat me."

"He didn't beat you enough," Josiah told him. "Now shut up."

There was a note on the desk stating that Pen and Bam were out chasing some petty thieves. They would be back first light.

The men took their baths, shaved, then got something to eat. Josiah turned up the lamp on the office desk and took pen and paper and began writing out his report. He left it on the desk when he went out back to use the privy. Sam picked it up and read, "Me and Bodine and Two Wolves picked up their tracks heading north from the burned-out ranch. We found the six of them the next morning. I think we was in Texas. We braced them, they jumped, we shot them. Killed five—I spoke words over them—and we brung Charles Gruen back to Nameit for trial."

"That pretty well says it all," Matt said, reading over Sam's shoulder.

"He's not a wordy man, is he?"

Dodge rode up and walked into the office. He looked at the outlaw sitting on his bunk in the cell. Back in the main office, he poured a cup of coffee. "John Lee is hirin' more men. I got that word this afternoon."

"How's his mouth?" Matt asked with a grin.

"Sore, so I'm told," the old gunfighter turned rancher said with a smile. "I'm told they can't tell about Nick's mouth until the swellin' goes down." He looked at Sam. "Watch your backtrail, boy. Nick's swore to kill you. And don't take him lightly. He'll kill you any way he can.

"I never take death threats lightly. I guess I should have shot him when he drew on me, or tried to draw on me, back in the saloon."

"You mighty right you should have," Dodge said. "But I understand why you didn't."

"You're out pretty late, Dodge," Matt said.

"Jimmy's on the prod. We're lookin' for him. He left home swearin' to kill John Lee. That was about noon today. Nobody's seen hide nor hair of him since."

Josiah had entered through the back door and stood listening until the foreman had finished. "Is the boy any good with a gun?"

Dodge shrugged. "Average, I'd say. He's not fast, if that's what you mean. But he's real good with a rifle."

"What brought this on?" Sam asked.

"No one knows. But he was real fond of Ed Carson. Funeral's at dawn, by the way. Ed always requested that."

"We'll be there," Matt said. "What do you want us to do about Jimmy?"

"Rope him if you see him. But I don't think you will. I think he's hid out plannin' on how to get a shot at John Lee."

Josiah sighed audibly. "If he does that, it'll have to be called murder, Dodge."

"I know it. And you boys will have to go after him."

"Damn!" Matt swore.

The service was a simple one, with the Reverend Willowby officiating. Halfway through the service, Sam looked up and saw a dust cloud rolling toward them. He dropped to his knees and put an ear to the ground, just as Willowby stopped in the middle of his sermon and looked disapprovingly at him.

Sam jumped to his boots. "Riders! A lot of them and coming straight for us."

"Not even John Lee would do something this horrible!" Ed's widow cried.

"Let them open fire!" Josiah yelled. "If they do that, we can take it to a court of law and stop John Lee."

"Get the women in the house!" Jeff Sparks called. "Move, people, move!"

The riders, fifty or more strong, all wearing bandanas over their faces, circled the ranch-house area, shooting at anything that moved. All of the smaller ranchers who had moved back into the area were at the funeral with their families, several of them with small children.

One woman went down, crying out as a bullet hit her in the shoulder. A young girl, no more than five or six, ran crying and screaming toward the circling gunmen. A horse knocked her sprawling. She did not move.

"You goddamn no-good Godless heathens!" Reverend Willowby roared, grabbing up a rifle from a saddle boot and opening up. He knocked one rider out of the saddle and shot another in the knee, the man screaming in pain, dropping his six-shooter and grabbing at his leg.

Vonny Dodge was down on one knee, both hands filled with Colts, and his aim was deadly. He was literally making each round count. The old gunfighter was showing his skills as he emptied saddle after saddle.

Nettie Carson screamed once and called out her dead husband's name as a bullet tore into her back just as she was climbing up the steps to her house. She sprawled face down on the porch and lay still.

"Oh, Sweet Jesus Christ, no!" Jeff Sparks yelled, watching Noah run to his mother's side, shooting as he ran. The other Flying V hands ran to cover Noah, all of them throwing lead as fast as they could.

"They're trying to torch the house!" Sam yelled "Come on, brother."

The men and women had managed to exit the lonely gravesite and make it to some sort of cover. The blood brothers ran around the side of the ranch house and began emptying saddles, the torches falling harmlessly to the ground.

The attackers tore down the corral and scattered the horses. Most of the horses of those who had ridden over had run off, frightened and panicked. Several buggies had overturned as the scared animals bolted, smashing the buggies into buildings, water troughs, other wagons. The attack broke off, the riders galloping away, leaving behind them a scene of blood and death and misery.

Josiah caught up with the brothers. "We'll see to the wounded first," he said, his face hard and his words grim.

"Then you boys will find out what it means to be called Texas Rangers."

Noah was sitting on the porch, his mother's hand cradled in his lap. He was crying soundlessly, tears streaking his tanned face. Lisa sat down beside him and put her arms around him, comforting him.

"The little girl's arm's busted," Tate called. "But other than that she seems to be all right."

"Some of you boys carry that wounded lady into the house," Dodge called. "Move."

Red was cussing, tying a bandana around his wounded leg. Compton was matching him word for word, a bullet-shattered arm hanging by his side. Jeff Sparks had a gash on his forehead and Denver had taken a round in the side and was down on the ground.

Doc Winters was busy, issuing orders and cleaning out the wounds. Other than that, there was little he could do to fight any infection that might set it. When he ran out of alcohol from his bag, he ordered vinegar from the house to be used.

"Acetic acid," he explained. "Just do it, it works."

Josiah walked over to Jeff. "We'll be catchin' our horses and ridin'. Ain't no point in stayin' around for the buryin'. Trail'll be cold by then."

"Are you going to call for more Rangers?"

"Nope."

"For God's sake, man—why not?"

"Three of us here now. Don't need no more."

"What about the wounded outlaws?" Dodge asked.

"I ain't got time to fool with nothin' like that. We got to get on the trail of them that's ridin' off."

Matt and Sam were bringing in their horses and selecting spare mounts.

"I don't understand," Jeff said.

"I do," Dodge said, his words flint hard.

"We'll borrow some food from the house," Josiah said.

"Bell," Dodge called. "Get that wagon tongue up over yonder. Lash it up high."

Bell's smile was savage. "Right, boss."

Matt and Sam were in the saddle when Josiah swung up into his. Barlow and Chookie and Parnell were building nooses as they rode out.

When there aren't any trees around, and the barn's been burned down, a lashed-up wagon tongue does just fine for a hanging.

Chapter 14

"They're headin' away from Broken Lance range," Sam said. "And those tracks say they're riding hard."

Josiah nodded his head in agreement. "They'll ride for miles in this direction, with one or two of them breakin' off ever' now and then, mixin' their tracks in with cattle or followin' a creek bed for a time. You agree with that, Matt?"

"Yes. We'll probably have to split up before very long. How do we play this, Josiah?"

"You bring 'em in upright and you'll be doin' a lot of paperwork and spendin' days listenin' to lawyers yelpin' back and forth. Personally, I'm a man who believes in law and order. I ain't never testified against an innocent man nor shot an innocent man. Now, I've come close, but some inner sense has always warned me off. We ain't dealin' with innocent people. Anyone who would attack folks at a funeral, shooting women and kids and interruptin' God's word is trash. There ain't no pity in my heart for trash. I've had high words of praise spoke to me. I've had medals given me by the governor. All because I'm supposed to be a good lawman. But I swear on my wife's grave I'll not bring none of this bunch in alive. If I have to take this badge off and stomp it into the dust I'll show no mercy to this pack of hyenas. Them's my words. You boys do what you want to do. I'm veerin' off here. See you."

Josiah Finch turned his horse and was gone, following two sets of tracks that had just left the main pack of outlaws and hired guns.

The brothers rode on in silence, both of them thinking of Mrs. Nettie Carson, shot in the back and lying dead in a pool of blood on her front porch.

"Two riders branching off here," Sam broke the silence. "See you, brother."

Matt rode on for another mile. Two more men left the main body and cut west. He let them go, continuing to follow the larger group. He saw where the group had stopped, perhaps to rest their horses, but more than likely to make plans. He would have to assume they were ambush plans. And in this country, where the terrain was so deceptive, an ambush would be an easy thing . . . if a man wasn't very careful.

Matt sat his horse for a time, thinking things over. They had passed no water since leaving the funeral site. Their horses would have to have water. And that meant the raiders would be forced to swing back west, toward the Pecos. Matt turned toward the river. If things worked out, he'd have a little ambush of his own.

Josiah faced the two men and they were scared. They didn't know how the Ranger had gotten ahead of them, and at this juncture, that really wasn't important. He had, and the outlaws' guns were in leather.

"Mornin'," one said, his eyes not meeting Josiah's gaze, but instead remaining fixed on the muzzle of the Ranger's .45, the hammer back.

"Man shouldn't ride no blue steel on a raid," Josiah said. "Horse like that's too easy to fix in a person's mind. Your hat's got a turkey feather stuck in it. That's stupid too. Stands out like a pimple on your nose. You're one that raided the funeral, I'm Josiah Finch, and that makes you dead."

Josiah shot him, the .45 slug knocking him out of the saddle. The second man grabbed for iron and Josiah blew him to hell. Josiah pulled saddle and bridle off the horses and turned them loose. Josiah took the dead men's ammo and hung their gunbelts on his saddle horn, after making sure all weapons were loaded up full. He left the raiders where they lay, baking under the hot Texas sun.

"Hope the buzzards don't get sick," he said, and rode out. He'd cut some more tracks in a little while. He wondered how the brothers were doing.

"Breed," the man said, "I don't know where you come from, but I'm gonna gut-shoot you and leave you out here to die."

Sam shot him, then shifted the muzzle and drilled the second man in the center of his chest. The first man was hanging onto the saddle horn and trying to quiet his bucking horse and lift his Hog-leg all at the same time. He didn't have anymore time left him. Sam's .44 barked again and the raider tumbled from the saddle.

Sam swung down and approached the raiders. Both were dead. He checked the brands on the horses; they were not familiar to him. He stripped saddles and bridles from their horses and turned them loose. Just as Josiah had done, he took their guns, looping the gunbelts on his saddle horn after checking to see they were loaded up full. He left the men where they lay. The carrion birds and wolves and coyotes would feed, and soon the bare bones would bleach under the relentless sun. The leather would rot and the spurs would rust.

Sam mounted up and rode away, wondering how his brother was doing.

* * *

Matt sighted in the rider in front and squeezed the trigger. The Winchester rifle boomed and the rider fell from the saddle to land in the cool sands on the east side of the Pecos. Before the large group of raiders could get out of range, Matt had emptied two more saddles. He punched rounds into his rifle as he walked back to his horse. Across the river, he left the saddle and looked at the hired guns. One was still alive, the .44 slug taking the man low in the left side and exiting out high on the right side, just under his arm pit.

"Lawmen ain't supposed to ambush people," the dying gunny whispered.

"I'm an unusual lawman," Matt told him. "You got any family you want me to notify?"

"You'd do that?"

"Yes."

"Got a sister in Arkansas. Fort Smith. Old maid, last I heard. Probably still is. Ugly as sin. Mabel Tucker. She'd like to know where I'm buried. You are gonna bury me?"

"Nope."

"You a cold man, Ranger."

"Not as cold as you're about to be."

"That's a fact."

"Who hired you?"

"Don't know his name. Man that contacted us was a go-between, I'm shore. Give us a hundred dollars apiece to hit the Flyin' V. Said there'd be a bonus if we killed the woman and the boy. Did we git 'em?"

Matt shook his head as waves of disgust washed over him. Even dying, the outlaw was not repentant. He started to ask another question, then saw that the man was dead.

He decided he would not write the old maid sister. She'd be better off forgetting this brother.

As Josiah and Sam had done, he turned the horses loose and took the guns. He was just starting to swing into the saddle when he heard hooves. He turned, pistol in hand.

Josiah was riding up from the south. "That's Heck Tucker," he said, looking at the nearest body sprawled on the sands. "He's a bad one. Reward on him, but you're gonna have to tote the body in to claim it."

"I think I'll pass on that."

"Don't blame you. He'd be ripe as a plum 'fore you got him in. You gonna bury 'em?"

"Did you bury yours?"

Josiah smiled. "Not likely."

"Let's see if we can find Sam." Matt swung into the saddle and they headed out.

Sam found them, joining them about a half-hour after they left the Pecos. "I heard shots."

"I got two, Matt got three," Josiah said. "How about you?"

"Two. I didn't recognize any of them."

"I did. They're ol' boys fresh from the cattle wars up in Kansas. Most of 'em anyways. John Lee's savin' his permanent people and hirin' out 'way far from here. What'd you boys want to do?"

"Trail them," Sam said.

"Might make good Rangers after all," Josiah said.

They caught up with them at a trading post on the Seminole Draw after days of hot, dusty tracking. The three were dirty, unshaven, tired, hungry, and about as sociably inclined as irritated porcupines.

"I was beginning to think you were lost," Sam said to Josiah, as they sighted the small settlement by the river.

"I ain't never been lost," the little man said. "Horse has, but I ain't."

Horse swung his tired head around and gave Finch a baleful look.

"We've been pushing them hard," Matt said. "And we know they're out of supplies, living on jackrabbits." He checked his guns. "Let's go get this over with."

"No way we can ride in unseen," Sam said. "You can bet they've got lookouts."

"I want something to eat I didn't have to shoot, skin, and cook," Josiah said. "And I aim to have it before or after we brace that trash over yonder. It don't make no difference to me. Let's go."

They made a half circle and came in behind the long, low building, reining up at the corral. Josiah patted Horse on the neck. "You just hold that saddle up for a few more minutes, ol' feller. I'll be out directly to relieve you of it and you can rest for a time."

The men loosened their guns in leather and walked around the front of the trading post. The windows were so dirty and fly-specked they could not see inside. The outside walls were pocked and pitted with old bullet scars, and parts of several arrows were still imbedded, grim reminders of the battles the post had endured. Bleached white by years in the sun, the skeletal fingers and wrist bone of a human hand hung outside by a piece of wire.

Josiah pointed to it. "Durin' an attack one Injun got close enough to ram his hand through a window. One of them inside lobbed it off with an axe. That was about ten years ago. Injun attacks sort of petered out for a time after that." Josiah pushed open the door and stepped inside.

The door they entered opened into the store section of the post, filled with everything that the owner figured somebody might want . . . someday. The bar was at the far end, to the right of the men. They could hear loud talk and rough laughter coming from that end.

"Maybe they didn't have guards out," Sam said.

"They figure they're a day or so ahead of us," Josiah said. "They ain't been figurin' on us ridin' all night to get here. You boys ready for a drink to cut the dust and some food for the belly?"

"Sounds good to me," Matt said, and took the lead, winding his way through the counters piled high with merchandise.

The men stepped into the dimly lighted bar area and the

laughter and loud talk stopped as abruptly as someone suddenly blowing out a lamp. Matt walked to the middle of the bar—several long planks supported by barrels—and leaned up against it.

Josiah took one end and Sam took the other. All three men were conscious of the hard eyes that stared at them from two tables pulled together in a corner of the room.

The barkeep, a huge grossly overweight man who both looked and smelled like he was only days away from his semiannual bath, lumbered out of a back room and pulled up short at the sight of the badges pinned to the shirts of the trio. His gaze cut to the men in the corner.

"Three whiskeys," Josiah said. "Then we'll talk about somethin' to eat."

"Got stew that's hot and fresh homebaked bread my old woman just took from the oven."

"Sounds good," Sam said "We'll drink first."

The barkeep looked at the identical three-stone necklaces on Matt and Sam. He looked hard at Sam, frowned, and said, "I ain't never served up no whiskey to Injuns. If you is an Injun."

"He's a breed," Josiah said. "Pour the rotgut."

"No offense meant," the fat man said, filling the shot glass in front of Sam, which Sam had carefully wiped out with a handkerchief.

"None taken," Sam said with a smile, then suddenly whipped out a long-bladed knife. His eyes hardened. The barkeep backed up as far as he could go. "But don't serve me over three whiskeys. It stirs up my Indian blood and I get vicious and might take a notion to start scalping."

"Two'll be your limit!"

Sam laughed, sheathed his knife, and picked up his drink. The three of them moved to a table, arranging the chairs so they could all look over into the corner.

"I don't recognize the brands on them horses out in the corral," Josiah said. "You reckon they might be stolen?"

"I wouldn't doubt it," Matt replied.

"We ain't ridin' no stolen horses," the voice came from a man in the corner. "Them horses was bought by us."

"They mighty tired animals," Josiah said. "You boys been pushin' hard since you left the Pecos. I think you ought to give them a rest."

"We ain't been close to the Pecos, and I don't recall askin' for your opinion on nothin'," another man at the corner table said. "So why don't you shet your trap?"

"Them's Texas Rangers, boys," the barkeep said.

"That don't spell crap to me," yet another man said. "And it damn sure don't give 'em the right to call us horse thieves."

"I think we hurt their feelin's," Josiah said.

"Maybe so." Sam picked it up. "But how do you hurt the feelings of a liar?"

"Good point," Matt said.

"You callin' us liars?" one of the raiders asked.

"I'm callin' you all liars," Josiah said. "You're liars, back-shooters, ambushers, and hired killers. You're scum, punks, and trash. We've trailed you all for days. And we've left a string of dead bodies from the Pecos to here, and the list includes Tom Johnson, Hale Rivers, Barry Jackson, and Heck Tucker. Now what do you have to say about that, you ugly bastard?"

The outlaws came up dragging iron. But the Rangers had anticipated that. They jerked first and the trading post thundered with gunfire. Matt, Sam, and Josiah had a six-shooter in each hand, two more tucked behind each gunbelt and they let the lead fly. The barkeep hit the floor and stayed down, the building trembling when his weight impacted the boards.

It was over in only a few heartbeats. Gunsmoke hung heavy in the low-ceiling post. The reverberating gunshots had caused old bird's nests, dirt, and droppings to fall from the ceiling. One raider crawled to his knees, blood on his face, hate in his eyes, and his hands filled with .45's. Six pistols roared as one and the slugs lifted the gunhand to his boots and flung him back against a wall, dead before he hit the wall.

"Holy Jesus Christ!" the barkeep bellered.

The trio of Rangers walked over to the blood-slick corner. Raiders were stacked up on top of each other, sprawled in death and near death. One of them looked up through the gunsmoke and cussed the trio.

"I'd hate to go meet my maker with them words on my lips," Josiah told him.

The outlaw added a few more.

"Where's the rest of your bunch of trash?" Josiah asked him.

"You go straight to hell!" the outlaw told him.

"It don't make no difference," Josiah said. "We'll find 'em if we have to track 'em clear to Canada. Who paid you to attack the ranch?"

The raider told the Ranger where to put his question. Sideways.

The Rangers loaded up while the raider cussed them. The barkeep was on his hands and knees, peeping around a barrel behind the bar. "I'll bury 'em for five dollars apiece," he said.

"I ain't dead yet, you fat pig!" the only surviving raider gasped.

"You will be in a little while," the barkeep replied. "And I can wait."

"First thing you do it git up and fetch us somethin' to eat," Josiah told him. "Then start draggin' this trash out the back. You take what they owe you and five dollars more per hole. And dig the holes deep or the coyotes'll eat 'em. Bring ever'thing else back in here. You hear me?"

"Yes, sir!"

Josiah turned to the brothers. "I figure we got ten back at the ranch. We've left ten more on the trail. They's six here. That means we ain't got but about twenty more to go. We ought to have this wrapped up in a week or so."

"I want a doctor!" the surviving gunslick said. "I'm bad hurt."

"You best hurry up and expire," Josiah told him. "I don't see how you're livin' now. You got more holes in you than a prairie-dog colony."

"I hope the Injuns git you all and stake you out over an anthill!" the raider gasped.

"What an unkind thing to say," Sam told him. "After all we've done for you."

"All you've done for me! You ain't done nothin' for me except kill me." The raider shuddered and closed his eyes.

Sam started to reply, then looked down at the man. He was dead.

"I'm hungry," Josiah said. "Let's eat."

Chapter 15

The Rangers caught up with five more at a tiny hamlet on the Blackwater Draw. The townspeople stood in silence and watched the lawmen slowly ride in, stable their horses, and slip their guns in and out of leather a time or two. One minute the few stores on the short street were window-lined with people. The next minute they were deserted.

"They'll be in that hole-in-the-wall saloon over there," Matt said.

"Probably," Josiah replied. "And they know we're here."

The batwings opened and five men crowded out, stepping into the street. One called, "We're tarred of you pushin' us. Damn tarred of it. We'll settle it here."

"Suits me," Matt called. He jerked iron and put a slug in the man's belly. The man went down to his knees and the others grabbed for guns.

Sam's first shot hit a man's gunbelt and exploded the cartridges in the belt. One slug struck the raider in the foot, another hit him in the groin, and several others exploded and tore a hole in his stomach. Sam's second shot ended his painful screaming.

Josiah had a Peacemaker in each hand and took two out,

the Colts thundering. Matt took careful aim and drilled the last man standing, knocking him up against a hitchrail. The raider's .45 went off and he shot himself in the knee. He pitched forward into a horsetrough and bubbled and gurgled for a few seconds.

"They come in with about ten more, Ranger!" a citizen said, running up. "Them others pulled out this morning. They headed west toward New Mexico Territory."

"Thank you," Josiah said, reloading. "Git someone to bury that trash and bring me what's in their pockets. We'll be over yonder in the saloon."

Over beer and stew, the men inspected what the raiders had in their pockets. Sam read a letter aloud. " 'Dearest Rob, I hate to be the bearer of sad tidings, but I feel it is best to tell you that Father has stricken your name from the family Bible and forbade your name to be mentioned in this house. He (and I) cannot understand why you left a loving family and chose a life of desperate company and painted women. We are all heartbroken. Your sister, Meg.' "

"Where's it from?" Matt asked.

"It doesn't say."

"Another unmarked grave," Josiah said. "Another family who'll wait to hear from a son gone bad. The West is full of them kind of stories."

Matt picked up a tintype and looked at it. "Very pretty lady. Young. Must be his sweetheart."

"She's better off without him," Josiah said. "What's that on the back?"

Matt turned the tintype over and looked at the scratchings. " 'Ruth Sessions. Kansas City. Age fifteen.' " He slowly placed the picture on the table.

Sam opened a folded sheet of paper and read, " 'In the event of my death, I wish to tell the whole damn world to go right straight to hell.' It's signed 'Billy Jackson.' "

"Heard of him," Josiah said. "Horse thief and murderer from over Louisiana way. We had warrants on that one." He clicked open a pocket watch and read the inscription. "To Jay from Mother. Love. 1871." He shook his head and sighed. "Another mother to sit by the door and wait for a son that'll never return. They never think about their mothers. I don't know what the hell they think about."

A citizen nervously approached the table where the men were sitting. "The man who'll be prayin' over the deceased, ah, wants to know if there is anything that should be said. I mean, you know what I mean."

Josiah looked up at him. "Might say they shoulda stayed in closer touch with their mamas."

They lost the trail cold shortly after entering New Mexico Territory. Someone had been driving a small herd of cattle and the raiders found out where the drovers were pushing the herd and got ahead of it.

Josiah sat his saddle and sighed. "Hell with it, boys. It'd take us days, maybe weeks, to pick up the trail. Maybe never."

The brothers looked at him in astonishment. Josiah Finch—giving up?

Sam put it together. "You got chewed out for crossing the Texas line last time, didn't you?"

Josiah smiled. "You might say that, yeah. I was told to keep my butt in Texas, for a fact. Come on, we'll cut south. I know a little tradin' post not too far from here. Folks keep talkin' about there bein' a town there someday. Damned if I can see it. Why would anybody want to build a town in New Mexico when the Texas line is only five miles away?"

The trading post was made of adobe and rock and looked like it had been there for some years. Matt said as much.

"Has been," Josiah said.

"Looks deserted," Sam remarked.

"Corral and stables are on the south side. This was supposed to have been a church, so I'm told. Injuns killed all the priests and the place was abandoned for years. Fellow name of Aquillo opened a tradin' post here years back. His son runs it now. I'm told it's nice and cool inside and the food is good."

They rode around the back of the place, looking it over, and pulled up short at the sight of a dozen or so horses in the corral.

"I recognize that black," Sam said.

"And that mustang," Matt said.

"We lucked up, boys," Josiah said with a grin. "Them raiders took a chance that we'd follow the herd and give them some breathin' room. Then they cut back south. And here they stopped and here we are."

The men rode into the barn and stripped their weary mounts of saddle and bridle. A worried-looking boy helped them.

"Bad hombres in the post, son?" Matt asked him.

"*Si,*" the boy replied. "They beat up my father and I'm thinking they want to do ugly things to my sister."

"Did they see us ride in?"

"No. They are concerned only with drinking and cussing and saying vulgar things to my mother and sister. They sent me out here and told me not to come back in until they called."

"Any other gringos in the store besides them, son?" Sam asked.

"No, señor. Just my mother, my father, and my sister."

Matt gave the boy a dollar. "You rub these horses down good and give them all the grain they can eat. And you stay in this barn and out of sight, you hear me?"

"*Si,* señor. Señor? There are twelve of them in there. They are very rough men, and they all smell very bad. There are but the three of you."

Since they were in New Mexico Territory, and Josiah said

his butt still hurt from the chewing he'd received, he had
taken off his Texas Ranger badge and Matt and Sam had
done the same. Josiah smiled at the boy. "We'll get your sis
and your mom and dad outta this mess, son. You can count
on that. You ever heard of the Wyoming gunfighter Matt
Bodine?"

Sam rolled his eyes and snickered at Matt's sudden discomfort.

"*Si,* señor! *Everybody* has heard of Matt Bodine."

Josiah jerked a thumb in Matt's direction. "That's Bodine
right there, boy."

The boy's eyes widened. He looked at Sam. "Then you
must be the half-breed, Sam Two Wolves?"

"That's right, son."

Back to Josiah. "You must be famous to be riding with
these men.'

"I'm Jesse James, son."

The boy drew back in fear. "No!"

"It's the truth. But I ain't here to rob nobody. Bodine and
Two Wolves wouldn't ride with me if I was here to do a
wrong. So don't you fret none about that."

"Stay in here now, boy," Matt told him. "Keep the horses
calm when the shooting starts."

They stepped out of the barn and slipped along, hugging
the adobe of the trading post. Sam looked at Josiah and
whispered, "Jesse James?"

"The man's got enough bad things being said about him.
Might as well have something good circulatin' too."

They dropped down behind a pile of stove wood as the
back door opened and a man stepped out, heading for the
outhouse. He walked to it without looking in their direction.

"He saw us," Sam said. "It's unnatural for a wanted man
not to look in all directions upon leaving a building."

"I agree," Josiah said. He picked up a piece of stove wood
and waited. The man stepped out of the privy and began his

walk to the post. He looked neither left nor right. Josiah stood up and tossed the chunk all in one motion. He missed the man's head by a good two feet.

But Sam was already up and running at the throw. Before the man could jerk iron or yell out, Sam was on him, his forward momentum knocking the raider down. Sam clubbed him on the head and dragged him back to the privy. Having nothing to tie the man up with, Sam jerked off the two-hole privy seat and shoved the man down in the pit. He landed with a thick splashing sound. Sam replaced the seat.

"What'd you do with him?" Matt asked, when Sam slid back behind the stove-wood pile.

Sam told him.

Josiah grinned. "Good place for him. But be sure to tell the people here to dig a new hole and fill this one in. It'll be ripe here 'fore long."

"You're becoming very inventive, brother," Matt said with a smile.

"I didn't know what else to do with him!"

"They'll be missin' him in a few minutes and somebody else will be out to check," Josiah said. "Anybody got a plan?"

"We sure can't go in shooting," Sams said. "And if we try to take them out one at a time, they'll get suspicious and hold the people hostage."

"That's what they're doin' now," Josiah said sourly. "But I know what you mean."

A bubbling, gurgling sound came from the outhouse.

"Wait here," Matt said. "I want to talk to the boy one more time." He was gone only a short time. When he returned, he laid out the interior of the trading post, drawing each room into the dirt. "The raiders are all in the saloon part. The boy's father was pistol-whipped and tossed in this small storeroom, tied up. When the boy was ordered out of the place, there was no one in the family's living quarters, right here."

"That's the window right there?" Sam asked, pointing to an open-shuttered window only a few yards away.

"That's it."

"Someone has to do it. So I'm gone." Sam ran from behind the woodpile, reached the house, stayed close to the wall, and peeked into the bedroom. He signaled that it was empty and then disappeared into the room, crawling through the open window. Matt and Josiah followed.

With Matt in the lead, the trio walked through the bedroom and into the hall. Sam and Josiah had guns in hand, hammers back. Matt carried a long-bladed knife for silent work. Loud talk and dirty laughter reached them, coming from the far end of the long building.

"Come on, baby!" a man's voice lifted above the laughter. "Dance for us. Hike up that skirt and show us some skin."

The sound of a brutal slap followed that, then a woman's crying.

"Sounds like we're just in time," Josiah said.

The men flattened against a wall as a door opened and a man staggered out, sloppy drunk and careless. He fell against a wall, turned, and saw Matt only a few feet away in the dark hall. He opened his mouth to yell. The warning died in his throat as Matt's knife buried to the hilt in his belly, the cutting edge up. Matt ripped the knife upward with all his strength, the razor-sharp edge slicing through bone and tearing into the heart. Matt grabbed the outlaw's shirtfront with his left hand and lowered the body to the floor, wiping his blade clean on the dead man's shirt.

The trio moved on, silently working their way toward the rough talk and drunken laughter. They had hung their spurs on their saddle horns and moved without a sound.

An older woman carrying a platter of food passed by the open door and spotted them. Matt put a finger to his lips and the woman nodded her head in understanding. Matt sheathed his knife and pulled his guns, cocking them. He held up a gun and motioned that when the shooting started, the woman should get down.

She again nodded her head and moved out of the way.

"Take them petticoats off, baby!" a man yelled. "And I mean take it all off like right now!"

"I'm first!" a man yelled. "I ain't waitin'no longer. Jerk 'er down from that table and lay 'er over yonder on the floor." The other thugs and trash began hollering and yelling obscenities as they lined up to rape the girl.

"Now or never," Matt said. "I'll go straight in. Sam, you cut right. Josiah, you take the left side."

"Let's do it."

With both hands filled with guns, spare six-shooters tucked behind their gunbelts, the trio ran toward the open archway and went in low and fast, splitting up. It took only a second for the men to find clear targets and they opened up.

The young girl was naked, except for a few rags the men had left on her as they ripped her clothing away. She was screaming in terror and thrashing on the floor, pleading with the men.

Josiah shot the man who was forcing the girl's legs apart through the head. He fell to one side, part of his head gone. The mother grabbed her daughter and dragged her against the wall under a table.

The walls seemed to tremble as the guns of the Rangers thundered out frontier justice and retribution. Standing tall, the Texas Rangers held court in the old trading post; the Colts in their hands were the judges and the juries and the lawyers, dealing out death sentences in smoke and fire and lead.

One big thug managed to clear leather and fire, the slug blowing Matt's hat off his head. Matt shot him twice in the belly. The man's boots flew out from under him and he pitched backward, dying with his head stuck in a spittoon.

Sam's .44's roared, belching fire, the slugs finding their targets—two more crud would exit this world.

Josiah shifted his Peacemakers and nailed one outlaw trying to leave the post and shooting a second man just as he was coming up with a rifle. The first slug hit the rifle and exploded several rounds, mangling the man's hands and bringing a scream of pain. His second slug stopped the screaming.

A raider dressed only in his filthy longhandles, but with his hands filled with .45's faced Matt. Matt fired, and splotches of crimson dotted the underwear. The outlaw sat down in a chair and died, his chin on his chest and his hands by his side, still clutching his pistols.

"We yield!" a man yelled, dropping his guns and flinging his hands into the air.

"Not damn likely!" the mother said, holding a dead outlaw's pistol in her hand. She shot the would-be rapist in the belly and doubled him over.

"Now that there's a hell of a woman!" Josiah said, admiration in his voice. He leveled his Peacemakers and began the final act of clearing the saloon of human crud.

The saloon fell silent, only an occasional moan touching the quiet. The men fanned at the thick gray smoke. Sam began propping open windows to help clear the air of gun smoke. Josiah tossed the mother a serape to cover her daughter's nakedness.

"I'll get the man," Matt said. "Sam, check for wounded, will you?"

"Personally, I hope we don't find any."

"As much lead as we slung around, I doubt it," Josiah said.

The trading-post owner was awake and mad clear through. His jaw was swollen where he'd been hit with a pistol, but other than that, he was all right. He was cussing in Spanish as Matt untied him.

"Two alive, so far," Sam called.

"I'll get a rope," the owner said, and Matt did not disagree. Mad as the man was, he'd be awful hard to talk out of a hanging.

In the body-littered saloon part of the post, the man turned to his wife. "Maria, get our daughter out of here. Take her to the bedroom. I have work to do."

"We will witness it," Maria said. "It is only right."

A hard smile appered on the man's bruised face. "As you wish, Maria."

Two of the outlaws, with only minor wounds, stared at Josiah. "You're a Texas Ranger. You cain't let this greaser hang us."

"I'm Jesse James," Josiah told him. "Personally, I think hangin's too good for you. Ought to turn you over to the 'Paches."

"You ain't Jesse James!" the other one hollered.

"The hell I ain't. Now, you best be makin' your peace with God. 'Cause you ain't got long for this world, scum."

Sam and Matt were busy dragging bodies out the back door.

"You cain't let him do this to us! It ain't right," the first raider bellered.

"I ain't got no authority to stop him neither," Josiah said. "I'm a wanted man myself, remember?"

"I'll see you in hell!" the second gunhand screamed.

"I don't imagine you'll be lonely there," Josiah told him. "I'll wave at you as I climb them golden stairs."

The outlaw cussed him as the post owner tied his hands behind his back and pushed him out the door.

"Where're you puttin' the bodies?" Josiah asked Matt, as he returned for another load.

"In the outhouse pit. I guess we'd better help them dig another pit and move the privy."

"That would be the neighborly thing to do," Josiah agreed.

"Halp!" the hired gun hollered as the noose was put around his neck.

"Maria will probably cook us up some fine vittles," Josiah said. "And I do like Mexican food."

The horse was slapped out from under the raider and he dangled and jerked.

Sam looked at the remaining raider. "You're next."

The man cussed him.

Matt poured a drink and held up the shot glass. "To your health," he toasted the raider.

The trused-up outlaw tried to kick him.

The post owner came in and jerked the outlaw to his boots. "Son of a *puta!*" he told him. "Child rapist. Let's see how well you die."

The outlaw spat in the man's face.

"Let's find some shovels and get this over with," Josiah said. "I'm hungry."

Chapter 16

The men worked on into the evening, digging a new pit and slinging the dirt from that hole over into the pit that contained the bodies—among other things.

It was well after dark before they finished and could take a very welcomed hot bath and then chow down. And eat they did, with Maria fixing a feast for them. After the boy had been put to bed, the post owner looked over at Josiah and smiled.

"I have seen pictures of Jesse James, sir. Not that it matters, for you all are saviors, but you are not Jesse James."

"But the boy don't have to know that," Josiah told him. "We're Texas Rangers, just slightly out of our jurisdiction."

"Jesse James it is, then, señor. I understand, knowing how little boys love to brag of their adventures."

"He wouldn't have had time to do much bragging," Sam said. "That bunch didn't have plans to leave any survivors behind when they left."

"They would have killed a child?" Maria asked.

"Just as quick as they'd kill anything else," Matt told her, then explained why the three of them were on their trail.

"Monstrous!" the woman said. "To attack a funeral and shoot and kill innocent people. If I felt any guilt at all for killing that one and enjoying seeing the others hang, it is gone now."

"No point in feeling guilty about what happened to that bunch," Josiah told her. "They was born to meet it."

Just to be on the safe side, Josiah crossed over what he believed to be the line and got back into Texas. "Some of them got away," he said. "But we cut the numbers down a goodly bit, I'd say."

"I'll add that the survivors will probably think twice before returning to Texas," Sam said.

"That's the way I like it," Josiah said with a smile.

Several days later, they swung down from their saddles in the yard of the Circle S. They had picked up a frame at the trading post and used one of the spare mounts as a pack horse, bringing in a lot of rifles and pistols from the dead outlaws. The horse didn't much like it, but after a few miles, he settled down.

"Any word from Jimmy?" Matt asked Jeff Sparks as he stepped out to greet them.

"Not a peep. The boy's either dead, or he's found him a deep hole and is just waiting' for John Lee to come into gunsights." He eyeballed the rifles and pistols Josiah spilled onto the ground. "You boys look like you hit pay dirt. In a manner of speaking," he added drily.

"Close to thirty, if my tallyin's right," Josiah said. "What was the final count here?"

"Nine, includin' the two we hanged."

"What's the word on John Lee?" Sam asked.

"Still hirin' any gun that'll ride for him. He's got him an army, for sure."

"He's also spendin' a lot of money," Josiah mused aloud.

"He's got it to spend, Josiah. John Lee is a very wealthy man."

"Pitiful," the Ranger said. "Some type of man gets some

money, he seems to go crazy about wantin' more. How's that foolish boy of his?"

"Crazier than ever. He was always vain about his looks, just like his father. But Matt fixed John's looks and Sam did the same to Nick. I'm told they're both a sight to see and listen to with no front teeth. And by the way, Bam and Pen are doing an excellent job as lawmen. I think they've finally found their callin'."

"They're both pretty good ol' boys," Josiah said. "They just was ridin' down the wrong trail for a time. And they both knew it."

"You boys get cleaned up. Conchita will have supper ready in a little while."

The next day was Sunday, so Matt and Sam were informed by Lia and Lisa, and they were all going into town for church.

"We are?" Matt questioned.

"We are," Lia settled it, and gave Sam a dirty look when he snickered at the expression on his brother's face. Lisa was spending more and more time with Noah, and that suited Sam just fine.

The hands would stay at the ranch. Conchita was a Catholic and wouldn't dream of setting foot in any Baptist church, so Dodge was staying behind too.

"I hope he's a good preacher," Josiah said. "I like one that makes sense, not none of them pulpit-poundin', fire-and-brimstone spoutin' fools. They make me want to shoot 'em."

"There will be no carryin' of guns in the house of the Lord," Jeff said sternly.

"Then I ain't a-goin'," Josiah said.

"Me neither," Matt and Sam said together.

"Well, pooh on you all," Lia said. "You can just stand outside the church and listen, then." She flounced off to get gussied up for the buggy ride into town.

"I'll stand outside, all right," Josiah said. "Outside the saloon. That Willowby feller is too pompous a windbag for my tastes."

The ride into town was uneventful, except for the heat and the dust. Summer was on the land in full force, and even early in the morning it was hot, just plain hot.

"Like hell must be," Lia said, looking at the Rangers. "For those who don't go to church."

"That woman's got marryin' on the mind, Matt," Josiah said. "You best walk light around her or 'fore you know it she'll have a nose ring on you and be leadin' you around like a hog."

"It would serve him right," Sam said with a smile.

The trio escorted the family to church and then adjourned to the saloon for coffee. It was too early in the day for beer to appeal to them. Gene wanted to go with them, but his mother and father and sisters gave him hard looks, and he went on into the church.

"The path to hellfire and damnation is littered with the souls of those who choose strong drink over the words of the Lord!" Willowby stood in the door and shouted at the Rangers.

"Go pee up a rope," Josiah muttered.

"Have you been saved, brothers?" Willowby thundered.

"Saved from havin' to listen to the likes of you," Josiah said darkly.

"Heathen!" Willowby roared.

Sam and Matt grabbed Josiah before the man could turn around and direct a few well-chosen words in the preacher's direction.

"That Willowby's a pest," Pen Masters said. The men sat at a window table in the saloon, drinking coffee. "He's about to bore me to death about bein' saved. But I tell you what: them boys who was at the funeral when the raiders hit say he's hell with a rifle and they ain't no back-up in the man."

"I'll give him that much," Josiah admitted. "The Broken Lance riders ever come into town?"

"A few at a time," Bam said. "They haven't caused no trouble, though. They have a few drinks, buy their tobacco and so forth, and leave."

"How's the prisoner?"

"Gettin' fat. I got a letter from a judge said he'd be over this way in a month or so. It's costin' the town a lot of money to keep him, and the merchants are complainin' about it. They tell me either try him, hang him, or cut him loose."

"Matt and Sam can write out depositions, and one of your boys can take him on the stage down to Fort Stockton. Let them worry with him for awhile."

"There ain't no stage on Sunday," Bam said, "but I can load him up tomorrow and be back the next day."

"We'll get pen and ink and write it out," Matt said.

"Take your time," Josiah said. "I got a hunch Willowby is gonna preach for about half the day. One of them ladies will get tired of it and wave a basket of fried chicken under his nose. That'll shut him up."

The brothers wrote out their depositions and Bam took the papers back to the office. At Josiah's orders, he did not tell Gruen he was to be moved. He did not want the outlaw to tell some midnight visitor—and he'd been having a few—and then have the stagecoach stopped at gunpoint in an escape attempt.

The Reverend Willowby droned on, his voice carrying all the way to the saloon. Josiah just shook his head. "I don't see how people go back for that every week. Once a year ought to be plenty."

"Riders pulled in at the livery," Sam said, after returning from the outhouse. "About a dozen of them."

"You recognize any of them?" Matt asked.

"No. But they don't look like they're here to attend church."

Boots sounded heavily on the boardwalk and the batwings pushed open, the saloon swelling with a dozen riders, dusty and trail-worn and all of them packing two guns. A big man in the lead looked over at the table and smiled.

"Pen. When'd you start totin' a star?"

"Cannon." Pen acknowledged the greeting and ignored the question. "You're a long way from Utah."

"Man goes where he can find work. I hate to see that badge on your chest."

"You'll like it even less if you break the law," Pen said shortly. "You know Bam, don't you?"

Cannon's eyes narrowed. "Bam Ford wearin' a damn badge too. What's the world comin' to?"

Bam ignored the man and looked square at another long-rider. "Riggs. When'd you get out of prison?"

"That ain't none of your concern, Bam. I done my time and it's over." He walked away from the group and up to the bar, ordering a whiskey.

Josiah turned his chair and eyeballed the group. One rider tensed at the sight. "Pate," Josiah said.

"Finch," the man said. "Didn't know the Rangers had a hand in anything around here."

Josiah smiled and jerked a thumb. "Meet Matt Bodine and Sam Two Wolves. They joined up with the Rangers."

Several of the men exchanged glances. Josiah Finch was bad enough, but Bodine and Two Wolves put a whole new light on the situation.

"Heard of both of 'em," another man said. "Two-bit gunnies from up Wyoming way. I ain't seen none of their graveyards."

"I have," Pen said quietly. "From Montana to Texas. They swing a big loop, Giddings. Don't get caught up in it."

Giddings snorted contemptuously and turned his back to the man, walking to the bar to stand beside Riggs.

Another of the men studied Matt out of cool eyes. Matt returned the stare. He knew him, but couldn't put a name to the face. Finally it came to him. "Hallett. Last time I saw you you were on trial for horse stealing up in Wyoming."

Hallett flushed, clenching his hands into fists, and managed to keep his temper in check. "You got a big mouth, Bodine. I was acquitted of them charges."

"Only after two of the witnesses turned up dead," Sam pointed out. "Shot in the back. Probably by one of your buddies there." He looked at the two men standing shoulder to shoulder by the man.

"You know them two?" Josiah asked.

"Perry and Striker," Sam said. "Two-bit rustlers and horse thieves."

"I don't take that kind of talk from no goddamned Injun!" Perry said.

Sam stood up. "Then by all means, do act upon your words, Perry."

Cannon stepped between them. "Not now, not here," he told the man. "Let it alone."

Cannon looked at the five lawmen seated around the table. "We're here to ride for the Broken Lance. Nothin' more than an honest day's work for good pay. That's all."

Pen Masters busted out laughing. When he wound down, he said, "Oh, that's a good one, Cannon. You never done anything honest in your life. And as far as you bein' a puncher, I seen you try to rope a steer one time. You dabbed the loop over another puncher and damn near strangled him. The only thing you can do with a cow is steal it."

This time it was Cannon who was held back. The man was mad clear through.

"You better hold on to him, Clint," Bam said. "The sun ain't never rose on the day the likes of him could take Pen Masters."

"They'll be a day of reckonin', Bam," another rider said.

"Not from you, Wheeler. Not unless you shoot me in the back."

One man who had yet to be heard from pushed through the batwings and shoved his way through the riders to face the lawmen.

Josiah looked up at him. "Waco Mason," he said. "I run you out of Texas once, Waco."

"I come back, Finch. You got no warrants on me, and neither does any other law office nowhere. And speakin' for myself, I ain't gonna take your crap. That tin badge don't mean nothin' to me. I come in here for a drink, and that's it."

"Nice little speech, Waco," Josiah told him. "I'm impressed." He smiled at him. "So go have your drink. There ain't nobody stoppin' none of you."

The other four around the table looked at each other. Josiah wasn't acting right to cave in this easy. Waco cocked his head to one side and squinted his eyes. All could tell he was confused by Josiah's easy manner.

Waco turned around and headed for the bar. Josiah pushed back his chair and stood up, a slight-built man whose eyes had turned as mean as a rattlesnake. "But if you ever talk to me again like that I'll kill you!"

Waco turned, facing the Ranger. The guns of both men were loose in leather. "You made sport of me like baitin' a bear back then, Finch. I swore I'd kill you, remember?"

"I remember. You had a gun then, Waco. Why didn't you use it?"

Waco stared hatred at the smaller man.

"Big brave boy like you," the Ranger taunted the man. "You boys know why I run him out of Texas when he got out of jail, don't you?" Josiah asked the crowd of gunnies.

They waited.

"He pistol-whipped the woman he was robbin'. Wasn't any need for it; he had her purse. He just wanted to hurt someone. Messed her face up real bad. I just go no use for a man who'd do somethin' that low."

"Maybe she asked for it," Hallett said, the words telling all what he was made of.

"She was eighty years old," Josiah said softly, but with contempt dripping from his words. "What could she have done to ask for it?"

Cannon grunted and looked with distain at Waco. He was a gunfighter, a horse thief, and a cattle rustler, but like so many Western men, would not harm a woman—unless he was paid to do it. "I don't think I want you ridin' with me no more, Waco."

"Oh, hell, Cannon," Josiah said. "Don't you boys know who you're workin' for? Me and Bodine and Two Wolves tracked the men John Lee hired to kill a rancher's wife. Yeah, that's right. So if you go to work for John Lee, there ain't none of you any better than this skunk here." He looked at Waco Mason.

Waco jerked iron. It was no contest. Josiah shot him before the hired gun could clear leather, the .45 slug taking him in the belly and knocking him back. Waco finally pulled his six-shooter out of leather and cocked it. Josiah shot him again, then a third time before the man went down to his knees. Waco's gun went off, the slug blowing a hole in the floor.

"Dammit!" Al swore at the damage from behind the bar.

Waco fell forward on his face, dead on the floor.

Before the first shot was fired, Matt, Sam, Pen, and Bam had risen as one, their hands by their guns.

"It's over," Cannon said. "He drew on you, Ranger. We're out of it."

"Tote him off and bury him," Josiah said. He returned to the table and sat down. Up the street, Willowby was still verbally hammering at his flock. "And if he ever shuts up," Josiah said, jerking his thumb toward the church, "I'm told he does a right nice funeral service. When he ain't interrupted by hired guns, that is," he added.

Chapter 17

John Lee waited exactly twenty-four hours after his new gunmen hit town to strike back at what he considered to be his mortal enemies. He had convinced himself, during his laudanum-induced haze while having his and his son's broken teeth extracted by a dentist he had brought in from El Paso, that *everybody* was his mortal enemy; that *everybody* was against him; that *everybody* was out to get him.

When he struck, he struck hard and mean and vicious. A small rancher who had moved back into the area and who was running about two hundred and fifty head of cattle experienced the full fury of John Lee's nightriders.

Matt and Sam and Josiah could sense death long before they reached the burned-out and still smoking ruins of what had been a house.

The nightriders had fired several hundred rounds, killing not only the rancher and his wife and two children, but also killing about a hundred head of cattle. They lay stinking and bloating under the sun, while overhead the buzzards slowly circled, waiting for a meal.

"The man's stepped over the line," Matt said, as he and

the others tied bandanas around their faces to block out at least some of the horrible odor.

"They scattered the rest of the herd," Sam said, "then got in with them, hiding their tracks."

"Pushin' the herd west," Josiah noted. "Towards that little crick about five miles away. That's where they'll get in the water and try to lose us."

Matt pointed to a piece of sacking on the ground. "When they leave the creek, they'll tie sacking on the horses' hooves to leave less of a trail. They're getting smarter and more vicious."

Jeff Sparks and some of his hands rode up. The men, grim faced, sat their saddles for a moment.

"Gilley," Matt said, "you and Parnell ride into town and get the minister. We'll dig some holes and then drag these cattle off aways. It's not going to be fun, but we got it to do. So let's do it."

Dr. Winters rode out with Willowby and looked at the bodies. "This child has been shot at least a dozen times," he said, standing up from the swollen body of a girl about ten or eleven years old. "I have never seen such a brutal and totally vicious, senseless thing in my life." He walked away and vomited.

"Was she raped?" Josiah called.

The doctor shook his head. "No. I don't believe so."

Chookie said, "It appears they rode this young boy down and trampled him to death. Then filled him full of holes. Fightin' growed-up men is one thing, but anybody who would do this to a child don't deserve nothin' better than a rope—and a slow hangin' at that."

Lia and Lisa rode up, with Dodge and Noah accompanying them. The girls took one look at the still-uncovered bodies and got a little green around the mouth.

"Stop this," Dodge said to Josiah. "And do it now. If you don't, we will."

"Now, Vonny," the Ranger said.

"I'm tellin' you flat out, Josiah," the old gunfighter told him, "John Lee ain't the only one who can nightride."

"I'll forget you said that, Vonny."

"I don't give a damn what you remember or forget. You either put a stop to this legal like, or we ride against the Broken Lance full force. I know some boys I can call in, and you know the type of men I'm talkin' about."

Josiah knew. Old buffalo hunters, ex-scouts for the Army, Indian fighters, and the like. Men now living quiet in their advanced age, but men who owed Vonny Dodge much—in many cases, their lives. Men who would come at a run if he called.

The tall old gunfighter and the Texas Ranger faced each other amid the stink of violent and senseless death. And to tell the truth—even though Josiah didn't think it would ever come to gunplay between them—Josiah wasn't at all sure he was faster than Vonny. Damn few men were.

"Give us time, Vonny." Matt defused the situation quietly. "Give us time to track and trail and try to build a case. Give us that much, at least."

The old gunfighter stared at the much younger man for a moment, then slowly nodded his head. "I'll give you a few days, Matt. I understand you boys need time. But be forewarned about this: I've talked it over with the hands. They're drawin' fightin' wages, and they're ready to fight. We got to bring peace to this country. And if we have to bushwhack John Lee and his no-count son to do it, then so be it. The end will justify the means."

"An eye for an eye and a tooth for a tooth!" Willowby hollered. "Thine eye shall not pity, but life shall go for life."

"Yeah, I know, Willowby," Josiah said. "Deuteronomy. See to the dead. Me and the boys will ride over to Broken Lance spread and talk to John Lee. Let's go."

Leaving the stench of death behind them, Sam said, "John Lee and his bunch just might shoot us on sight."

"Doubtful," Josiah replied. "Don't none of them boys

want the Rangers in here full force. And that's what would happen if one of us was shot."

The three of them were shocked at John Lee's appearance. The man's eyes were wild and his person unkempt. The swelling had gone from his mouth, but he whistled when he talked, due to the gap in his teeth. And he didn't talk as much as he ranted and raved.

"Shut up," Josiah finally told him. "Just shut up your mouth and listen to me."

John Lee stood on the front porch of his grand house and glared at the Rangers. His son stood by his side, his hands by the butts of his guns. He appeared to be at least as crazy as his father.

"You're just a few days away from a full-scale war, John Lee," Josiah told him. "Maybe only hours away. We're tryin' to keep the lid on the pot, but I don't know how long we can do it. Now you started this senseless crap, and you can stop it. Fire all these damn gunhands you got hangin' around you. Go on back to ranchin' and leave other folks alone. They got as much right to be here and to live in peace as you have. You got more than enough for one man. You got plenty. Pull in your horns and do it right now, John Lee."

With much whistling and spitting and slurring of words, John Lee told Josiah where to go, what route to take getting there, and what he could do with his tin badge once he got there.

"And that goes for me, too," Nick whistled.

"And you can't prove that I done a damn thing wrong, neither," John Lee added. "If you had any proof, you'd be arresting me, not running your mouth."

"And that goes for me, too," Nick said.

"All right, John Lee," Josiah told him. "I tried. God knows I tried. And that's all a mule can do, is try. One more raid on your part, and you're gonna open the gates to hell, and I mean it. I don't know why you can't see that."

"Unless you got a warrant for my arrest," John whistled,

"I suggest you get the hell off my property. All of you! Like right now."

"I will be seein' you, John Lee," Josiah said. "Bet on it. I just hope it ain't lookin' at you down the barrel of a gun."

"Get off my property!" John screamed, spraying spit.

The men turned their horses and rode off, back toward Nameit.

"Has he lost his mind?" Bam asked over coffee in the marshal's office.

"His bucket don't go all the way down into the well water," Josiah said, "but he's got sense enough to know what he's doin' is wrong. I been in insane asylums, he ain't got the look of them folks. You can feel sorry for them people; there ain't no pity in my heart for John Lee, his son, nor any man who'll ride with them."

"What now?" Pen asked.

"We do some nightridin' of our own. Startin' tonight. And while my officers might frown on this—frown, hell, they'll fire me if they get wind of it—we got to fight fire with fire. So this is what we're gonna do . . ."

Josiah, Matt, Sam, Pen, and Bam were dressed in dark dusters, riding horses they had brought back in from the dead outlaws now residing in the crap pit back of the trading post in New Mexico. They wore bandanas around their faces and their hats were pulled down low.

"Would you believe, after all the things that's been said about me," Pen said, "I ain't never wore a mask in my life, nor have I ever stole anything." He thought for a moment. "Exceptin' that time when I hadn't eaten in a week and I rustled me a beeve."

Josiah smiled under his mask. "After the war, they was thousands of cattle roamin' the Texas countryside, belongin' to nobody. I've roasted me a chunk of somebody's beef over a fire a time or two myself."

"Josiah!" Sam said, disbelief in his voice. "You, of all people. I'm shocked."

"I know you are, Sam. 'Course, when you was growin' up in the Cheyenne village with your daddy and mama, y'all never dined on no stolen beef, did you?"

"Ummm," Sam said. "Well . . ." He trailed off with a laugh.

"We been sittin' here for two hours," Bam said, after consulting a pocket watch. "Maybe John Lee ain't gonna send no nightriders out this evenin'?"

"Quiet!" Sam said, holding up a hand. He dropped down and put his ear to the ground. "Here they come. A lot of them, riding straight from Broken Lance range."

The men mounted out and adjusted their bandanas. They put the reins in their teeth and filled their hands with .44's and .45's. No one had to speak. They had gone over this plan several times, and there was nothing legal about it. If they found Broken Lance gunnies riding that night, they were going to ride among them and empty some saddles, and to hell with what the law books said. It was like some folks were fond of saying: There ain't no law west of the Pecos.

"Now!" Josiah said through clenched teeth and knee-reined Horse. Horse jumped on command and the men were riding hell-for-leather into a crowd that outnumbered them ten to one.

When they got into range, the lawmen could see raiders were wearing dark dusters and eye-slit hoods over their heads. They opened fire and the night was pocked with flashes of muzzle blasts, and the air was filled with the screaming of horses, the painful shouting of wounded men, and the churning of dust from more than two hundred steel-shod hooves.

The lawmen emptied their guns during the first charge, holstered them, and pulled out two more from belts looped on the saddle horns and wheeled around, heading back into the fray.

Matt's horse knocked one nightrider to the ground, then

mangled him under his hooves. Sam fired pointblank into a hired gun's face and the face blossomed in crimson. Bam emptied two saddles and Pen, out of ammo, began smashing and slashing any head that came into arm's length. Josiah screamed like a Comanche and that was the cue to get gone, and the men vanished into the dust-stormed night, leaving behind them death, horrible wounds, and mass confusion.

They headed for Nameit, changed mounts along the way, where they had put spare horses that afternoon, and were seated in the saloon having a late supper and a mug of beer when the wounded men began trickling in.

Vonny Dodge was seated alone at a table, a bottle of whiskey in front of him. He had greeted the lawmen with a curt hello, and that told them the old gunfighter wanted to be left alone. They left him alone.

John Lee stormed into the bar, followed by his son, his foreman, and a dozen gunhands.

"Finch!" John thundered and whistled. "Some of my men were coming into town this evening for cards and drinks and were bushwacked by a bunch of masked road agents and thugs. I've got ten or twelve dead and at least that many wounded. What do you intend to do about it?"

Josiah sopped up the last of his gravy with a hunk of bread, popped it into his mouth, and chewed reflectively. He swallowed and said, "Well, sir, I would suggest you take them to see Doc Winters."

"Goddammit, Finch!" John Lee yelled and sprayed spit through the gap in his teeth, top and bottom. "Don't you get smartmouthed with me. I demand that you and your . . . fellow Rangers there investigate this atrocity."

"Yeah, we'll do that, John Lee. Just as soon as we conclude our investigation of who killed Ed Carson and his wife, who shot up the Circle S ranch, who killed the Flyin' V hand, Sonny, and who massacred that rancher and his wife and children the other day. I 'spect we'll get around to your problem about this time next year. If you're lucky. But now, if you don't feel we're actin' quick enought to suit you, you can write Ranger HQ in Austin. I'm sure they'll send more men in here."

John Lee was so angry he looked like he was going to bust a gut trying to contain his rage. His face actually turned a dark shade of purple.

"Let's do it, Papa!" Nick whistled and slurred. "Come on, let's do it."

"Shut up, boy!" the father warned him.

Vonny Dodge laughed at them. "What language are you two speakin'? Sounds to me like a drunken Digger Injun tryin' to quote Shakespeare."

Nick turned, his face flushed. "Don't you make fun of me, you old fart!"

"You better hold the reins tight on that kid of yours, John Lee," the old gunfighter said. " 'Fore I take them fancy guns of his and feed 'em to him."

"I'd like to see you try!" Nick yelled.

"Oh, I won't try, boy," Vonny said. "I'll do."

"Back off, Nick," John Lee told his son. "Just back off."

Pukey Stagg stepped around father and son. "This is what you're payin' us to do, Mr. Lee," he whispered, his lips barely moving. "I'll handle this one."

"As you wish," John Lee said.

"What do you want?" Vonny asked the gunhand.

"Git up, old man," Pukey ordered.

"My pleasure, boy," Vonny said. He downed his glass of hooch and pushed his chair back, standing up and stepping away from the table.

"I git word that you're Vonny Dodge," Pukey said.

"That's right, punk. That's me. Who are you?"

"Stagg."

"Oh, yeah," Vonny said. "The one called Pukey. It sure fits. You look like puke."

"You'll die for insultin' me, you old buffalo turd!"

Vonny laughed at him.

Pukey stood tensed, slightly hunched over, his hands hovering over the butts of his guns. Vonny stood tall and relaxed, a slight but hard smile visible under his handlebar mustache. This was nothing new to the old gunfighter. He'd played this scene out dozens of times before Pukey was even a gleam in his daddy's eye and had left men lying in their own blood on dirty barroom floors from the Cascades to the Mississippi River and from Calgary to Texas.

"I ain't never had to draw on no old man," Pukey said. " 'Specially one who looks like he needs a crutch to help hold him up." He laughed confidently. "You sure you don't need a nurse to help you haul that Hog-leg out of leather?"

"You don't worry about me, Pukey," Vonny told him. "You best be concerned about someone carin' enough about you to write your mama, tellin' her where her bad-seed boy is buried."

"Your old bones will be dust in a rotten box long before that happens, old man," Pukey snarled.

"Are you talkin' to build your confidence, punk?" Vonny asked. "Come on, boy, pull them guns and let's get this over with. I got supper to eat yet."

A sudden flash of worry passed Pukey's face. This old coot wasn't at all scared. He just stood there, smilin' at him. "Draw, damn you!" Pukey yelled.

"After you, boy," Vonny said.

"I'd be made fun of the rest of my life if I drew first agin an old geezer like you. Hell, old man, jerk iron if you got the strength to do it. I won't even start a draw 'til you're clear of leather."

"You're a fool, Pukey," Vonny told him, the smile gone from his lips and the words flying like chipped ice from his mouth. "You're just like every damn punk I've ever seen. Big guns, big mouth, and a yellow streak runnin' wide down the center of your back. Why don't you hang them guns on a peg and go on back home and spend the rest of your days gatherin' eggs and sloppin' hogs and milkin' cows and the like? You don't want this, punk. You really don't want it."

"You can't call me no coward!" Pukey yelled.

"Boy, I just done it. And you took it. Now wear it and ride on out of here."

Pukey cussed him until he was breathless. Vonny stood staring at him, unblinking.

"Yellow clear through," Vonny finally said.

Pukey grabbed for his guns.

Vonny shot him. He pulled iron and plugged Pukey before the man's fingers closed around the butts of his guns. Smiling, the legendary old gunfighter twirled his .45 and holstered it.

The slug knocked Pukey back, his shirt front blossoming crimson. He put a hand out on a table to steady himself and pulled his left-hand gun.

Vonny let him clear leather before he drew his left-hand .45 with the same smooth, practiced motion. He put his second shot into Pukey's guts. Pukey's fancy guns clattered to the floor. The hired gun doubled over as the pain hit him and he slowly sank to his knees, a groan escaping his lips, as one hand went to his chest, the other hand to his belly.

Vonny twirled his left hand .45 and popped it back into leather.

Josiah grinned and said, "Hot damn! I always wanted to see that, and tonight I seen it."

"Awesome," Pen whispered.

"At least," Sam agreed.

"Anybody else want to play my game this evenin'?" the old gunfighter threw out.

"The old goat beat me," Pukey said. "The old coot really beat *me*."

"By God!" Tanner said, stepping around John Lee and son. "Stagg was a friend of mine. You'll follow him into the grave, old man."

With a motion that was almost too quick to follow, Vonny

jerked both .45's and blew Tanner back on his boot heels. The gunny stumbled backward, staggering toward the bar. He hit and grabbed the edge, holding on for a moment.

"Damn you, Dodge!" he gasped, his right hand snaking his .44 from leather.

Vonny shot him again, Tanner jerking as the slug tore into his chest. But he would not fall. He managed to get off a round, the slug blowing John Lee's hat off his head. The rancher yelped and hit the floor. Tanner fired again, the slug hitting Jack Lightfoot's boot and knocking the heel off of it, sending Lightfoot slamming to the barroom floor, yelling in shock.

Tanner lurched forward, pulling his left-hand Colt from leather and cocking it. His eyes were glazed over and everything was blurry. He fired, the slug knocking a hole in the ceiling.

"Jesus H. Christ!" a muffled yell came from overhead.

Tanner fired his right-hand Colt, the slug striking Pukey in the head and Pukey had no more worries on this earth.

"Somebody shoot that crazy fool!" John Lee whistled from his belly-down position on the floor.

His brave son obliged his daddy's wishes. Nick jerked out a pistol and shot Tanner through the heart.

"That's it!" Al said from behind the bar, coming up with a sawed-off shotgun, the hammers eared back. "the next man pulls iron and I fire this blunderbuss smack into the crowd of you Broken Lance boys. Now settle down and get the hell out of my saloon."

"Your saloon!" John Lee hollered. "I put up the money to build this damn place. Where it used to be," he added.

Al fired one barrel into the ceiling.

"Holy Crap!" the resident upstairs yelled as the buckshot tore a hole in the ceiling.

"Get out of here!" Al yelled.

"I'm goin', I'm goin'," the man on the second floor yelled. "Just let me get my damn pants on!"

Chapter 18

After the shootout at the saloon, it was all out that the foreman of the Circle S was the legendary gunfighter Vonny Dodge, several of John Lee's hired guns pulled out. The old gunfighter still had his stuff and knew how to use it. And with Matt Bodine, Sam Two Wolves, and Josiah Finch looking like they were in this to the end, it just added up to more than the hired guns cared to face.

John Lee stood on his front porch and cussed the men as they rode out, his ignoramus son by his side, sneering at the riders.

Cindy spent most of her time in her room in the mansion, alternately cussing her husband and her condition. She ate constantly and had picked up about fifty pounds. Cindy was now about as wide as she was tall, and no joy to be around.

The ambush of the nightriders and the deaths of a dozen of the men had taken more of the steam out of the hired guns of John Lee. John Lee still had a small army at his command, but the men who made up the army were now very wary about riding at night. One Broken Lance rider had ridden up to a small rancher's house to ask permission to let his horse have a drink. Before he could open his mouth, the rancher blew him out of the saddle with a shotgun. The rancher let the horse drink anyway.

The men of Broken Lance could still ride into Nameit for whiskey and tobacco, but they did so cautiously. Now when they appeared, the townspeople also appeared, with shotguns and rifles and pistols in their hands. They spoke when spoken to, be it a nod of the head or a word, but let it be known they were more than willing and certainly ready to empty a lot of saddles in a very short time.

John Lee did a lot of cussing and stomping around his house. But for the time being, that was all he did. But all that was about to change.

A week after the ambush in the night and the shootout in the saloon, John Lee stepped out on his porch for an after-supper cigar and a brandy. John Lee turned his head just as the rifle boomed, the slug tearing the cigar out of his mouth. The second shot tore a good-sized chunk of wood out of a support porch, and the third shot thudded into the house.

By that time the men of the Broken Lance had the rifleman spotted, circled around him, and managed to take him alive. The missing Jimmy had surfaced.

The men roped him and dragged him to the house.

"I almost got you, you murderin' son of a bitch!" Jimmy yelled at John Lee.

"But now I got you," John Lee said, a wicked grin on his face. "What do you think I ought to do with you?"

Jimmy stood and stared at the man.

"Now, the reasonable thing to do would be to turn you over to the law, wouldn't it, Jimmy?"

"Probably. But you've never done a reasonable thing in your life, Lee."

John Lee stepped off the porch and slapped the young man. "You mind your manners when talking to me, punk."

Jimmy spat in his face.

John Lee hit him twice in the face, a hard left and right

that bloodied Jimmy's mouth. Jimmy took the blows as stoically as possible; he knew the worst was yet to come.

John Lee stepped back. "But if I was to turn you over to the law, you'd get off. I know how much the other people in this area are envious and jealous of me."

Jimmy had to laugh at that. "Envious and jealous? Of you? No one is envious and jealous; they just hate your guts, is all."

That got him more blows to the face.

John Lee stepped back and caught his breath. "I'm gonna see how well you die, boy. Personally, I think you're just like your old man: a yellow-bellied coward. But we'll see." He turned to his foreman. "Strip him buck-assed naked and tie him to a post down by the barn. Then get me a bullwhip."

Pen Masters pounded on Matt and Sam's hotel-room door. "Open up, Matt! Hurry up. It's me, Pen."

Matt lit the lamp and clicked open his pocket watch. One o'clock in the morning. "Okay, Pen," he called. "Let me get my britches on." He almost fell down getting into his jeans and Sam tripped over his boots trying to pull on his britches. Matt flung open the door. By this time, Josiah had left his room and joined Pen in the dark hall.

"What's up, Pen?" Matt asked.

"Jimmy. He's alive, but just barely. Somebody dumped him at the edge of town. Buck neeked. John Lee horsewhipped him. He ain't got long, boys. Come on."

It was hard to recognize the bloody form as anything human. John Lee had spent hours beating him, stopping only to rest his arm and finally handing the whip over to others. Dr. Winters looked up at the men and shook his head.

"It's a miracle he's still alive, much less able to speak. I don't give him long, and I told him so."

Matt knelt down beside the cot, swallowing back the bile building in his throat.

"John Lee done it," Jimmy whispered. "He . . . enjoyed doin' it. When he'd . . . get tired . . . some other would take . . ." He closed his eyes and Matt thought he was gone. But somewhere deep inside the young man he found the inner strength to continue. "I had three good shots at him and . . . missed . . . all three. They took turns . . . whippin' me. Cindy watched 'em 'till . . . she got hot and went on back in . . . inside the house. She's as crazy as all the others."

Jimmy turned his head as the doctor tried to give him a sip of laudanum. "I . . . I'm past pain," Jimmy said. "Leo Grand's got my rifle. I seen him . . . admirin' it. I . . ."

Jimmy died in mid-sentence. Doc Winters leaned over and closed the young cowboy's eyes with gentle fingertips. He looked up at Josiah. "Surely, surely now you can arrest the man?"

Josiah shrugged. "You heard Jimmy say he tried to bushwack John Lee. Life's hard out here, Doc. You gotta understand that. This ain't Philadelphia where you can call a uniformed police officer if you get in a jam. I ain't sayin' it's right what John Lee done to the boy, but a jury probably would once a slick lawyer got done with them."

"This is a strange and barbaric land," Doc Winters muttered, laying a white cloth over Jimmy's face.

"Not really," Matt told him, standing up from his squat. "There's a saying out here, Doc: A man stomps on his own snakes and saddles his own horses."

"I don't understand that."

"A man settles his own troubles, Doctor," Sam said. "Out here, the sheriff might have a county to patrol that's as big as some Eastern states. The law might be five or six day's ride away from a trouble spot. You just settle matters yourself out here, and usually frontier justice is administered to the right party. We're trying to bring law and order here, Doctor. We're really trying. But it's still years away. Any way you look at it, Doctor, frontier justice is damned effective."

"That would never be tolerated back in New York City," the doctor said.

"Yeah?" Josiah looked at him. "Them New York folk will be sorry for that decision someday, too, I betcha."

Matt looked at Sam, and his brother nodded his head. They both took off their Texas Ranger badges and handed them to Josiah. He smiled and handed them a piece of paper. "Got that when the stagecoach run this noon. Read it."

Sam took it and read it. He grinned. "Your request for a leave of absence has been approved."

"I don't understand," Doctor Winters said. "Of all the times to ask for a leave of absence! Good God, man. We need your authority figure here, now!"

"You need my guns, Doc. Sometimes the law just don't work the way it ought to." Josiah took off his badge and put it in an inside pocket of his vest. "And when that happens, it's time to step outside the law to beat the lawless at their own game. That's the way it is, Doc."

He nodded his head. None of the three men felt the doctor really understood, but he was trying.

"Let's go, boys," Josiah said.

Outside, Matt asked, "You got a plan, Josiah?"

Josiah nodded his head. "We crowd them. We push them. We make them pull iron agin us. We knock their numbers down ever' time we come up on a bunch of them. We hit them first and we hit them hard. Don't think about the law. 'Cause we ain't much better than them from now on out. Let's go on back and get some sleep. Tomorrow is gonna be the start of a busy time, I'm thinkin'."

It started early. Jeff Sparks had just ridden in with a wagon to fetch the body of Jimmy back to his place for burying in the family plot. He was at Doc's office. And he was mad clear through. Killing mad.

Three of the Broken Lance riders came riding into town as if nothing eventful had happened. It made Matt mad just looking at them. One of them, Blackie, was an arrogant son.

Blackie and the two others reined up in front of the saloon, and that was where Matt was standing, leaning up against a support post at the edge of the boardwalk.

Blackie's eyes flicked to Matt's shirt front as he dismounted. He narrowed his eyes at the absence of a badge. "What's the matter, Bodine, you git tarred of lawin' or turn yeller?"

"You want to find out right now, Blackie?"

That stopped Blackie where he stood in the dirt. He smiled. "You callin' me out, Bodine?"

"In a word, yes."

Blackie stepped away from his horse, moving into a position more directly in line with Bodine. As most men who depend on their guns to keep them alive, Blackie had slipped the hammer thongs from his .45's the instant his boots touched the ground. He waved at the two who had ridden in with him.

"Stay out of this. This is a personal matter," Blackie said.

Bodine stood on the boardwalk, putting him about a foot and a half higher than Blackie.

Pen and Bam stood in front of the marshal's office window, watching the scene. Josiah was across the street, leaning against a post, watching. Sam was at the other end of the short block from Josiah, waiting and watching.

"I can't believe you'd actually call me out, Bodine," Blackie said with a smile. "You bein' such a high-minded sort of law-and-order feller. A principled sort, I guess you'd say."

"All that's changed since scum like you hired on with John Lee," Bodine told him.

Blackie tensed, a flush creeping up from his neck to cover his face. "Scum, Bodine?" he asked, his words softly offered.

"Just like what you'd find on a stinking pool of bad water, Blackie."

"What's goin' on here, Bodine?" the hired gun asked. "How come you sudden on the prod?"

Blackie's two riding buddies were standing silent and listening, sensing that the rules of the range war had suddenly changed, and not to their advantage.

"The law is oftentimes inadequate, Blackie," Bodine replied. "Especially when decent people have to deal with the filth of the earth—like you."

The hired gun thought about that for a few seconds and got mad. "Why, damn your eyes, Bodine. I'm gonna kill you."

Bodine shot him. His draw was lightning quick and his aim right on the mark. The .44 slug struck Blackie just to the right of center chest, turning him around in the dirt and numbing his right arm. Blackie had not even had time to drag iron.

"Jesus," one of his fellow guns-for-hire whispered. It was the first time he'd ever seen Matt Bodine in action, and he hoped he would never have to face the Wyoming gunfighter. He wasn't in Bodine's class and knew it.

Blackie pulled his second gun from behind his gunbelt, and Matt drilled him again, putting the slug a couple of inches above Blackie's ornate silver belt buckle. That slug sat Blackie on the ground, on his butt. The gun fell to the earth with a small plopping sound and lay in the dust by his leg.

The newly arrived undertaker and his assistant came rushing out of their half-completed building to stand on the edge of the boardwalk. The undertaker carefully measured Blackie with a practiced eye and concluded they had a pine box that was just right for him. It might be a little snug around the shoulders, but Blackie wouldn't mind the tight fit.

With blood staining his lips, Blackie gave a macabre grin. "You're good, Bodine. But they's a surprise in store for you. He'll be gettin' here any day now. Wish I could hang round and see it." He fell over on his side and turned his head in the dirt to stare at Matt. His left hand was close to the .45 he'd pulled from behind his belt.

"I like surprises, Blackie," Matt told him. "Makes everyday seem like Christmas."

Blackie moved his hand closer to the butt of the pistol. "You won't like this one, Bodine. Monty Brill stands to earn big money by killin' you." He closed his eyes against the pain that suddenly hit him, rolling over him in hot waves. He sighed and opened his eyes. His world was getting all fuzzy and blurry. The .45 only inches in front of him had turned into three pistols. He didn't know which one to grab.

He didn't have to worry about it. He died in the dirt.

Matt turned to face Blackie's buddies. "You boys rode in with him. That makes you both just as crap-sorry as he was."

"We can ride out," one of them said, a thin sheen of sweat making his tanned face shiny. "You just tell us which direction you want us to head, and we'll do 'er."

His buddy looked around him and silently cussed. Bodine faced them. To their right was Josiah Finch. Sam Two Wolves stood watching to their left. Right behind them was Pen Masters and Bam Ford. All in all, it made for a lousy situation.

"And I'm supposed to take your word that you'll keep riding and not return to Broken Lance range?" Bodine asked.

"You'll not see either of us again, Bodine," the third man spoke. "In two days we'll be in Fort Stockton, and we won't even look back."

"When's Monty Brill due to arrive?"

"Today or tomorrow."

"Coming alone?"

"Beggin' your pardon, Bodine, but he don't need no help." That was a fact. Bodine knew one thing for fact about

Monty Brill: he was supposed to be the fastest gun west of the Mississippi. He been hired to kill dozens of men, and he had done it without ever taking lead.

Matt looked across the street toward Doc Winters's office. Jeff Sparks and some of his men had stepped out at the sounds of shooting. They stood on the boardwalk, looking at the bloody scene in the street.

"I'd not like to face the law on the wrong side of it," Jeff called to Pen and Bam. "If you boys get my drift."

Pen looked at Bam. "There was that matter of them runaway kids down by the river."

"Sure was. We best go have a look."

The two remaining lawmen walked toward the livery to get their horses.

No one spoke a word until they had ridden out of town.

"What the hell . . . ?" one of Blackie's buddies said.

"I think we're in a world of hurt," his partner whispered.

"I think we're dead," his friend replied.

Jeff Sparks hanged them both from the hay hoist at the livery. The tortured and blanket-wrapped body of Jimmy lay in the bed of a wagon only a few feet from where the gunmen now swung.

"But there was no trial!" Dr. Winters protested. "You just . . . *hanged* them."

"They rode for John Lee," Al told the doctor. "And that's the way it's going to be from now on. If you don't have the stomach for it, Doc, then you best catch the next stage out."

"I have a back room full of shot-up gunhands from the other night. I can't leave them. They'd die."

The look he received from Al told him without words that that probably would be the best thing that could happen to them.

The doctor shook his head at Western justice and walked back to his office.

The undertaker looked up at the swaying bodies of the hired guns. "You go back and extend that long box by about a foot, Ralph. Get some of that scrap lumber from out back. And do a better job of it than last time. I don't want the end fallin' off and his bare feet pokin' out like before. It wouldn't have been so bad 'ceptin' his damn feet was dirty!"

Chapter 19

"So he's hired Monty Brill," Josiah said. The men sat at a table in the saloon, drinking coffee. They were leaving for the Circle S in about a hour to attend the funeral of Jimmy, to be held just at sunset.

"Do you know him?" Sam asked.

"Never laid eyes on the man. All I know about him is he's killed about thirty men face-to-face. He's never had a warrant writ out on him. He'll deliberate bump a man at the bar, and they'll be a few cuss words exchanged, and one man will call the other out into the street. Brill always collects in advance in some manner—never in person—and minutes after the shootin', he's gone."

"Any idea what he looks like?" Matt asked.

"I've heard a dozen different descriptions. But the one that keeps comin' back is that he's a tall, rangy sort of man. Very soft-spoken and well-mannered. Never uses profanity and is very polite around the ladies. Not much of a drinker. He's no backshooter. He'll face you head on and throw down. And he's fast."

"Age?" Sam asked.

Josiah shook his head. "Anywhere from forty to fifty.

Monty Brill's been around a long time. He's faced a lot of men and made a lot of money by killin' for hire, and there ain't nobody that I ever heard of ever got no lead in him. Don't nobody seem to know where he calls home. But several have said it's up in the Dakotas."

"Then maybe Dodge knows him?"

"Could be. It won't hurt to ask."

Sam looked at the clock over the bar. "It's time to head for the Circle S."

Jeff had sent heavily armed punchers out from the ranch to prevent any replay of the tragedy that had occurred during the funeral services at the Flying V. It was an indication of how badly conditions had deteriorated just west of the Pecos.

When Jimmy had been buried and the last words spoken and the final prairie flower placed on his grave, the men and women returned to the house, the men to gather on the front porch and the ladies inside, fixing coffee and food.

"Monty Brill?" Vonny Dodge said. "Yeah, I know him. Or, rather, I knew him, years back, when he was just earnin' his reputation. You talk to him and he comes across like a nice fellow. But he's all twisted inside his noggin. He enjoys killin'. And he don't always charge for it. Sometimes he just strikes out on his own to stalk and kill somebody. It's like it's something he has to do; something that just builds up inside him like steam in a kettle. Folks say he's killed thirty men." Vonny shook his head. "More like a hundred and thirty. Maybe more than that. He comes into town, Matt, you kill him first time you see him. Don't ponder on it none. Just plug him and keep pourin' the lead into him until you're sure he's dead."

Matt shook his head in the rapidly fading light. "You know I can't do that, Vonny."

"Well," the old gunfighter said, "if I'm in town, you won't have to worry about it. I'll do it."

The men sat in silence for a time, enjoying each other's quiet company and the peacefulness of the purple-shadowed close of day. Even some of the revengeful fire seemed to have been banked in Vonny Dodge, but all knew that while the flames were not visible, the coals were still white hot inside the man, and it would take but a whisper of a breeze to fan them into a hellfire of a killing inferno.

Vonny abruptly excused himself and walked off into the night, heading to his bachelor quarters off from the main house.

On the ride back to town, Matt said, "Vonny's up to something, I think."

"I got the same impression," Sam said. "The death of Jimmy is affecting him more than he's letting on."

"Them few days he gave us back yonder at the burned-out ranch is over," Josiah added. "I seen that the other night in the saloon. From here on out, any time Vonny comes up on a Broken Lance rider, he's gonna kill him. And he'll be lookin' hard, bet on that."

"You think he's passed the word to the hands?" Matt asked.

"Oh, yeah. John Lee don't know the narrow corner he's worked hisself into. But he's gonna be findin' out shortly."

As they were speaking, Vonny Dodge and half a dozen Circle S hands were quietly saddling up and getting ready to ride.

Jeff Sparks and his son stood on the porch of the ranch house and watched them walk their horses out of sight before mounting up.

"What if Cindy catches a bullet during this sneak attack, Papa?" Gene asked.

"I'd hate that, boy," the father said. "It'd be a hard thing. And I'd have to live with it for the rest of my life. But she made her choice when she turned her back on her family. Personally, I think Noah would seriously consider shootin' her hisself if he got the chance. And that's an awful thing to say."

"He told me that just the thought of her havin' Nick's baby makes him sick to his stomach," Gene said.

"It don't make me feel real good. But let's hope that nothin' happens to the unborn child. It ain't the baby's fault."

Vonny personally led the attack on the Broken Lance spread. The riders went in hard and fast and caught everyone by surprise. They set one of the bunkhouses on fire with thrown torches and managed to set the shed out back of the main house blazing while Tate, Lomax, and Cloud tore down the corral and sent the horses scattering in a wild stampede.

Bell pulled sticks of short-fused dynamite from a sack on his saddle horn and really got the fireworks started when he tossed a stick into the well and ruined their drinking water. He bounced another stick off an outhouse door and blew it apart. Its occupant was blown several feet into the air and came down with his pants around his boots and splinters driven deep into his bare butt. He would not be sitting a saddle for several days.

Chookie tossed a stick of dynamite onto the front porch of the mansion and caved in the overhang, the porch roof collapsing and blocking the entire front portion of the house.

John Lee was having a brandy in the dining room when the attack came. Beavers rode past the lighted area and stuck a sawed-off shotgun through the open window, blowing the chandelier that John Lee had brought in from St. Louis into a million pieces and sending the rancher diving for the floor, crawling under the table.

The charge that ruined the front porch lifted the table off its legs and turned it over, the supper dishes and chicken and dumplings slopping all over John Lee and a silver serving platter conking him on the head. Cussing and hollering and screaming, John Lee looked up just in time to see Gilley level a six-shooter at him through the open window. John Lee, slipping and sliding in the dumplings and the chicken and the apple pie got his butt out of the way just as Gilley fired, the slug knocking a hole in the expensive table.

Nick ran out the back door, his hands full of six-shooters and Chookie dabbed a loop over the young man and jerked it tight. Screaming like a Comanche, Chookie dragged the rancher's son through the yard until Nick impacted against the side of a horse trough and the force of the sudden stop tore the saddle horn off.

Two Broken Lance riders faced Vonny with Colts in their hands. Vonny smiled a hard smile and John Lee could scratch two more hands off his payroll sheet.

Just before the Circle bunch rode off into the night, Chookie tossed a bundle of taped-together sticks of dynamite into the now-empty barn. The charge blew a huge hole in one wall and collapsed that side of the barn. With a ear-splitting creak, the other side slowly caved in, until the barn roof was sitting flat on the ground.

Whooping and hollering, the Circle S attackers rode off into the night, knowing that it would take several hours for the Broken Lance men to round up their horses and launch any kind of pursuit.

John Lee staggered out of the house, still slipping and sliding on his slick-soled boots, dumplings in his hair and a piece of boiled chicken hanging out of one ear. In a futile gesture of rage and frustration, he emptied his pistols into the air, hitting nothing.

Nick slowly got to his boots, a huge knot on his head where he had impacted with the watering trough. He had lost his fancy guns and he was addled, for a moment not knowing where he was, who he was, or what the hell had happened. Cindy stuck her head out of an upstairs window and brought her reluctant husband back to reality by squalling at him.

"Aw, shut up," Nick said. But he was catching on fast to married life. He did not say it loud enough for his wife to hear.

"Round up the horses," John Lee said. He was so angry his voice trembled. And he was having trouble hearing out of one ear. He reached up and pulled a piece of boiled chicken out of it. "We're striking back—tonight!"

His foreman said, "They'll be expectin' it, John. and they'll be waitin' for us."

"Not at the Flyin' V, they won't. Those were all Circle S riders that hit us."

Max nodded his head. "I'll get us saddled up and fetch a sack full of dynamite. I'll have one of the boys cap and fuse it while we're roundin' up the horses."

"Pay-back time," John Lee muttered and whistled and sprayed spit. "You boys had you a good time this night, now I'm going to have me a better one."

But Vonny had warned young Noah what was going to happen right after the funeral, and Noah had turned his ranch into a fort, with riflemen ready in the best positions around the area. While there was only seven of them counting Noah, seven men with rifles could do a tremendous amount of damage. In addition to the riflemen, Noah and his crew had worked hard in painting rope black and then stringing it from barn to bunkhouse, house to barn, and corral to bunkhouse. The painted rope was just high enough to catch a mounted man in the chest or in the throat, and it was stretched tight.

"Here they come!" Burl called from the barn loft. "And they're comin' hard."

"Let 'em hit the ropes!" Noah called. "And then open up."

"For a youngster," Mark raised his voice to be heard from the loft to the bunkhouse, "that boy's got a lot of nerve and good sense."

"And after what happened to his ma and pa," Pete called, "I reckon he's fightin' with a heart full of hate for John Lee."

Nick was leading the assault against the ranch. He came riding in with both hands filled with guns and knee-reining his horse. He was the first to hit the ropes and the rope caught him across the chest, lifting him out of the saddle and hurling him against Lew Hagan, slamming both men to the ground and knocking the wind from them. They both lost their guns. Their horses galloped on and kept on going.

Bradshaw had sticks of dynamite looped together and

hanging around his neck when he hit the rope and was knocked from the saddle. He rolled and came to his boots, looking wildly around him. Burl lined him up in rifle sights and pulled the trigger, the hot slug striking the cap.

The explosion concussioned the night, and when all the bits and pieces finally fell back to earth, there wasn't enough left of Bradshaw to write home about.

Nick was running wildly, disgust and fear moving him; part of Bradshaw had splattered all over him. He ran into the barn, and Mark rolled a bale of hay over the edge of the loft. The bale hit Nick on the back and knocked him to the rough floor, where he banged his head on the floor and was out cold.

A hired gun called Peck had run his horse into the back of another horse who had refused to go any farther, sensing that something was wrong up ahead and had stopped quite abruptly. The rider on the reluctant horse had gone sailing through the air, crashing into the corral and shot dead.

Peck left his saddle almost as suddenly as the now-dead gunny had and upon hitting the ground had started crawling on his hands and knees, getting the hell gone from that area. He'd been in too many fights not to know when one was going sour.

John Lee had his horse stumble and fall, spilling him from the saddle. He lost his hat and one gun and ran into the south end of the barn and stepped on the tines of a rake. The handle flew up and busted him directly on the snoot, breaking the nose. The blood flew as John backed out of the barn and caught up a loose horse, swinging into the saddle.

" 'Et's 'o," he hollered.

"What the hell did he say?" Lightfoot asked Lopez.

" 'Et's 'o!" John squalled, his words slurred because his nose was spreading all over his face, and he didn't have any front teeth to begin with.

"I'm gone!" Leo Grand said, and those close to him followed suit, riders heading out in all directions.

In the confusion, no one noticed Nick was not among them.

Noah and the hands roped the bodies of the dead by the ankles and dragged them to a gully about a quarter of a mile from the house. Two men were not seriously hurt and they were hog-tied and tossed back to the ground just as Nick was shoved out of the barn.

Noah pulled his .45 and cocked it, the sound loud in the night. He put the muzzle against the head of one of the hog-tied gunhands. "Tell me the names of those who whipped Jimmy to death, or die right here."

The hired gun didn't even take a breath. "John Lee and his son Nick, the foreman Max, and—"

"That's enough," Noah told him, holstering his pistol. "Gary, get me that quirt that Mex rider left here a couple of years back. Burl, you and Teddy strip Nick bareass and turn that barrel over yonder and tie him across it. I want his butt shinin' up."

"You got it!"

The short-handled quirt had four long, tightly braided lashes and was a cruel whip. Nick started hollering as the men tore his clothes off him and tied him belly down across the barrel. The two tied-up gunnies were thinking: Better him than me.

"Jimmy had the courage to crawl into town and live long enough to tell us who did it to him, Nick," Noah said. "And I doubt he screamed once while you and your sorry father and the others were whipping him to death. I don't think you're one tenth of the man Jimmy was."

He laid the lashes across Nick's bare butt with all the strength in his strong young arm, and John Lee's son started howling.

Chapter 20

Nick passed out long before Noah's arm gave out. He finally dropped the quirt when he could no longer lift his arm and his chest was heaving with exhaustion.

Nick's buttocks were a mangled, bloody mess.

"Throw a bucket of water on him and then pour salt in those wounds," Noah ordered.

Awake after being doused with two buckets of water, Nick started screaming again when the salt was applied freely to his backside.

Noah cut the hog-tied pair loose. "Strip right down to the buff," he told them. "Boots, socks, and all."

"We didn't have nothing to do with that kid gettin' whipped!" Giddings said. He was almost sick to his stomach after looking at Nick's ruined sitter.

"I never said you did. But if my arm wasn't wore out I'd give you both a good hidin'. Now strip!" he yelled. "And get that damned Nick on his feet."

"I cain't walk!" Nick whined.

Noah jerked iron and put two slugs very, very close to where Nick lay on the water and blood-soaked dirt. Nick jumped to his feet, screaming from the pain in his mangled buttocks.

"Now walk!" Noah told the three. "You ought to make the town by daylight."

The three butt-naked men began walking, Nick whining and blubbering and sobbing as his bare feet moved him along.

"One thing about it," Noah said with a smile. "There sure ain't no place between here and town for them to steal any clothes. Nameit is gonna be quite the place to be come daylight when those three come strollin' in."

John Lee sat in his bedroom and didn't know what to do. He didn't think Nick had been hit, but the boy was still missing. He probably was taking the back trails home. John Lee placed a warm damp cloth over his busted hooter and moaned in pain at just the slightest pressure. One of the hands had set it, and that procedure had brightened up John Lee's evening considerably.

It never entered John Lee's mind that if he would disband his army of hired guns and thugs and outlaws, Jeff Sparks would be more than willing to forgive the past and live and let live—even though Jeff Sparks had told him that very thing. John Lee had stepped over the edge. He was insane. He had stepped into the murky waters of that form of insanity that allowed him to appear normal in most instances, even though his mind was full of snakes.

He leaned back in his chair and through the pain began planning yet another stroke against his enemy—which included everybody west of the Pecos. He silently cursed Jeff Sparks, Matt Bodine, Sam Two Wolves, Josiah Finch, Vonny Dodge, Noah Carson and everybody else he could think of. He fell into a nighmarish sleep just as dawn was breaking.

* * *

A shout brought another shout until everybody in the town of Nemeit had turned out, standing on the boardwalks in various dress watching the three naked men come limping into town. Nick Lee was bawling like a little baby, tears running down his dusty cheeks—his face, that is—his buttocks swollen to twice their normal size, each step sending excruciating pain through his body. The men had cut small leafy branches from a cottonwood tree and that helped to conceal their privates. They were a sight to behold; even Doc Winters could not hide his smile.

Matt and Sam stood beside Josiah and chuckled at the big tough gunhands, as bare-butted as a baby.

"Hey, Nick," a citizen called out. "What's the matter, boy, did someone take them fancy guns of yourn and spank your be-hind?"

"I'll kill you!" Nick squalled. "I'll kill every one of you. You can't laugh at me. I'm Nick Lee."

That brought catcalls and hoots of derision from the people-lined boardwalks.

"Our feets is tore up awful bad," Giddings called to the crowd. "Can anybody give us some aid?"

"The same kind of aid you thugs give the people you burned out and kilt!" a woman yelled.

"Yeah," a man called. "Go to hell!"

Nick collapsed on the street.

Doc Winters stepped out to help him. The townspeople did not challenge his right to do so. He was a doctor, sworn to take care of the sick. But no one made a move to help him. Winters glanced over at Matt. Matt shook his head. Winters cut his eyes to Sam. Sam shook his head. He looked at Preacher Willowby. The man was unmoved by Nick's pitiful condition.

"As far as I'm concerned," Willowby said, "you can stone the Philistine."

"We don't blame you for helpin' him, Doc," a woman called out. "But we ain't gonna touch the lousy no-good."

With his face in the dirt, Nick screamed, "I'll kill all of you. I'll burn your damned houses down and kill your kids and your dogs and cats and horses. You're all inferior to me and my pa. You're jealous of what we got!" Nick ranted and raved and snorted and blubbered and whistled his threats.

Giddings looked around him at the faces of the men and women. Hard faces, unforgiving faces. There ain't no way we're gonna do nothin' but die fightin' these folks, he thought. John Lee is not gonna win this fight. But he had taken the man's money, and he would stick it out.

Providing he could get some clothes, that is.

His partner, Tidwell, said to Doc Winters, "We'll pay you, Doc. We're owed wages."

"Get Nick on his feet and carry him to my office."

"If we do that, we got to drop these branches," Giddings said.

Doc Winters was catching on fast to frontier justice. "That is not my problem, boys. If Nick wants to crawl, then he can get to my office on his hands and knees."

It was a strange and both comical and tragic scene being played out on the dusty street.

"Goddamn you all to the hellfires!" Nick screamed, crawling to his hands and knees, snot dripping from his nose and sweat from his dirty face. "I'll get you for this. I swear on my mama's grave I'll kill all of you."

Giddings and Tidwell manged to hold onto one thinly leafed branch with one hand and with the other hand managed to get Nick to his swollen feet and begin to walk to Doc Winters's office.

Not one person offered to help. The blood from the rock and briar and cockleburr-mangled feet of the men left dark stains in the dust as they staggered on. Nick screamed and shouted and cussed the townspeople.

"That boy's as nutty as his pa," Josiah said, then predicted, "It'll be over in a week to ten days. John Lee will

never let this go unavenged. He'll hit this town with everything he's got, and that's a-plenty."

"He can't tree this town," Sam said. "No one has ever
treed a Western town."

"That's a fact," the Ranger said. "But I'll bet you a pair of
boots he'll damn sure try."

John Lee retreated further into the darkness of madness
when he went into town to fetch his pride and joy home.
Giddings and Tidwell had been forced to walk from the town
to the Broken Lance range (no one would sell or loan them a
horse) and had arrived in midafternoon, exhausted and
wrapped only in ragged sheets from Doc Winters office. A
wagon had been dispatched immediately, with John Lee and
his small army riding with it.

Max went in first, alone, and paled at the sight that greeted
him. Every man in the town was visible and heavily armed.
There were riflemen on rooftops, riflemen in the alleys, riflemen on the second floor of buildings.

"One wagon, one driver, and you and John Lee can come
in," Pen told the foreman. "Anybody else gets shot out of the
saddle. Take that back to that jerk you work for."

Max nodded, turned his horse, and delivered the message.

"It's a death trap in there, John," he told his boss. "The
slightest wrong move on our part and we're dead meat in the
street."

"We'll get Nick," John said. "We'll deal with the town
and the scum in it later."

John Lee almost bawled at the sight of his wonderful boy.
Nick had been heavily sedated with laudanum and was mumbling incoherently. His buttocks had swollen to the size of a
water barrel, and he screamed when they picked him up and
toted him out, laying him facedown on a bed of hay.

"Take him home," John Lee told the driver. John Lee stood alone in the street and looked at the people looking back at him. There was no fear in their eyes. The king and his court jester son had been dethroned. The only one who did not realize that was his royal majesty John Lee.

John Lee looked at Matt Bodine and Sam Two Wolves standing only a few yards away to the left of the doctor's office door.

"Think this is funny, don't you, boys?" John Lee asked in a low voice.

"Hysterical," Sam told him.

Matt replied, "That stupid son of yours was some sight to see, lying in the dirt crying and blubbering like the coward he is."

John Lee started to verbally fire back when he realized what the blood brothers were doing: they were deliberately baiting him, trying to force him into drawing. His gaze shifted at the sounds of a slow-walking horse. At the far end of the street, a man dressed in a black suit pulled up at the hotel's hitchrail and swung down from the saddle.

Monty Brill had arrived.

John Lee picked up the reins and got into the saddle. He looked down at Matt Bodine.

"It isn't over, Bodine."

"I know that. But it could be if you'd just listen to reason for a change."

"I run this area," John Lee said. "I always have and when this is over, I shall again."

"No, you won't," Sam told him. "The people will never stand for that. Law and order has arrived, and it will prevail. Men like you can't survive it."

John Lee sneered at the brothers. "There is no law west of the Pecos, boys, and after you're gone, and that stupid Ranger gets called elsewhere, everything will return to the way it was."

"You're forgetting Pen Masters and Bam Ford, aren't you?" Matt asked.

"Who can prove where a shot out of the dark came from?" John Lee replied. He laughed at the expression on the brothers' faces. "You'd like to kill me, wouldn't you, boys? Sure you would. But you just can't do it. You just can't draw down and put lead in a man who's just sitting his horse looking at you. That's the difference in us, boys. That's why I'm going to win this fight. Because if I had the drop on the both of you, and thought I wouldn't get shot all to pieces by these town-folk, I could easily kill the both of you and not give it a second thought."

"You're a madman, John Lee," Sam told him. "You need to be in an insane asylum."

The rancher smiled at the brothers and turned his horse, riding slowly out of town.

"The town is going to have to be guarded at all times," Matt said. "For sure he'll try to burn it down."

"We have more pressing matters to deal with, brother. You saw the man who rode in?"

"Yeah. That's probably Monty Brill. I'll face that situation as it comes."

"Are you going to let him call the shots?"

Matt smiled. "Not hardly, brother, not hardly."

"Then . . . ?"

"Watch." Matt pulled on leather gloves as they walked.

The brothers crossed the street and walked toward the saloon. Josiah fell in with them. Vonny Dodge and several hands from the Circle S rode in, just as the sun was a boiling ball of fire sinking in the west. Vonny studied the strange brand on the horse's hip and stepped up on the boardwalk just as Matt and the others reached the saloon.

"That's a Dakota brand. I recognize it from years back. It's got to be Monty's horse," the old gunfighter said. "Let me handle this one, boy."

"You just stay out of this, Vonny. It's me he's after, and I'll handle it my way."

"You go in shootin', boy," Vonny told him. "Just like you would a rattlesnake. Don't give him no chance at all. Listen to me. I know what I'm talkin' about."

"I got a better idea," Matt said. "There's gonna be plenty of shooting soon enough."

"What's your plan?" the gunfighter-turned-rancher asked, questions in his eyes.

Matt grinned. "Monty Brill's a bad man with a gun, right?"

"That he is, son. One of the best."

"Watch this." Matt pushed over the batwings and stepped into the saloon.

The man in black stood with his back to Matt. But he was watching him in the mirror's reflection.

Matt studied the man. About forty or forty-five, and looked to be in excellent physical condition. He lifted his eyes to the mirror's reflection to meet the eyes watching him. Cold eyes. Killer eyes. He began his walk to the bar.

"A cold beer, Al," Matt said, never stopping his walk.

"I'll have another whiskey," the man in black said.

"Forget the whiskey, Al," Matt told him. "Mr. Brill won't have time to finish it."

Brill turned, a strange smile on his lips, his hands dropping to the butts of his guns. Matt was right on the man and hit him. A solid straight right that landed like a sledgehammer. Matt jerked Brill's guns from leather and tossed them on the table.

"Now, Brill," Matt told him. "Let's see how good you are with your fists."

Chapter 21

With a snarl coming from his freshly blooded lips, Brill charged Matt, both fists balled and ready.

Matt tripped him, sending the man crashing to the floor. Matt kicked him in the belly, and Brill grunted and rolled away, coming up to his boots. The men circled each other warily. Brill was just about Matt's size, and he knew how to box; Matt could tell that by the way he moved.

Brill threw a left, Matt slapped it away, and Brill tried to follow that with a right. Matt busted him in the mouth again and followed that blow with a left that clubbed Brill's ear and backed him up.

Men had crowded into the saloon, forming a silent circle around the combatants.

Brill got through Matt's defenses and landed a solid left hook that stung. Matt backed up until his head cleared. Brill followed him and pressed his luck, thinking he had Matt on the run. It was a bad mistake. Matt deliberately lowered his guard and Brill took the opportunity. Matt slipped the punch and landed a left and right to Brill's head. Brill spat out part of a broken tooth and shook his head.

Matt popped the man hard in the gut, then stepped around

and hammered at his kidneys. Brill backed up and Matt pressed him hard, landing body blows that bruised and shots to the head and jaw that stung and brought blood.

Brill swung a wide looping right. Matt stepped inside it and butted Brill with his head, the gunfighter's teeth snapping together, bringing a howl of pain from the man and a spray of blood from his lips. Brill looked around him frantically, seeking a way out. There was none, the crowd had closed ranks.

Matt bulled in, swinging hard fists and connecting with Brill's jaw and mouth and belly.

"Time!" Brill panted. "I evoke gentleman's rules."

"I'll honor it," Matt said, backing up. "Even though you're no gentlemen."

"I'll have a beer, barkeep," Brill said. "You'll join me, Bodine?"

"I'll pass."

Al pulled a mug for the man and slid it down the bar. Brill drank half of it, then wiped his bloody mouth with the back of his hand. He turned and looked at Bodine, noticing that Bodine was not even breathing hard.

"You're going to beat me to death, aren't you, Bodine?"

"I'm interested in how you know me."

"Oh, I've known how you look for over a year. I do that, you know, plan ahead, figuring that someday someone would want you dead. I'm usually right. Are you going to answer my question?"

"I'm not going to beat you to death, Brill. I'm just going to stomp you, then break both your arms at the elbows, so you can never again use a gun." Matt had been watching Brill as he moved closer, the half-empty beer mug in his hand.

"That would be a death sentence for me, Bodine."

"How many death sentences have you handed out, Brill?" Brill smiled disarmingly and swung the heavy mug.

Bodine jumped to one side, picked up a chair, and splintered it across Brill's shoulders, knocking the man down.

"No more gentlemen's rules, Brill," Matt told him. "Get up on your feet and fight."

Brill got up. He got up with a knife in his hand he jerked out of his boot.

Sam laughed. "You didn't do enough research on my brother, Brill. Matt grew up in a Cheyenne camp. He knows more about knife fighting than any white man I ever saw."

Matt reached behind his left-hand gun and pulled out a long-bladed, razor-sharp Bowie. "You should have passed up this job, Brill."

"I almost did, Bodine," Brill said, then slashed.

Bodine parried and slapped the man, the back of his hard-gloved hand sounding like a gunshot when it impacted.

Again and again, Brill tried to cut Bodine. Each time Bodine anticipated the move, as he had been taught by Cheyenne warriors. Brill's face was shiny with sweat. He sensed his own defeat—knowing that Bodine was playing a deadly game with him—and his eyes turned wild.

"Finish it, damn your eyes, Bodine!" he yelled.

"All right," Bodine said, and opened up Brill's left arm all the way down from elbow to palm, slicing through tendons and ruining the arm.

Brill screamed.

"That's one hand that'll never hold another gun, Brill," Bodine told him.

"Goddamn you!" Brill cursed him as the blood flowed from the long incision.

Bodine brought his knife down on Brill's right shoulder, the heavy blade slicing through flesh and bone, forever ruining the arm.

Brill howled in pain and fell to the floor, the knife falling from suddenly useless fingers.

"Get the doc," Vonny said, his hard old eyes holding no

pity or compassion for Brill. "I want this scum to live. I want him to live in fear for the rest of his days. Lookin' over his shoulder for the kin of some of his victims."

"Kill me!" Brill screamed.

"No way, Brill," Matt told him.

Dr. Winters pushed through the crowd and took one look at the bloody Brill. He lifted his eyes to Matt, seeing the red-stained blade in Bodine's hand. "Frontier justice again, Matt?"

"Just plain ol' justice, Doc. And believe me, he had it coming."

It was late when Dr. Winters joined Matt and the others for supper.

"Brill will live," Winters said, taking a chair. "But he'll have absolutely no use of his right arm and limited use of his left hand. You've ruined him, Matt."

"That is exactly what I intended to do, Doc."

"Don't shed no tears over that one, Doc," Josiah told the young man. "He's ruint no tellin' how many lives with them guns of his."

Dr. Winters slowly met the eyes of all the men seated around the table in the café. "I should be shocked. Appalled. I would have been a month ago. But now . . ." He trailed that off into silence.

"Why not now?" Vonny asked.

"I've been listening to those dying gunmen over in my of-fice. Listening to them talk about the evil things they've done over the years. They're not repentant. They're dying boasting of the blackest criminal acts I have ever heard of. Murder and rape and torture and the foulest of deeds. I've had to leave several times. It was . . . disgusting, sickening. I see now why you men hold no compassion for that ilk. I understand it. My college professors would be dismayed at my new attitude, but they can go to hell. They're out of touch with reality."

Vonny picked up his hat and set it on his head. He patted

the doctor on the shoulder. "You'll do, Doc. You'll do to ride the river with."

He walked out the door and swung into the saddle, his crew with him.

"Was that a compliment?" Dr. Winters asked.

"Of the highest kind," Sam told him.

Matt and Sam and Josiah hung around town for a week, playing cards and talking and relaxing, knowing that the lid was going to blow off the pot, but not knowing when. Only that it would be soon. Vonny and some of the Circle S hands rode into town several times that quiet week. They had nothing to report. Everything was quiet on both the Circle S and the Flying V range.

"Too quiet," Chookie said over beer and cards one evening. "Gives me a creepy feelin.' You know that crazy John Lee is goin' to pull something, but you don't know when. Makes a man jumpy."

The truth was, John Lee didn't know what to do. He was just about out of ideas. When the news reached him about Monty Brill, he was shocked, as were most of his fighting men. For Matt Bodine to have first stomped the renowned gunslinger-for-hire and then cut him up like a side of beef, crippling him forever, was something that caused a lot of the men on John Lee's payroll to seriously think about hauling their ashes out of this country. Several already had.

Kingman, the gunhand who had taken lead from Bodine several years back, summed up his feelings while drinking in the bunkhouse one night during the lull in the fighting. "I ain't runnin' from Bodine. I aim to see this settled here and now, once and for all. The chips just ain't been fallin' right, is all. We got the guns, we got the men. It'll all come in line for us. It's just a matter of time, that's all."

"Yeah," Leo Grand agreed, cutting his eyes to Dan Ringold. "You 'posed to be some kind of hotshot with that rifle you're always cleanin' and lovin' on. Why don't you do what you're bein' paid to do and put lead in Bodine and that Injun brother of his?"

"The boss ain't told me to do that yet," Ringold replied. "When he does, I will."

Giddings and Tidwell, still having to soak their feet in liniment and brine several times a day after their long and unintentional commune with nature, looked at the sniper. "Could it be, Ringold, that you're just scared of them two?" Giddings asked.

Ringold turned cold mean eyes at the man. "I'm hired to do one job of work and one job of work only, Gimpy. Don't crowd me."

The bunkhouse door opened and the foreman walked in. "Ringold, the boss wants to see you."

Ringold smiled and stood up. "Now I get to go to work." He walked out behind Max, heading for the mansion, which was still undergoing repairs after the bombing and shooting raid.

Bodine swallowed the last of his beer and started to walk out of the nearly deserted saloon. The night man was getting the bucket of water ready for his swamper to mop up. At the batwings, Bodine hesitated, then stepped to one side, standing by the wall. Sam and Josiah had turned in early, and Pen and Bam had made their nightly rounds and were getting ready to hit the bunks. Matt walked back to the bar.

"I'll use the back way this evening, Jack," he told the bartender.

Jack nodded, thinking nothing of it. Maybe Bodine had to use the privy.

Bodine cut to his right once outside the darkened storeroom. He pressed up against the outside wall for a moment, adjusting his vision from the lamplit barroom to the night, wondering what had triggered the sudden feeling of danger.

He slipped his guns in and out of leather. Something

dangerous was out there in the darkness, some predator lurking. But who, or what?

The town was very quiet, most of its citizens long abed. Matt did not move. He listened. Heard nothing. He reached down and removed his spurs, sticking them in a back pocket of his jeans. He shifted positions, darting across the dark alleyway. He pulled his right-hand .44, thumb on the hammer. He did not want to cock it yet, did not want to make the slightest noise that might give away his position. A back door opened and Matt flattened himself against the building. A man tossed out washwater, stood for a moment breathing in the night air, then stepped back and closed the door.

Matt moved quickly and silently, working his way down the back of the line of buildings. A dog barked from across the street, not a bark of greeting, but a bark of annoyance at something or somebody in its territory. It yelped after the sound of something striking the animal. Something thrown to chase it off? Bodine wondered. Probably.

He peeked around the corner of the closed café, first inspecting the rooftops, and after finding nothing amiss, carefully studied each pocket of darkness on ground level. He put his left hand over the action to muffle the sound and cocked his .44. He began working his way toward the street side of the alley, staying close to the café's outer wall.

A slight shifting of a shadow from across the deserted street stopped him. He stood very still, knowing that to a hunter, movement attracts more notice than noise. The silhouette of a man appeared from out of the gloom. A man with a rifle in his hands. Matt waited motionless. The man seemed to be studying the other side of the street. If he was after Bodine—and Matt was sure he was—he had seen Bodine appear at the batwings, hesitate, and then back off. He had heard the saloonkeeper closing the doors and knew that Bodine had sensed something amiss and exited the place through the back door. The hunter would also know that he was now the hunted.

It was a wide street, not yet hard packed, due to the newness of the town, but it was rutted and uneven from wheels and hooves. It would too chancy for a shot from a short gun. Matt had to get closer. He began moving toward the front of the alley, carefully putting one boot in front of the other, testing the ground ahead of him with the toe of his boot before moving the other boot, not wanting to step on a bottle or can or sleeping cat's tail.

He froze when the shadow across the street abruptly moved back into the blackness, away from the alley front.

Matt waited, his eyes straining to pierce the gloom. He saw no more silhouettes. The dog barked again, but this time it was farther up than before, off to Matt's left. The man was shifting positions, and that would put him behind the general store; Matt hoped he was right in that assumption. Taking a deep breath, Matt ran across the street, exposing himself and expecting the shock of a bullet with each step. None came. He jumped the boardwalk and landed in the now-vacant alley, going down on one knee and catching his breath, breathing through his mouth to cut down on the noise of sucking in air.

The little dog continued to bark. Matt knew which dog it was: the little mutt that Bam and Pen had taken to feeding. A likeable little dog. Matt liked him even more now. He moved to the end of the building and pressed against it, listening and waiting. The dog stopped yapping.

Matt stepped around to the back of the store and stayed close to it as he worked his way up the row of buildings and houses. He saw the little mutt sitting by a back step, looking at him. Matt knelt down and the mutt ran to him, wagging his tail.

Matt petted the dog with his left hand and then patted the ground beside him. The dog plopped down. Matt put his mouth close to the dog's ear and whispered, "Good boy. Good boy. You stay here."

The dog stayed put and Matt moved on. He stepped into the next alley and saw the form of the rifleman near the mouth of passageway. Matt walked on for a few yards, then softly called, "Looking for me?"

The man spun around, startled, but not so startled that his rifle wasn't level and pointed at Matt's stomach, hammer back.

Matt shot him twice, the booming of the .44 enormous in the quiet night, the magnified sound bouncing off the walls that were left and right of the men.

Dan Ringold got off one shot, the muzzle pointing straight up as he was falling back, the shock of the twin .44's knocking him backward. The .44-40 boomed in the night, the slug hitting the night air and nothing else.

Matt walked up to the man and kicked the rifle out of his reach just as Pen and Bam were running across the street, pistols in their hands. They wore longhandles, boots, and their hats.

Matt knelt down and took Dan's pistol from leather, handing it to Pen. "How about it, Dan," he asked, just as Josiah came running out, Doc Winters right behind him, Josiah in his longhandles and the doctor in a robe. "Tell us that John Lee sent you to kill me."

"Sorry, Bodine," Dan spoke past gritted teeth against the pain. "You know the rules of the work."

Doc Winters tore open the rifleman's shirt. He stared him in the eyes. "You're lung-shot, man. Don't go out with a confession wedged behind your lips. Help us bring an end to this terrible war."

Dan smiled up at the man. "You got a ridin' horse, Doc?"

"What?" Winters asked, momentarily confused. "Ah . . . no, I don't."

"You do now. My horse is tied out back of the livery. He's a good horse. You're a compassionate man. I know you'll take care of him. And he ain't stolen neither. The bill of sale is in my saddlebags. He'll take you down a lot of trails, Doc."

"Why . . . ah, thank you," Winters said. "You're very kind."

Dan laughed painfully. "First time anybody ever called me that." He looked at Bodine. "How could you have known I was waitin' outside for you, Bodine?"

"You know how it is in this business, Dan. We play our hunches."

Dan nodded and closed his eyes. He would play no more deadly hunches on this side of that dark river.

"I'll fetch his horse for you, Doc," Pen said. "And he wasn't kiddin' none. That sorrel's a fine animal."

Dr. Winters shook his head. "What a strange gesture from such a violent man."

"I heard he was trained to be a schoolteacher," Josiah said. "I guess he got tired of it."

"Well, he can rest forever now," Sam summed it up.

Chapter 22

When Dan did not return, John Lee knew the rifleman was not ever going to come back. He sat on his not-quite-repaired front porch and drank coffee, watching the sun come up to chase away the cool pleasantness of early morning.

Max walked over from his quarters to join his boss. He poured a cup of coffee and sat down. "Gonna be a hot one, boss."

"Yes, it is, Max. For a fact."

They sat and sipped in silence for a few moments. Max finally said, "Boss?"

John Lee looked at him.

"You wanna pull in our horns and put an end to all this?"

"You think we can't win, Max?"

"Yes, that's what I think."

"You want to go to prison, Max?"

"Hell, no!"

"Well, that's what'll happen to us if we quit now. We've got too many deaths behind us, Max. Think about it. Do you believe that Ranger will just accept our backing down and ride on out of here and forget all about everything that's happened? That's not the way they operate, and you know it.

Could you ever ride into Nameit and be at peace with your back turned to some of those people? I couldn't."

"No," the foreman said after a few heartbeats. "I reckon I couldn't either, boss."

"We've lost some battles, Max. But the war isn't over yet. What are the men saying?"

"As long as you pay, they'll fight. That's what they do, and they'll stay as long as you got the money to pay them."

"How many men do we have left?"

"Forty-one, counting you, me, and Nick."

"That's a lot of men, Max. Dammit, that's an army!" He looked at his foreman. "Max, did you say forty-one? What happened? Ths time yesterday we had over fifty men on the payroll."

"Some rode out this morning, boss. I paid 'em off and they hauled it. All the culls are gone, boss. The ones left are professional fighting men."

"Do you have any kind of a plan at all, Max?"

The foreman shook his head. "Not a clue, boss. Ever'time we do something, they come one up on us. Bodine's done crippled Monty Brill and killed Dan Ringold, I reckon. 'Least he ain't come back, and he ain't the type to run. So I figure he's dead. The cook's complainin' that we're near out of food, and we shore can't buy it in Nameit. So that means a run to the settlement."

"Who says we can't buy in Nameit?"

"Well . . . nobody, I guess. I just figured that you'd—"

"You figured wrong, Max. Get the wagons ready. Two men on each wagon and two men per wagon as guards. You and me will ride in, too. We're going to town, Max."

Max smiled. "I pick the best, boss?"

"You pick the best, Max."

John Lee and Max took the point. Driving the first wagon was Leo Grand and Trest. The guards were Lew Hagan and

Bob Grove. On the second wagon were Jack Lightfoot and Gil Lopez. Their guards were Dusty Jordan and a man called Winslow. When they reached the town, John Lee halted the parade and rode in alone, straight up to the marshal's office and sat his horse, staring at Pen Masters and Bam Ford.

"Mornin'," Pen said. "You want something?"

"I'd like to buy supplies," John Lee said. "If you have no objections to my spending money in your town."

"No objections at all," Bam said. "How many men are with you?"

"I have two wagons. Two men to a wagon and two outriders per wagon. My foreman and me."

That was reasonable. Indians still raided every now and then, and a body couldn't get careless when carryin' food and other supplies.

"Your money's good here, John Lee," Pen told him. "You might want to pay your last respects to Dan Ringold; he's over yonder at the undertaker's place. He tried to bushwack Matt Bodine last night. He didn't make it."

A small nervous tic appeared under John Lee's left eye. Other than that, he did not change expression. "I didn't even know he'd left the ranch. What a pity. Did he have enough money on him to bury him?"

"Oh, yeah. Plenty of cash in his pockets for that," Bam said. "And he done a right nice thing before he passed on. He give his horse and his rig to Doc Winters. Wasn't that a grand gesture on his part?"

"Lovely," John Lee spoke through clenched teeth—and not many of them.

John Lee turned his horse and rode back up the street, conscious of the many eyes upon him. He could feel the raw hatred from the onlookers' eyes. At the wagons, he said, "Ten thousand dollars to the man who kills Matt Bodine, five thousand for the Indian's death. I'll pay cash money and give you the fastest horse on Broken Lance. You men talk it over and decide who does the deed. Let's go in."

"He's up to something," Josiah remarked, standing between Matt and Sam. "And I got a hunch it involves you boys."

"It's sort of funny," Bodine said. "John Lee thinks that killing me and Sam would solve all his problems. He can't understand that we're just a small part in this play. Our deaths wouldn't stop the momentum of the people. It might even quicken it. I wonder why he can't see that?"

"Because he's nuts," Josiah's reply came quickly. "Doctors probably have a better word for it, but I don't know what it is. 'Nuts' is good enough for me."

"Look who he's got driving those wagons and acting as outriders," Sam said.

Matt had picked up on that. John Lee was not using any of his regular hands. The men accompanying him on this day were all top guns. "You can bet that John Lee will stand clear of any action. He's not ready to bet the whole pot just yet."

"Lightfoot and Lopez will double-team you," Josiah said. "That's the way they work. You boys stay together. I'll watch your back."

"Look there," Sam said, shifting his eyes to the other end of the street. "Here comes Vonny and a few of the hands."

Josiah cuckled. "This thing just might get settled today."

"I wish," Matt said. "Sam and me have a lot of country to see yet."

"You boys sure you don't want to stay in Texas and join the Rangers? We could use you."

"I'm not cut out for carrying a badge," Sam said. "And Bodine doesn't have the patience for it."

Josiah smiled as he watched the wagons turn down the alley to the loading dock behind the general store. Josiah liked Matt and Sam, this pair of young hellions. They sort of reminded the Ranger of himself, back in his younger days.

"I wonder if they'll have a drink and then brace us, or just come straight on with it?" Sam mused.

"There's your answer," Josiah said, as Lightfoot and

Lopez stepped out of the store. "John Lee and his foreman have retired to the saloon. They're out of it."

Hagan and Grove appeared in the mouth of the alley and stepped away from each other.

"Here it comes," Sam said. "It's double-team all the way around, brother."

Vonny Dodge stood in the center of street, a street that had suddenly become void of traffic of any kind. The tall old gunfighter's hands were by his sides, inches away from his guns.

"I reckon it's time, boys," Josiah said. "Vonny's closest to Lightfoot, so we'll leave him for Vonny. I'll take Lopez. Matt, Hagan is yours. Sam, take Grove."

"There's four missing," Matt pointed out. "Over there in the store somewhere or in the alley. Don't forget them when the shooting starts."

Men began moving the last of the horses from the hitch-rails to get them out of the line of fire.

"You know why we're here, Bodine," Lightfoot called from across the street. "Ain't no need in pussy-footin' around it."

"You're mine, Lightfoot," Vonny called. "Turn and face the man who's about to kill you."

Josiah, Matt, and Sam stepped off the boardwalk and into the street. They stepped away from each other to offer less of a target mass.

"All mouth and nothin' to back it up, old man," Lightfoot said to Vonny, turning to face him. "You should have stayed in your rockin' chair, you old coot. Now I'm gonna fit you for a pine box."

"Then do it, punk," Vonny told him. "Don't just stand there flappin' that stupid mouth of yours."

There had been a slight breeze blowing. The breeze died out and the sun beat down. Somewhere nearby a horse stamped its hoof against the ground. A dog barked. The faint sounds of a baby crying drifted up the street.

Preacher Willowby and his wife stood in the doorway of

the church watching. Dr. Winters began laying out surgical instruments, preparing his operating room for customers. He made a mental note to order more laudanum.

Monty Brill lay on a cot near the window, his face flushed from pain and fever. "Fools," he whispered. "Ain't no man ever going to beat Bodine. You could empty a .44 in him and he'd still find the wherewithal deep inside himself to kill you."

"Then what made you think you could kill him?" Dr. Winters asked.

The badly crippled gunman forced a smile. "I didn't know whether I could or not. But I had to try. God, I'd rather be dead than live like this."

Doc Winters looked out the window. "What are they waiting for?"

"Those boys of John Lee's are buildin' up their nerve, talkin.' They're stallin'. They all know they're lookin' death in the face."

"Each one trying to trick the other into drawing?" Winters questioned.

"Something like that, Doc. Something like that."

"It's so quiet out," Winters muttered, staring out the open window.

"Always is at a time like this." Monty's voice was low.

Matt never took his eyes off Lew Hagen. They were the only two men left in the world, and both of them knew the other's reputation. At this distance, about thirty feet, Matt could see the sweat dripping off Lew's face. No point in delaying it any longer, Matt thought. He opened the dance by drawing and shooting Lew in the belly. The street exploded in gunfire and gray smoke.

Lew was down on his knees, clawing at his pistol, disbelief in his eyes at Bodine's speed. Matt shot him again, the slug striking him in the center of his chest and finishing it for Lew Hagen.

Vonny's guns spat fire and lead and smoke and Lightfoot sat down in the center of the street. He pulled the trigger of first his right-hand Colt and then the left, the slugs blowing holes in the dust. Lightfoot sighed and fell backward, dying with his eyes open, looking up at the clear blue Texas skies.

Bob Grove was down, the front of his shirt bloody. Sam shot him again and the gun fell from his fingers. "Damn Injun's fast," he said, then fell over on his face.

Gil Lopez was down on his butt in the dirt, gut-shot twice by Josiah. He lifted his .45 and eared back the hammer. Josiah put another round in him and Lopez began his dying with a very strange look on his face. "No," he said. "No."

"Yeah," Josiah corrected. "It ain't supposed to happen to you, is it, Gil?"

"No," Lopez said. "I shall not die on this day."

"I wouldn't put no bets on it," Vonny said, looking around for the others.

"I want a priest," Gil Lopez said.

"How about a Baptist preacher, amigo?" Sam asked him.

"Are you serious?" Lopez said, then fell over dead.

Leo Grand stepped out of an alley and took aim through the swirling gunsmoke. He put a round into Josiah, the slug knocking the Texas Ranger down. Matt shot him four times, the shots sounding like artillery fired by a precision team. Leo was dead before he hit the dirt.

The Oklahoma gunfighter, Trest, stepped over Leo's body. "By God, I'll end it," he said.

Matt, Vonny, Sam, and Josiah all fired at once. Trest's boots flew out from under him and he landed on his rear, his back to a building, his guns by his side.

"Git them other two!" Josiah said, his voice strong. "It's just my leg. Go on!"

But Winslow and Dusty Jordan, seeing how the battle was going, had ducked into the saloon through the back door and were sitting with John Lee and his foreman when the men slammed open the batwings and stepped inside.

"Quite a show, boys," Max said, lifting a mug of beer in a mock salute. "You put that on for our benefit?"

"Yes, very entertaining, indeed," John Lee said, but unable to keep the disappointment and the bitterness from his tone. Six more of his men now lay dead in the dirt.

"Looks like your Texas Ranger friend is all right," Max said, tilting his chair back and looking out the window. "Doc Winters is with him, and he's limpin' off toward the office."

"It'll take more than the scum John Lee hires to kill that Ranger," Vonny said. "How about it, John?" Vonny laid down the challenge. "You and me in the street, face-to-face? The fastest gunhand walks off."

John Lee would not meet the old foreman's eyes. He stared into his beer mug.

"Stand up and fight, you yeller-bellied bastard!" Vonny roared.

John Lee sat his chair.

"Scum," Vonny verbally crowded him. "Stinkin' no-count yeller pile of horse droppin's. That's all you are, John Lee. You have to hire your fightin' done. You ain't man enough to do it yourself."

Max pushed back his chair and slowly stood up. "You'll not talk to John Lee like that in my presence."

"Well, then, you'll just have to do," Vonny told him, then jerked iron and shot the Broken Lance foreman in the chest.

Max swayed on his feet for a moment, feeling the hot stickiness running down his chest, his life's blood ebbing from him. "But you're old!" he whispered.

"Naw," Vonny told him, twirling his Peacemaker and settling it back into leather. "I'm just good, Max!"

Max tried to life his pistol out of leather. He gave up. It was just too much effort. His legs could no longer support him, and he sat down in his chair and looked at John Lee. His face was very pale. "I reckon I'm dead, boss." Max slowly put his head on the table and closed his eyes. His hat fell off and hit the floor with a very small sound.

"Hot damn!" Josiah yelled from the batwings. "I got to

see it again! You're finer than frog hair with them Peace-makers, Vonny."

"Will you *please* come on to the office!" Doc Winters pleaded. "I've got to get that slug out of your leg."

"Shoot that damn John Lee," Josiah urged. "Lemme see you twirl them guns again. I ain't never got the hang of twirlin' guns. I give it up when I damn near blowed my toe off one time."

"Please, Mr. Finch," Doc Winters said. "You have got to get off that leg!"

"You worser than a old woman, Doc," Josiah told him. "Hell, I got more bullet scars on my hide than an Injun's got arrows. Stop tuggin on me, I'm comin' along."

"I 'spect our supplies is loaded by now, boss," Winslow said. "We best be gettin' on back."

"Yes," John Lee said in a low tone. He could not take his eyes off his dead foreman. "Please . . . remove Max from this place and put him in a wagon. Do it gently. He's been with me for many years."

John Lee stood up, moving like a man in severe pain. He looked at Vonny, opened his mouth to speak, then closed it. He shook his head and walked toward the batwings.

"Have a shootin' iron in your hand next time I see you, John Lee," Vonny told him. "Either that or leave this part of Texas."

John Lee turned slowly. "You dare to give me orders?"

"Yeah, I'm givin' you orders. I'll not kill you now," Vonny told him. "I reckon even men like you and Max is capable of feeling a man's comradeship to one another. I'll let you put him in the ground and get drunk a night or two. Do your grievin' for a friend. After that, get gone or face me."

"You . . . !" John Lee started to bluster. Winslow quickly dropped Max's feet and grabbed his boss by the arm. "Not now, boss. Now now."

"Yes," John Lee regained control of himself. "I shouldn't

respond to anything this . . . rabble has to say. You're quite right, ah . . ." He looked at the man. "What is your name?"

"Winslow, boss."

"Certainly. I knew that. It's . . . the shock, I suppose." He held Max's hat in one hand. "Come on." He pushed over the batwings and walked out.

"It's just about over," Bam Ford said. He and Pen had been about two miles from town when the shooting started and had just entered the batwings in time to see Max get his long overdue comeuppance.

"It will be the next time I see John Lee," Vonny said. "Even if he's standin' alongside God!"

Chapter 23

John Lee buried his friend—his only friend—and then retired to his grand house, sitting on the front porch, drinking not whiskey, but coffee. Nick, his behind resting on several thick pillows, sat with him.

"When do you think you'll be able to ride, boy?" his father asked him.

"Another week or ten days, Papa. We goin' to attack the town?"

"I am, you're not."

"What do you mean?"

"I want you gone from here, boy. I'll arrange for drovers to come in and move the herd. These damn gunhands bleeding me dry couldn't manage a herd of goats, much less several thousand head of cattle."

"We're sellin' out, Papa?"

"No. Were moving out. Heading west to start over. We're finished here. I could go on and fight for the next year and all I'd be doing is spending money." John Lee paused, recalling the words of Vonny Dodge and the gunfighter's terribly cold eyes.

"Where are we goin', Papa?"

"Montana, maybe. Wyoming. I don't know. Someplace away from here."

The son shook his head. John Lee looked at him. "What's the matter?"

"I was born right here, Papa. Not in this house, but on this land. It's ours. I ain't leavin'. Besides, Cindy ain't in no condition for a move."

"That's true," the father said.

"You're just depressed 'cause Max is dead, Papa. Look, Bodine and Sam and the Ranger can't stay here forever. They're drifters. We just lie low for a time and they'll move on. We'll rebuild our crew and in a month or six months or a year, we'll hit that damn town so hard they'll not know what happened to them. Then it'll be right back the way it was 'fore all these outsiders come in to screw it all up."

"It'll never be the way it was, boy," John Lee told his son. "Get that notion out of your head. I'm under a death sentence put on me by Vonny Dodge. I'm on the downswing of life, boy. You've got years ahead of you. You've got to live, you and Cindy and the child. Cindy can't stand no long trail drive, but she could be taken to Fort Worth and looked after there. You go with her. You're not in good enough health to help me in what I got to do. I'll arrange for drovers to move the herd, and then when you and Cindy are able, you come on following. You and me, we'll plan tonight where we start over. I've had my say, boy. That's the way it's going to be. Now leave me for a time."

After his son had gone back into the house, John Lee warmed his coffee and set about cleaning his guns. No man talked to him the way Vonny Dodge talked to him that day and lived. When all the plans were firm, and the drovers moving the herd, and the boy and Cindy were in the buggy and gone, John Lee would gather his fighting men and seek his revenge. That was the way it had to be. Vonny Dodge had thrown down the challenge, and John Lee had to pick it up. That was the code.

John Lee called for one of his few working hands to come to him. "Ride for the settlement, Booker. Start passing the word that I want drovers. We're moving the herd. Get them back here as soon as possible."

"Right, boss. I'm gone."

John Lee's eyes were bleak as he stared out over his land. "A week, Vonny. Ten days, maybe. Then one of us is dead."

"Stage driver just told me that John Lee's hirin' drovers," Pen said, sitting down at the table in the saloon.

"Drovers or gunhands?" Josiah asked, his wounded leg propped up on a chair.

"Cowboys," Pen said. "John Lee's gonna move the herd. Cindy's done pulled out for Fort Worth in a fancy buggy, and Nick is supposed to follow her pretty quick."

"That stage driver was full of information, wasn't he?" Sam smiled.

Bam stepped out of the saddle in front of the saloon and knocked the dust from his clothing before stepping up on the boardwalk and entering the saloon. He'd been out chasing a horse thief for the better part of two days. He ordered a beer and sat down wearily.

"You catch him?" Pen asked.

Bam nodded his head. "I caught him. He pulled iron. I shot him. Planted him this mornin'." He took a long swig of beer. "Lots of news out on the trail. John Lee's movin' his herd to Montana, by way of Kansas. He's plannin' to sell most of his beeves to the Army and take the best north for breedin' stock. He's gonna start the herd in a couple of days."

"I can't believe he's giving up," Josiah said.

"He ain't," Bam said, after draining his mug and wiping his mouth with the back of his hand. "I run into Rodgers on the trail. He left the Broken Lance. Said John Lee seemed like he was gonna pull something wild. He doesn't know what, but said some of the boys is talkin' about hitting the town and lootin' it and then settin' it on fire. And John Lee is all the time talkin' about killin' Vonny Dodge."

"John's good with a gun," Pen said. "Don't sell him short on that. I don't know whether he's as good as Vonny—I doubt it—but the man is no coward."

"Nick won't last in Montana," Matt said. "He'll be dead within six months. It takes some doing to live up there."

"I agree," Sam said. "If the weather doesn't kill him, some cowboy will. And it's my opinion that Cindy will never leave Fort Worth. She isn't cut out for homesteading in Montana." He looked at Bam. "You think Jeff Sparks and Vonny know about this move?"

"Oh, yeah. Rodgers told me that Circle S and Flyin' V punchers are watchin' ever' move the Broken Lance boys make. John Lee's still got about thirty or thirty-five randy ol' boys with him. They could hurt this town for a fact. They'll not tree it, but they could do enough damage so's it might not recover from it. We got to think about that."

"And stay close," Josiah said.

"Yeah." He looked up at the sounds of hooves striking the sun-baked earth of the street. "Here comes Jeff and some of his crew now."

The owner of the Circle S pulled a table close to the men and he and Vonny and Gene sat down, ordering beer. The other hands with him went to the bar. "You men heard the news about John Lee?"

"That's what we were just talking about," Matt said. "What do you make of it?"

The rancher sipped his beer and looked thoughtful for a moment. "I think that John Lee has sent his stupid kid and equally stupid wife out of harm's way. I think he is going to throw the dice for the jackpot or bust."

"A suicide raid?" Sam asked.

"Exactly."

"I hadn't thought of that," Josiah said. "But now that you brung it up, you just may be right."

"He's gone around the bend," Vonny said. "And I think he knows it. I believe that durin' any right-thinkin' time he might have, he knows he's slap-dab crazy, and he's chosen this way to go out rather than be placed in some institution for the feebleminded."

"Then he's doubly dangerous," Matt said. "You can usually predict what a normal person will do. There is no way of telling what a crazy man might do."

"Especially one who is on a suicide mission," his brother added.

"So what do we do?" Pen asked.

"Wait," Josiah said. "There's ain't nothin' else we can do, 'ceptin' warn the townspeople to get ready."

The town made ready without being obvious about it. Every water barrel that could be found was filled, and buckets and pails were stashed closeby in the event of fire. The manager of the general store sold out of .44's and .45's and had to reorder. But everyone knew by the time the reordered ammo arrived, their fates would have been long settled.

Men were assigned positions from which to fire. Women knew where to go with their kids from any part of town. Anyone handy with a hammer and saw was busy building thick shutters with gun slits to close and cover their windows in the hope that while the walls sure wouldn't stop a bullet, the shutters might.

One bright hot morning, one of Noah's hands came fogging into town and jumped down in front of the marshal's office. "The drovers have started the Broken Lance herd north," he panted, wiping the sweat from his face with a bandana. He used his hat to knock the dust from his clothing. "One of Jeff Sparks's spies he sent down to the settlement come back last night sayin' that John Lee's men done bought ever' box of bullets in town."

"Nick Lee?" Matt asked.

"Gone. Pulled out yesterday in a buggy. I think we done seen the last of that squirt."

"Don't bet on it," Josiah said. "He's just as crazy as his old man. And when he learns of his old man's death—and John Lee is gonna die, and soon—Nick'll be back with murder in his eyes."

"I tend to agree with you, Josiah," Sam said, noticing the badge was once more pinned to Josiah's shirt.

"Thank you," the Ranger said with a smile. "I asked to come off leave, since it's all up to John Lee now. I'll be sure to arrest any survivors of the raid."

"Here's the plan from our end of it," the young Flying V hand said, and laid it out.

Almost everyone was sure that John Lee and his men were coming hellbent for the town to loot it and destroy what was left. But the ranchers had to also plan on the unexpected, that being that John Lee and his raiders just might attack their ranches first. Noah only had a few hands, and he could not risk sending any of them in to help the town.

Jeff was keeping ten at the ranch and sending the rest into town. Those were Chookie, Barlow, Gilley, Parnell, and Beavers. They rode in late that same afternoon the Flying V hand delivered the message and the plan.

Vonny had already ridden in alone. The old gunfighter had tied his guns down and had a rifle in his hand and a bandoleer of ammunition slung across his chest. He pretty much stayed to himself, restlessly pacing the boardwalk, stopping occasionally to build a smoke.

He finally settled down and came into the marshal's office and took a seat. "When do you figure they'll hit us?" he asked Matt.

"Just before dawn. They'll make us sweat—or so they think. They'll think we'll be all tired and grainy-eyed from being up and tense all night. At least that's my thinking on it."

"I agree with it," Josiah said. "And I think it'll come in the morning. I get the impression that John Lee is not a very patient man. We'll take turns watchin' from the rooftops this night, and an hour before dawn, we'll roust everybody out of bed and be ready to meet the attack."

"How's your leg?" Vonny asked.

"It pains me some. But I can gimp around on it." He grinned. "I'll be right in the middle of it, boys. Don't none of you fret about that."

The town shut down early that night. By the time the sun had vanished over the horizon and the evening's shadows began cooling the land, most of the townspeople had eaten their supper and turned out the lamps.

The men would stand two-hour watches through the night, thus insuring that everyone would get enough rest while still maintaining a tight vigil over the town.

Doc Winters had laid out the tools of his trade before looking in on the few patients he still kept on cots in the back room of his office. He didn't think any of the gunmen left were going to make it much longer, and he, quite unprofessionally on his part, didn't really give a damn whether they lived or not. If peace was ever going to come to the frontier, men like these would have to be accounted for. And if accounted for meant stopping a bullet, that was fine with young Dr. Winters. He checked the double-barreled shotgun he'd asked for and received from the marshal's office, leaning it up against the wall by his bed. A sack of shells was on the floor beside the butt of the sawed-off. Doc Winters was quickly adjusting to life west of the Pecos.

He went to bed and was asleep in two minutes.

At four o'clock, all the men of the town were in their assigned positions and waiting for the attack.

"If my addition is correct," Sam said to Matt, "I figure John Lee's got thirty-five men, counting himself."

"Add about ten or fifteen more to that," Matt replied. "His regular hands will probably come in, too."

"I completely forgot about them. You're right. If John Lee fails this day, those men would have a tough time finding work anywhere in Texas. It's do or die for them, too."

The office door opened behind them and boots thudded on the boardwalk as Pen Masters joined the brothers. "I heard what you was sayin', Matt. Yeah, they's a good fifteen regular hands out on the Broken Lance, all loyal to John Lee. They're not known gunhands, but they're rough ol' boys who ride for the brand. They'll be comin' for a fact."

Matt looked up and down the street. He knew that everybody was up, but as instructed, no lamps were lit. The town appeared to be sleeping in the predawn hours.

Vonny joined them, the old gunfighter standing tall and straight and ready. "We got about an hour 'fore dawn. Say forty-five minutes 'fore they hit us. Time for a biscuit, one more cup of coffee, and a smoke. I'll do that and get into position. Good luck to you boys and keep your wits about you." He smiled. "Like we used to say up in the mountains—'and keep your powder dry.' "

He walked off into the darkness.

Bam called from the office. "Coffee's ready, and the cook at the café sent over some doughnuts. You can't beat a breakfast like that."

The men poured coffee and grabbed up the doughnuts, still warm and sprinkled with sugar.

Sam stepped out on the boardwalk and chanted something in a low voice.

"What's he sayin'?" Bam asked.

"That's a Cheyenne war chant," Bodine told him. "He's telling John Lee to come on, and that it's a good day for him to die."

Chapter 24

John Lee and his men struck the town hard, just as dawn was busting the darkness. They had walked their horses in close, then mounted up and charged, several of the raiders carrying lighted torches to fire the town. Those men were the first to die, for the townspeople knew that in these tinder-dry conditions, if one or two of the closely built buildings were to catch fire, the entire town would go.

One house was fired, but the women quickly formed a bucket brigade and caught the flames before they could do anything except very minor damage.

The raiders all wore long dusters and masks over their faces, their hats pulled down low. It was impossible to tell one from another.

One raider charged out of the alley between the general store and the café and rode his horse up onto the boardwalk. Matt blew him out of the saddle and slapped the frightened horse on the rump, sending it racing riderless up the street to the edge of town.

The wounded raider raised up on one elbow and leveled a .45 at Bodine. Standing on the boardwalk on the other side of the alley, Sam finished the man with a .44 slug to the head.

Two raiders came riding straight up the street, guns blazing. Matt, Sam, Bam, and Pen fired as one, and two more horses lost their riders. The hired guns lay motionless in the dirt.

Doc Winters stepped out of his office and took aim with his express gun. A rampaging raider took both barrels in the chest, the charge blowing him out of the saddle and very nearly tearing him in two. Doc Winters reloaded and crouched down behind a horse trough, saying some very uncomplimentary things about crazy ranchers, hoodlums, hired thugs, and the like. He eared back the hammers and waited for another target.

"Stand or deliver, Campbell," Vonny yelled at one raider who had lost his mask. Campbell turned and Vonny shot him out of the saddle. The hired gun staggered to his boots in the street, and Vonny gave him another taste of law west of the Pecos. Dexter Campbell would never hire his gun out again, unless it was for the devil.

Copper's horse panicked and threw him. He jumped to his boots and ran into the back of a building, crashing through the back door. A housewife was waiting with a pot of scalding coffee. She threw it in his face, and Copper screamed as his face seemed to catch on fire. He staggered howling out the back just as the woman's husband ran through the house to the back door, took aim with his .40-90 Sharps rifle, and blew a hole in the man large enough to stick your fist through.

A teenage boy, hiding in the loft of the barn at the livery, grabbed up a pitchfork and threw it at a masked man just below him. The tines caught him in the chest and drove right on through. The raider died without uttering a sound, pinned to the dirt of the street.

Harry Street wheeled his horse at the sight of Matt Bodine standing on the boardwalk, a .44 in each hand. He leveled his .45 at Bodine. He never got to pull the trigger. Josiah

drilled him clean between the eyes. The huge man toppled
from his saddle into the dust.

Giddings and Tidwell charged up the street and dismounted,
intent on looting the general store. The manager of the store
met them at the door with a shotgun. His first blast ended
any trouble Tidwell might have had with indigestion, and the
second blast ruined Giddings's complexion by taking off
part of his face.

"Heathens," the store manager said, and closed the front
door.

Dusty Jordan was shot off his horse by Pen Masters. Bam
put a slug into Winslow just as the outlaw put the spurs to his
horse. The horse jumped, and Winslow lost his balance, tum-
bling from the saddle. He landed headfirst in a horse trough,
knocking himself out, and drowned.

Matt recognized Kingman and called to him. The man
charged Matt with his horse, riding up onto the boardwalk.
Matt reached up, jerked the gunman from the saddle, and
threw him through the big front window of the saloon. Kingman landed on a table, crushing it, and came up cussing. He
turned and for one very brief moment, in the dim light, saw
Al standing by the bar, a shotgun in his hands. The twin muzzles of the shotgun blossomed in flames, and that was the
last thing Kingman ever saw.

Mark Hazard's horse was shot out from under him, the
gunman falling to the ground. In the excitement and noise of
the battle, he did not notice that the muzzle of his .45 jammed
deep into the ground, filling the barrel. He rose to his knees
and took aim at Sam. When he pulled the trigger, the pistol
exploded, and Mark lost a hand and part of his face. He lay
screaming on the ground, bleeding to death.

The townspeople, once all the outlaws were inside the
town, rolled wagons across the road and many of the alley-
ways, containing the raiders. Dave Land, seeing any escape
by horseback blocked, jumped from the saddle and ran into
the church. Reverend Willowby met him with a rifle and pro-

ceeded to read to him from the Scriptures, punctuated by .44-40 rounds.

Dean Waters tried to jump a wagon. His horse, smarter than the rider, refused, and Dean went flying, butt over elbows. He cleared the wagon and hit the ground on the other side. A woman stepped out of her quarters and conked him on the head with a poker, then hit him again for insurance.

Doc Winters shot Lou Witter in his big butt with buckshot as the raider was lumbering across the street. Witter hit the ground, squalling, his rear end ruined and his pants smoking from the hot buckshot.

Jack Morgan came face to face with Matt Bodine, and Matt laid a .44 across the man's face twice, breaking his jaw and knocking him out.

Riggs exited his saddle and tried to make a run for the alley. Chookie's rifle barked, and Riggs fell like a rag doll to lie still in the street. Pate ran into the guns of Barlow and Gilley, the slugs turning him around and around in the street. Wheeler came nose to nose with Parnell, and the Circle S cowboy's .45's belched fire and flame. Wheeler sat down on the ground and quietly expired.

Matt ran around to the back of the saloon and spotted John Lee. The man was standing alone, his guns in leather, his hands by his side.

"Don't let it end this way, John Lee," Matt told him. "You're a sick man. Maybe the doctors can help you. I won't draw on you."

The sounds of battle were fading as the last of the raiders were either killed or surrendering to the townspeople. Dust and gun smoke hung heavy and choking in the morning air.

"Come on," Matt urged. "It's over. Give it up, John."

"Kill me," the rancher urged.

"No," Matt told him, seeing Sam quietly slipping up behind the man. "I won't shoot you. You're a sick man."

"Then I'll kill you," John Lee said.

Sam laid the barrel of his .44 across the back of John Lee's head, and the rancher crumpled to the ground.

One final shot was fired in the day's battle. A dying outlaw in Doc Winters's office shot Monty Brill in the head. When asked why he did it, he said, "I wanted to go out knowin' I kilt one of the fastest guns around."

"But he wasn't armed!" Doc Winters said.

"So what?" the outlaw said, then closed his eyes and died.

Chapter 25

Of the nineteen hired guns that surrendered, twelve survived the day and night, the others dying of their wounds. Two more died the following day. The local undertaker did his best to keep the smile off his face.

When the Rangers arrived to take the men off for trial—it was state now, something about conspiracy and the shooting of a Texas Ranger and about two dozen other charges—Ranger headquarters decided to come in force. They sent two Rangers.

John Lee was a babbling broken man. He was in chains not so much to keep him from hurting other people as to keep him from hurting himself. His herd had been stopped in New Mexico and turned back. There was going to be a lot of settling up, and the herd was impounded until everything was over.

Josiah told Noah Carson and Jeff Sparks to "look after the herd and don't let nothin' happen to it." It was said with a smile and received with one.

Someone set the John Lee mansion on fire a couple of nights after the battle in Nameit. The mansion, the bunkhouse, and all the other buildings burned slap to the ground. But the Rangers never did find the safe that was in John Lee's study, and Nick just dropped out of sight—flat disappeared. Without his wife. Cindy, it was later reported, was taken in by some of Nick's mother's people over in Louisiana. No one who lived west of the Pecos ever saw her again.

The town of Nameit endured, although its name was soon changed. It's still right there about two, three miles west of the Pecos River on a old trail that's been a federal highway for years.

Vonny and Conchita got married. So did Lisa and Noah. Lia was busy casting her charms for Doc Winters; odds were he'd take the bait before long. Gene took to sparkin' the daughter of a rancher, and he was in love, walking into walls and falling off his horse and everything else that went with it.

Rawhide O'Neal, Dean Waters, and Carl Jergens were hanged. The others got long prison sentences.

Taylor and Cloud went back to work down south. Barlow stayed on and took over as foreman of the Flying V. Chookie and Parnell and Gilley and the others drew their time and drifted, as cowboys are wont to do.

Pen Masters and Bam Ford joined up with the Texas Rangers.

At the crossroads, Josiah Finch sat Horse and looked at Matt Bodine and Sam Two Wolves. "Well, boys, where are you off to this time?"

"We'll drift, see some country. We might run into you again," Matt said.

The Ranger shook hands with them both, and with a smile, said, "Boys, you can say you been to Hell, and you been to Texas. Which one do you prefer?"

With a grin, Sam told him.

Josiah chased them both for about a mile, cussing and hollering, but with a big grin all the time, knowing it was all in fun. The last he saw of Matt and Sam—for this go-around— was the blood brothers on the crest of a small rise, hats in their hands, waving them.

"Texas, by God!" Matt yelled.

AFTERWORD

Notes from the Old West

In the small town where I grew up, there were two movie theaters. The Pavilion was one of those old-timey movie show palaces, built in the heyday of Mary Pickford and Charlie Chaplin—the silent era of the 1920s. By the 1950s, when I was a kid, the Pavilion was a little worn around the edges, but it was still the premier theater in town. They played all those big Technicolor biblical Cecil B. DeMille epics and corny MGM musicals. In Cinemascope, of course.

On the other side of town was the Gem, a somewhat shabby and run-down grind house with sticky floors and torn seats. Admission was a quarter. The Gem booked low-budget "B" pictures (remember the Bowery Boys?), war movies, horror flicks, and Westerns. I liked the Westerns best. I could usually be found every Saturday at the Gem, along with my best friend, Newton Trout, watching Westerns from 10 A.M. until my father came looking for me around suppertime. (Sometimes Newton's dad was dispatched to come fetch us.) One time, my dad came to get me right in the middle of *Abilene Trail,* which featured the now-forgotten Whip Wilson. My father became so engrossed in the action he sat down and watched the rest of it with us. We didn't get home until after dark, and my mother's meat loaf was a pan of gray ashes by the time we did. Though my father and I were both in the doghouse the next day, this remains one of my fondest childhood memories. There was Wild Bill Elliot, and Gene Autry, and Roy Rogers, and Tim Holt, and, a little later, Rod Cameron and Audie Murphy. Of these newcomers, I never missed an Audie Murphy Western, because Audie was sort of an antihero. Sure, he stood for law and order and was an honest man, but sometimes he had to go around the law to uphold it. If he didn't play fair, it was only because he felt hamstrung by the laws of the land. Whatever it took to get the bad guys, Audie did it. There were no finer points of law, no splitting of legal hairs. It was instant justice, devoid of long-winded lawyers, bored or biased jurors, or black-robed, often corrupt judges.

Steal a man's horse and you were the guest of honor at a necktie party.

Molest a good woman and you got a bullet in the heart or a rope around the gullet. Or at the very least, got the crap beat out of you. Rob a bank and face a hail of bullets or the hangman's noose.

Saved a lot of time and money, did frontier justice.

That's all gone now, I'm sad to say. Now you hear, "Oh, but he had a bad childhood" or "His mother didn't give him enough love" or "The homecoming queen wouldn't give him a second look and he has an inferiority complex." Or "cultural rage," as the politically correct bright boys refer to it. How many times have you heard some self-important defense attorney moan, "The poor kids were only venting their hostilities toward an uncaring society?"

Mule fritters, I say. Nowadays, you can't even call a punk a punk anymore. But don't get me started.

It was, "Howdy, ma'am" time too. The good guys, antihero or not, were always respectful to the ladies. They might shoot a bad guy five seconds after tipping their hat to a woman, but the code of the West demanded you be respectful to a lady.

Lots of things have changed since the heyday of the Wild West, haven't they? Some for the good, some for the bad.

I didn't have any idea at the time that I would someday write about the West. I just knew that I was captivated by the Old West.

When I first got the itch to write, back in the early 1970s, I didn't write Westerns. I started by writing horror and action adventure novels. After more than two dozen novels, I began thinking about developing a Western character. From those initial musings came the novel *The Last Mountain Man: Smoke Jensen*. That was followed by *Preacher: The First Mountain Man*. A few years later, I began developing the Last Gunfighter series. Frank Morgan is a legend in his own time, the fastest gun west of the Mississippi . . . a title and a reputation he never wanted, but can't get rid of.

For me, and for thousands—probably millions—of other people (although many will never publicly admit it), the old Wild West will always be a magic, mysterious place: a place we love to visit through the pages of books; characters we would like to know . . . from a safe distance; events we would love to take part in, again, from a safe distance. For the old Wild West was not a place for the faint of heart. It was a hard, tough, physically demanding time. There were no police to call if one faced adversity. One faced trouble alone, and handled it alone. It was rugged individualism: something that appeals to many of us.

I am certain that is something that appeals to most readers of Westerns.

I still do on-site research (whenever possible) before starting a Western novel. I have wandered over much of the West, prowling what is left of ghost towns. Stand in the midst of the ruins of these old towns, use a little bit of imagination, and one can conjure up life as it used to be in the Wild West. The rowdy Saturday nights, the tinkling of a piano in a saloon, the laughter of cowboys and miners letting off steam after a week of hard work. Use a little more imagination and one can envision two men standing in the street, facing one another, seconds before the hook and draw of a gunfight. A moment later, one is dead and the other rides away.

The old wild untamed West.

There are still some ghost towns to visit, but they are rapidly vanishing as time and the elements take their toll. If you want to see them, make plans to do so as soon as possible, for in a few years, they will all be gone.

And so will we.

Stand in what is left of the Big Thicket country of east Texas and try to imagine how in the world the pioneers managed to get through that wild tangle. I have wondered about that many times and marveled at the courage of the men and women who slowly pushed westward, facing dangers that we can only imagine.

Let me touch briefly on a subject that is very close to me: firearms. There are some so-called historians who are now claiming that firearms played only a very insignificant part in the settlers' lives. They claim that only a few were armed. What utter, stupid nonsense! What do these so-called historians think the pioneers did for food? Do they think the early settlers rode down to the nearest supermarket and bought their meat? Or maybe they think the settlers chased down deer or buffalo on foot and beat the animals to death with a club. I have a news flash for you so-called historians: The settlers used guns to shoot their game. They used guns to defend hearth and home against Indians on the warpath. They used guns to protect themselves from outlaws. Guns are a part of Americana. And always will be.

The mountains of the West and the remains of the ghost towns that dot those areas are some of my favorite subjects to write about. I have done extensive research on the various mountain ranges of the West and go back whenever time permits. I sometimes stand surrounded by the towering mountains and wonder how in the world the pioneers ever made it through. As hard as I try and as often as I try, I simply cannot imagine the hardships those men and women endured over the hard months of their incredible journey. None of us can. It is said that on the Oregon Trail alone, there are at least two bodies in lonely, unmarked graves for every mile of that journey. Some students of the West say the number of dead is at least twice that. And nobody knows the exact number of wagons that impatiently started out alone and simply vanished on the way, along with their occupants, never to be seen or heard from again.

Just vanished.

The one-hundred-and fifty-year old ruts of the wagon wheels can still be seen in various places along the Oregon Trail. But if you plan to visit those places, do so quickly, for they are slowly disappearing. And when they are gone, they will be lost forever, except in the words of Western writers.

The West will live on as long as there are writers willing to write about it, and publishers willing to publish it. Writing about the West is wide open, just like the old Wild West. Characters abound, as plentiful as the wide-open spaces, as colorful as a sunset on the Painted Desert, as restless as the ever-sighing winds. All one has to do is use a bit of imagination. Take a stroll through the cemetery at Tombstone, Arizona; read the inscriptions. Then walk the main street of that once-infamous town around midnight and you might catch a glimpse of the ghosts that still wander the town. They really do. Just ask anyone who lives there. But don't be afraid of the apparitions, they won't hurt you. They're just out for a quiet stroll.

The West lives on. And as long as I am alive, it always will.

Turn the page for an exciting preview of the next book in
William Johnstone's BLOOD BOND series,

GUNSMOKE AND GOLD,

now available

wherever Pinnacle Books are sold.

Chapter 1

"Two riders comin'," the cowboy said, knocking the dust from him with his hat. "They look like hardcases to me. Be here in about five minutes. I grabbed a look-see from the rocks and come in the back way."

The knot of men followed him inside the saloon and up to the bar. The cowboy ordered a mug of beer and drank half of it before setting the mug on the bar. He wiped his mouth with the back of his hand.

"What brands?" he was asked.

"None I ever seen before. Fine horses, though. Real fine."

"Then it's happenin'," another said. "The damn nesters and sheepmen has hired guns."

"Aw, now, hell!" another man spoke from a table. "Don't none of us here know that for a fact. Simmer down. It's probably two drifters lookin' for work."

"With tied-down guns?" the messenger asked softly.

"Some men tie 'em down, others don't," the voice of moderation said. "We'll look 'em over when they get here."

"Suppose they head over to the Plowshare?" he was asked.

"Then we'll know, won't we?"

Matt Bodine and Sam Two Wolves rode into the town,

reined up at the start of the long street, and gave the town a once-over.

"We have our choice of watering holes," Sam said. The Red Dog and the Plowshare."

"And a fine hotel," Matt replied with a grin.

"I'm more interested in a long hot bath, a shave and a haircut, and something to eat. You see a barber shop?"

"Not yet. Let's ride on in and have a beer at one of the saloons.

"The Red Dog looks like it's doing a land-office business. Want to try the Plowshare?"

"Why not? It looks quiet. Maybe for once we can have a beer without getting into trouble."

"That would be a novel experience," his blood-brother replied dryly.

They rode on in.

"I knowed it!" the cowboy said. "Swingin' down in front of that damn sheep-dip bar."

The man who had tried to calm everybody stood up and watched the strangers. The town's two saloons were located directly across the street from each other. He grunted as he watched Matt Bodine slip the hammer-thongs from his guns the moment his boots touched the ground.

"Gunhands, all right. Shorty, you'd best ride for the ranch and tell Pete it's started."

"Right, Mr. Dale. I'm on my way."

"Frisco, get to the Circle X and tell Blake."

"I'm gone, Mr. Dale."

Mr. Dale looked around for a rider from the Lightning Arrow spread. There was nobody in the bar who worked for Hugo Raner. Well, he'd hear soon enough.

Matt turned at the batwings as the two cowboys jumped in their saddles and lit out of town like it was a double pay-day at the ranch.

"Curious," he muttered.

"Maybe we need a bath more than we think?" Sam said good-naturedly.

Matt laughed at his half-breed Cheyenne brother and pushed open the batwings. Sam's father had been a great and respected chief, his mother a beautiful white woman from the East. Matt and Sam had met while just children, and soon Matt was spending as much time in the Cheyenne camp as he was at home on the ranch. They grew up together and Matt was adopted into the Cheyenne tribe and became a true Human Being. Sam's father had been killed during the battle at the Little Bighorn, after he had charged Custer, alone, unarmed except for a coup stick. Matt and Sam had witnessed the slaughter—something they had never told any-one—and when they rode down from the ridges to stand over the carnage, it had affected them deeply. They decided to drift for a time, to blunt the edges of the terrible memory before they returned to their ranches along the Wyoming-Montana border.

Both were not without resources, for Sam's mother had come from a wealthy family and was fairly well-off for the time. Matt owned a huge and very profitable cattle and horse ranch—as did Sam—so while they might look like saddle bums, they certainly were not.

They were handsome and muscular young men, both in their mid-twenties; both with a wild and reckless glint in their eyes. Sam's eyes were black, Matt's were blue. Sam's hair was black, Matt's was dark brown. Both were big men, but very agile for their size—over six feet tall and weighing about one ninety each. They could pass for full brothers and had many times. Sam had inherited his mother's white fea-tures; only his cold obsidian eyes—which could sparkle with high humor at a moment's notice—gave him away.

Medicine Horse, Sam's father, when he knew war was coming and knew he must fight, had ordered his son from their encampment and ordered him to adopt the white man's ways and to forever forget his Cheyenne blood. Medicine Horse made his son repeat the pledge, knowing that even after his death, Sam August Webster Two Wolves would not disobey.

Both young men wore the same three multicolored stones around their necks, the stones pierced by rawhide.

And both young men were highly respected when it came to gunfighting. It was not a title they sought or wanted, but they were called gunfighters. Of the two, Matt Bodine was faster, but not by much. Matt had been at it longer than Sam.

Matt had killed his first man when he was fourteen defending his father's ranch. The man's brothers came after him when he was fifteen. They were buried that same day. At sixteen, rustlers came when Matt was nightherding. Two more graves were added. He lived with Cheyennes during his seventeenth year and then went to work riding shotgun for gold shipments. Four men died trying to rob the shipments. Later, two more called Matt out in the street. Neither man cleared leather.

After that he was a scout for the Army, when they asked him to be. He saved his money and bought land. His ranch was one of the largest in the state.

Sam Two Wolves was college-educated, while Matt was educated at home by his mother, who was a trained schoolteacher. Matt would be considered well-educated for the time.

There were four men in the saloon, including the barkeep. Both Matt and Sam noticed how tensed-up the men became as the brothers walked across the room to the bar, spurs jingling with each step.

Matt smiled at the barkeep. "Howdy," he said. "How about a couple of beers?"

The barkeep hesitated, then nodded and pulled two mugs of beer.

"All the business seems to be across the street," Matt remarked. "What's the place have, dancing girls?"

"Mister," one of the men seated at a table said, "you sure you're in the right saloon?"

Sam smiled at the man. "Is there a right place and a wrong place to get a beer in this town?"

"There sure is," another man said. Both brothers noticed he wore low-heeled boots and had his gun stuck behind his belt instead of in a holster.

Farmer, the brothers concluded. Then the name of the saloon sank in. The Plowshare. A saloon for farmers and sheepmen, probably.

"Well," Matt smiled the word. "If we have one beer in here and the second beer across the street, we'll please everybody, right?"

A man smiled in return. "A reasonable person might think so, but around here lately, reason seems to have flown the coop."

"Was I you boys," yet another man said, "I'd have my beer and then ride on. You been marked just by coming in here."

"Marked?" Sam asked.

"Range war shapin' up around here. Cattlemen and hands use the Red Dog. Farmers and sheepmen use this place. You was seen comin' in here. Them across the street probably think we hired you. You're marked."

"Sheep and cattle can get along, if both sides use some sense. Sheep have to be moved regular to keep from overgrazing. Hell, so do cattle." Matt took a sip of beer.

"A reasonable man," the barkeep said. "What a breath of fresh air around here."

"Are you boys lookin' for work?" the fourth man asked.

"Not really," Sam told him. "We're just drifting. Seeing some country. We both own spreads west of here."

"Cattlemen?"

"Yes," Matt answered. "There are farms all around our spreads. We get along just fine."

The farmer shook his head. "I wish that were the case

here. There are three big ranches in this area. The Box H, owned by Pete Harris; the Circle V, owned by Blake Vernon; and the Lightning Arrow, owned by Hugo Raner. They control—or think they do—hundreds of thousands of acres. We came in—the homesteaders and a few sheepmen—and filed on our land legal and proper. We've stayed and proved it up according to law. Built us a school and a church. We didn't expect all the hostility we're now facing."

Sam and Matt took their beers and moved to a table by the window.

"We put up wire to protect our crops, the cattlemen tear it down. If we try to irrigate—when we need it—the cattlemen dam up the water."

"Do you share the water?" Sam asked gently.

"Absolutely. We don't want it all, just a small portion of it. This really isn't an issue of water or land—no matter what the cattlemen say. It isn't. It's a question of who is the most powerful. Raul, one of the sheepmen, petitioned the government for grazing rights, and got it, in writing. Hugo Raner told Raul he didn't give a damn what was written on some piece of paper. Said if Raul didn't move his sheep, he'd kill them, then he'd kill Raul"

"And? . . ." Matt asked.

"Raul's lost several hundred sheep. He's written for some of his relatives to come up here and join him. They'll be along any day now."

"Basque?" Sam asked.

"Yes. They're good people. Gentle people. But if they're pushed, they'll fight."

The farmers filed out, leaving the place empty except for the bartender and the brothers by the window.

"The hotel have a dining room?" Matt asked.

"Yep," the barkeep said. "Good one. Nice rooms, too. But I doubt if Mister Dale will let you boys register there."

"Mister Dale?" Sam questioned.

"Owns this town. Well . . . he don't own it outright. He settled it. He's the mayor, owns the bank and the real estate office and some other businesses. He saw to it that Jack Linwood got the sheriff's job—rigged the election. You boys heard of Jack Linwood?"

"Yeah," Matt said. "Supposed to be a fast gun."

"There ain't no supposin' to it. He's fast. I've seen him work more'n once. And his deputies is scum. Buster Phelps, Sam Keller, and Wes Fannin."

"If the situation is as tense as the farmers say it is, don't you think you're talking a bit too much?" Sam asked.

The man smiled. "Name's Chrisman. I come in here two days behind Dale. I own this place, free and clear. I also own me a little spread west of town. Run a few head of cattle."

"What is the name of this town?" Matt asked.

"Dale. What else?"

The brothers saw to their horses and walked over to the hotel, carrying their saddlebags, bedrolls, and rifles. They had no trouble checking in, although the desk clerk's eyes bugged out when he read their names. As soon as the brothers had climbed the stairs to their rooms, the clerk sent a boy running across the street to the saloon.

"Matt Smith and Sam Jones," Mister Dale said. "Yeah. I'm sure those are their real names."

"I can run them out of town," Sheriff Linwood said, leaning against the bar, sipping a whiskey. "That'd be the easiest way to handle it."

"We don't know for sure who they are, so for now we'll leave them alone," Mister Dale said. "And I mean alone. Let them clean up and have a drink and eat and I think they'll probably pull out in the morning."

"And if they don't?" Pete Harris asked.

Mister Dale shook his head.

"I don't like it, them goin' straight to that sheepcrap and nester saloon," a cowboy said. "It's like they knew what they was doin.' "

"We'll see," Mister Dale said. "If they don't pull out in the morning, we'll . . ." he paused, ". . . Take the appropriate action." He looked at Jack Linwood. "Understood?"

Jack nodded his head. He was liking this job less and less. He'd used his gun many times, but he was no cold-blooded killer. And if Dale thought that, the man was flat-out wrong.

Chapter 2

Their boots were polished by a boy in the shop. Now, bathed and shaved, the hair cut off the backs of their necks and around their ears, and smelling like dandies (it was only a dime more to get that genuine imported aftershave splashed on), the brothers dressed in their last clean sets of clothing and left the rest to be washed and ironed by a lady who lived on the edge of town—recommended by Chrisman.

They stepped into the hotel dining room. The place was about half-full of early diners. "The town's gentry, so to speak" Sam muttered, looking around him.

"Hush," Matt told him. "You'll get us thrown out of here."

"I'll leave that up to you, since you're the expert at starting trouble."

"Thank you."

The brothers took a seat, very conscious of the sly gazes being tossed their way by the young ladies in the room; and they did look dashing. Matt was dressed in a red checkered shirt and dark jeans, a black kerchief at his throat. Sam had dressed in a sparkling white shirt, a red kerchief at his throat, and dark jeans. The brothers set some feminine hearts to palpitatin'.

Outside, the wide street rumbled under the hooves of hard-ridden horses.

"It's Rusty and some of the boys from the Lightning spread," a Box H hand said. "Damn! They're headin' into the hotel. I bet Shorty cut across their range headin' to home and told 'em."

"Stop them!" Mister Dale said.

"Too late. They're in the hotel."

"Where's Linwood?"

"I dunno. I haven't seen him or any of his men in a couple of hours."

"Damn!" Mister Dale said.

"Maybe Rusty and them boys will just end it right now," a Box H hand called Coop said.

"We can always hope," Mister Dale said.

The dining room fell quiet; not even the tinkle of silverware or the rattle of coffee cups being placed in saucers sounded. Sam looked over his shoulder and grimaced.

"Why do you always get us into trouble, brother?" His dark eyes were twinkling.

"I see them. And we just got cleaned up."

"Yes. But at least we won't have to fight on a full stomach. It's not good for the digestion."

"That really makes me feel better, Sam. You sure do know how to cheer me up."

"Thank you," Sam replied modestly.

"You two slicked-up dudes yonder!" Rusty called. "Outside. I want to talk to you."

Matt was facing the archway. He sized up the cowboy. Pretty good-sized ol' boy. Late thirties, he'd guess, and all muscle and gristle and bone. The three with him were about the same size, with hard-packed muscle and callused hands from years of wrestling steers and handling rope.

"Here we go," Sam muttered, not knowing what Matt was going to do, but knowing full well he was about to irritate someone.

"Are you speaking to us, Jackass Mouth," Matt called, "or are you braying at an early moon?"

About half of the men and women in the big dining room did their best to hide smiles. And that told the brothers that the big ranchers in the area were not all loved, providing these hands came from one of the Big Three, and both brothers were sure of that.

"You say that to *me*?" Rusty yelled.

"You're the only person in the room braying like a jackass," Matt told him. "As a matter of fact, you sort of resemble a jackass. In a way."

Rusty was so mad he looked like he was about to explode.

Sam turned around and stared at the red-faced foreman of the Lightning spread. He shook his head. "No, brother," he said loud enough for all to hear. "A jackass is much better looking."

Several men and women laughed out loud.

"By God!" Rusty yelled. "You people don't laugh at me. I'll tear this damn town apart."

"Oh, shut up," Matt told him. "Go away. We're trying to order supper."

Rusty marched over to the table, his men right behind him. They ringed the table. Real close. Sam smiled. "By God, saddlebum, you'll learn when a Lightning man tells you to do something, you'll do it."

"I doubt it," Matt said.

Rusty reached down, clamped a hand on Matt's good shirt, and jerked him to his boots. He tore the shirt. Bad mistake.

Matt knocked the bejesus out of the foreman. The blow sent the man stumbling across the room, crashing into tables and sending diners scrambling to get out of the way, but staying close enough to watch and enjoy the fight.

Sam rammed his chair back, knocking a puncher sprawling, and a split-second later he jammed the square-cornered table into another Lightning hand's groin. The hand dropped to his knees, his face white with pain, both hands holding his crotch, his mouth open in a silent scream. Sam came up fast and grabbed a chair, splintering it over the fourth puncher's head and knocking him to the floor.

"Get that dirty son, Tulsa," the puncher on his knees moaned as Tulsa was getting up off the floor.

Sam got set, a strange smile on his lips.

Matt had backed Rusty into a corner and was concentrating on beating the stuffing out of him. The initial blow had caught the foreman off-guard, and had been powerful enough to stun him. Now Matt was going to finish it.

Rusty swung and Matt ducked that one and the left that followed it. He grabbed the man's left forearm and slung him across the room. Rusty wiped out a row of tables as he spun out of control, Matt right behind him. Rusty hit the wall and looked confused for a moment. He wasn't used to people doing this to him. Then Matt was all over him as Sam yelled, "Hurry up, damn it. Quit showin' off."

Matt hit the foreman a combination of blows that rocked the man's head from side to side, bloodying his mouth, busting his nose, and pulping one ear. He finished the foreman with a thundering right to the man's belly. Rusty coughed up bile and slumped to the floor, out of action.

Matt screamed like a panther, and that nearly scared the women in the room out of their corsets. It frightened some of the men, too. It also startled the hell out of a Lightning hand named Buck. What really got Buck's attention was when Matt hit him in the mouth with a fist that looked about the size of a brick and was just about as hard. Pearlies flew from the man's suddenly bloody mouth. Matt hit him two more times, then clubbed him on the neck on his way down to the floor.

Sam was dealing his opponent some real misery. The man's eyes were glazed and his mouth and nose were smashed and bloody. One ear was badly swollen, and all in all, he looked like he really wished he had stayed back at the ranch. Sam hit him one more time and the man kissed the floor.

Then Matt and Sam turned on the man who had met the corner of the table. Together, as one man would later say, "Them boys beat the hell outta that Lightning hand."

Matt left Tony to Sam and looked around just as Rusty was staggering to his boots. Matt grabbed the man by the seat of his pants and his shirt collar and ran him squalling and bellering across the room, using the path Rusty had earlier cleared. Matt threw him through the window.

Rusty hit the boardwalk and kept on going. He impacted against the south end of a hitchrail, did a real nifty little flip, and landed in a horse trough.

Matt stepped through the broken window, dragged the man out of the trough, and retrieved Rusty's poke-sack from his pocket. He stepped back into the dining room. Mister Dale and the others had lined up on the boardwalk in front of the Red Dog, disbelief in their eyes.

But it wasn't over yet.

Matt counted out a few bills and held them up while Sam was gathering money from the other bully-boys. "This is for my shirt, folks." He put that in his pocket. He tossed the rest onto a table. "That will pay for the expenses, along with what money we pull from these other galoots."

"Ripped my brand new trousers," Sam griped. He counted out enough for a new pair of pants and tossed the rest of the money onto the table. There was over a hundred dollars in gold and greenbacks.

The brothers looked at each other and grinned. They then proceeded to toss the other Lightning out the shattered window. It made quite a pile when they were through.

They returned to their table, righted it, found chairs, and sat down. "Now," Matt said. "Can we please have something to eat?"

*   *   *

Hugo Raner stood on his front porch and watched as his foreman and three of his top hands came riding in at sunset. They were sure sorry lookin'.

"What the hell happened?" he shouted.

Rusty dismounted carefully and painfully. "I don't know who them hombres is, boss. But they're ringtailed-tooters. I ain't never had my ashes hauled this bad in all my life."

"For God's sake, men. How many were there?"

"Two," Tulsa said sheepishly.

"*Two!*" Hugo roared. "The townspeople join in with them?"

"No, sir. They just laughed and had them a good time."

Hugo Raner flushed. "Nobody laughs at my hands. That's the same as laughing at me."

His son stepped out to see what all the shouting was about. He stared at the beat-up top hands. Carl fancied himself a fast gun, and in truth he was good, very quick. He was also cocky, arrogant, and cruel to both humans and animals.

"You men see a doctor?" Hugo asked.

"Yeah, boss," Buck lisped the words through the gap where his front teeth used to be. "Nothin' broken."

"Get cleaned up. Supper's over but the cook saved you some grub. Tomorrow we'll all ride into town and see what this business is about."

"Right," Carl said, a cruel glint in his eyes.

Mister Dale walked over to the hotel and watched as workmen boarded up what was left of the big window in the dining room. He shook his head and walked into the lobby. He nodded at the desk clerk and stood under the archway, looking at the two strangers sitting in the nearly deserted dining room, having an after-supper coffee and cigar. Mister Dale decided there was only one way to get to the bottom of this. He walked over to the table.

"Gentlemen," he said with a smile. "Do you mind if I sit down?"

Matt pushed out a chair with the toe of his boot and the

man sat down. He waved to a waitress and she poured him coffee.

"That was quite a fight, boys," Mister Dale said.

"So-so," Sam replied.

"Some friendly advice from an older man?" Dale was about forty, the brothers guessed.

"It's free, so go ahead," Matt told him.

"Were I you boys, I'd pull out first thing in the morning," Mister Dale said.

"We like it here," Sam said.

The mayor smiled. "Hugo Raner owns one of the biggest spreads in all of Colorado. He has about thirty hands. I'm sure he and his boys will be riding in first thing in the morning. You boys wouldn't want to endanger women and children by engaging in a gunfight on Main Street, now, would you?"

"If there *is* a gunfight," Sam said, "it won't be us who starts it. So the logical thing to do would be to ban this Hugo person and his hands from town."

Mister Dale chuckled. "Logic. Well, yes, I suppose you're right. But Hugo and his men live and work and spend their money in this town. You boys are just drifters. You'll spend a few dollars and then drift on. You catch what I mean? By the way, I'm Mayor Dale."

"I'm Matt and this is my brother, Sam."

"Smith and Jones?"

"We're half brothers," Sam told him.

The mayor nodded his head. "Boys, don't play dangerous games with me. You won a fistfight. Fine. No real damage done. The people I talked with said the Lightning crew started it. All right. No charges will be filed." His face tightened and his voice became hard. "Now let's get down to the nut-cuttin'. I own this hotel and dining room. You boys spend the night, sleep well, then get out of here come morning. You catch my drift?"

"Oh, yeah," Matt said. "We'll check out in the morning."

Mister Dale smiled. "Fine, boys. Fine."

"Is there a boardinghouse in town?" Sam asked.

The mayor sighed, losing his smile. "You don't seem to understand. I can have you arrested for vagrancy."

Matt tossed a sack of gold coins on the table. Sam did the same. Matt said, "I'd sure like to see that charge stand up in a court of law."

Mister Dale carefully opened each sack. The banker in him surfaced. His eyes glinted at the dull gold shining at him. "That's a lot of money for a couple of saddlebums to have. I just might ask the sheriff to lock you up until we can decide if that money is stolen."

"We both own ranches in Wyoming," Sam told him. "And there are papers in our saddlebags to prove it. I would imagine our spreads are as large—or larger—than those around here. Try again, Mister Mayor."

Mister Dale sugared and creamed his coffee. He sipped and added more sugar. "Two ranchers passing through," he said softly. He shook his head. "We all make mistakes. Why did you go into the Plowshare instead of the Red Dog?"

"The Red Dog looked full," Matt said. "We chose the quieter saloon."

Mister Dale chuckled. "Things are tense here, gentlemen. My apologies for the behavior of Hugo's boys, and for my ordering you out of this hotel. Stay as long as you like." He tapped one sack of gold. "I'd bank that money, boys. That's a tidy sum to be carrying around."

"We might do that," Sam told him.

The mayor stood up. "Smith and Jones," he muttered. "Why not?"

He walked out of the dining room.

Bodine and Sam looked at each other and grinned.

* * *

Hugo brought every hand he could spare into town. They made quite a show of it and succeeded in raising a dustcloud that a tornado would have been hard-pressed to match.

Mister Dale met the rancher on the boardwalk in front of the Red Dog and briefly explained the situation.

Hugo Raner shook his big head. Everything about Hugo was big. He was a bear of a man. "That don't make a damn to me, Dale," he said. "I aim to see those two horsewhipped. Now get out of my way."

"Just calm down a second," Mister Dale said. "And think about what you're planning. Smith and Jones came into town looking for a room and a meal. That's all. They are respected Wyoming ranchers and have the funds and the papers to prove it. Your men were out of line. What we don't need now is trouble that will be carried out of this area. We don't want outside authorities to catch wind of this upcoming war. Now think about that, Hugo."

The big man thought for a moment and then sighed. He removed his hat and ran thick, blunt fingers through his dark hair. "All right, Dale. All right. I see what you mean. It was a misunderstanding all the way around."

"There they are, boss." Tulsa spoke from the saddle.

Hugo looked at the two men coming out of the hotel. His experienced eyes took in Matt's two guns and the way the man walked. He shifted his gaze to Sam. "They're gunfighters, Dale. Both of them. And that one has some Injun in him. *Injun!* Jumpin' Jesus Christ, Dale, they're ranchers, all right. But I'll tell you something else: that's Matt Bodine and Sam Two Wolves!"

THE MOUNTAIN MAN SERIES BY
WILLIAM W. JOHNSTONE

Available Wherever Books Are Sold!

Visit our website at **www.kensingtonbooks.com**